PRAISE FOR
THE BET SERIES

The Bet

"I haven't laughed this hard while reading a book in a while. *The Bet* [is] an experience—a heartwarming, sometimes hilarious, experience...I've actually read this book twice."

—RecommendedRomance.com

"If you need a funny, light read...I promise you this is a superb choice!"

—MustReadBooksOrDie.com

"Friends to lovers stories...is there anything better? And when told in a fun, light manner, with a potential love triangle with lovable characters, well, how can you not enjoy it?"

—TotallyBookedBlog.com

The Wager

"Rachel Van Dyken is quickly becoming one of my favorite authors and I cannot wait to see what she has in store for us in the future. *The Wager* is a must-read for those who love romance and humor. It will leave a lasting impression and a huge smile on your face.

—LiteratiBookReviews.com

THE *Bet*

THE *Bet*

RACHEL VAN DYKEN

FOREVER

NEW YORK | BOSTON

Forever
Hachette Book Group
1290 Avenue of the Americas
New York, NY 10104
Hachettebookgroup.com
Twitter.com/foreverromance

Printed in the United States of America
OPM

First published as an ebook

First mass market edition: January 2016
10 9 8 7 6 5 4 3 2 1

Forever is an imprint of Grand Central Publishing.
The Forever name and logo are trademarks of Hachette Book Group, Inc.

The publisher is not responsible for websites (or their content) that are not owned by the publisher.

The Hachette Speakers Bureau provides a wide range of authors for speaking events. To find out more, go to www.hachettespeakersbureau.com or call (866) 376-6591.

ACKNOWLEDGMENTS

After writing fifteen or sixteen (I've lost count!) of these, it never gets old. I still find myself staring at the screen going, "Holy crap, I'm really an author and I'm really doing what I love!" It's incredible and I can only thank God every second of every day that He's allowed me this awesome opportunity to live in my computer and make up stories.

Thank you to Laura Heritage for being basically the best editor/friend/cover artist a gal could ask for. You do such an excellent job. I seriously don't know what I would do without you. Oh, and p.s., thanks for tutoring me on how to use commas. Also, thanks for not getting mad when I forget. Every. Single. Manuscript.

Readers. You guys rock my face off. Seriously. I would dance for you right now if it wouldn't be totally awkward and slightly inappropriate. Thank you so much for your continual support and encouragement! As always, help a girl out . . . write reviews, good or bad, doesn't matter. I'm happy either way! There's always room for improvement, right?

Follow me on Twitter @RachVD or hang out with me on Facebook: Rachel Van Dyken Author.

Happy reading . . . see ya at The End.

THE *Bet*

PROLOGUE

1997 Portland, Oregon

Kacey, wait up!" Travis ran after her, tears streaming down his face from laughing so hard. Kacey was his best friend, but only in his heart. In real life, she hated him; he just didn't know why. At eight years old he did the best he could to show her he liked her, but she always ended up getting her feelings hurt.

Girls were dumb.

His younger brother, Jake, finally caught up to them. "Why'd you do that, Travis?" He shoved him in the side.

Travis's tongue suddenly felt thick in his mouth. He wanted to explain the reasons behind tripping Kacey—really he did—but the words wouldn't come.

He hated his stutter. It made it so hard to talk, and it happened only when he was either trying really hard or in front of Kacey.

"Ugh!" Jake kicked the dirt with his foot. "Now she won't even kiss me!"

"Kiss you?" Travis yelled, horrified that his brother would even say the word *kiss*, let alone think about doing something like that with Kacey. Besides, why would his six-year-old brother get a kiss over him? "She doesn't even like you like that." He crossed his arms.

Travis at least knew that much—girls didn't like boys. They liked men, and he was well on his way to being a man. In fact, he had just found a hair on his chin. He'd most likely be shaving by the end of the week. He puffed up his chest and scowled at his brother.

"Oh yeah? Well, she hates you." Jake stuck out his tongue. "She told me so, plus…" He shoved his hands into his pockets and took a deep breath. "I'm gonna marry her."

"Are not!"

"Am too!"

"Are not!" Travis pushed his brother to the ground. "I'm older. She's going to marry me."

Jake stuck out his tongue, then brushed the dirt off his pants. "Wanna bet?"

"Yeah!" Travis sneered. "I do. A million dollars!"

"Fine!" Jake spit on his hand and held it out. "Shake on it. Blood oath."

"But there's no blood," Travis pointed out.

"Duh! Mom would kill us if we used blood. It's just as good. Kacey said so."

"Fine." Travis spit on his hand and smacked it against his little brother's.

Jake grimaced. "Gross."

"Grow up." Travis rolled his eyes and searched the backyard for Kacey. He hadn't meant to trip her. Well, actually he had, but he had a really good reason for it.

He knew for a fact that Kacey loved princess stories. She would talk about how girls are supposed to be treated like princesses, and boys are supposed to be princes.

But how was he supposed to be a prince when there were no dragons to slay?

How could he prove himself when there were no monsters?

Good thing he was the smartest kid in his class. He knew just what to do. He just had to cause the trouble and then save her from it.

First, he set her doll on fire, but that didn't work out as planned. In fact, the doll was now sitting in the garbage can. How was it his fault that the fire extinguisher didn't work?

Next, he put a snake in her sleeping bag. When she woke up screaming, he rushed to her side to grab the snake but then couldn't find it! Jake ratted him out, and Kacey was so angry she cried.

In one last final attempt to impress her, he tied her shoelaces together so she would fall and then knelt down on his knees to help her.

But she was so mad she slapped his hands away, threw off her shoes, and ran away crying.

Girls.

He would never understand them.

After all, he was trying to help her *every time*.

And every time she just pushed him away more.

Which meant only one thing. In order to win the bet, he would just have to try harder. And he knew just how to do it.

"Hey, Jake? Do you know where any rocks are?"

ONE

Kacey searched his eyes for any hint of amusement. He couldn't be serious, not Jake. Jake never took anything seriously. She quickly raised her hand to feel his forehead and inwardly shuddered. Why God had blessed such an arrogant man with the face of a movie star was seriously beyond her realm of understanding.

But there he was, a regular Adonis, staring back at her as if his eyes didn't make mortal women uncomfortable.

"Are you drunk?" she whispered, leaning in closer, all the while cursing the expensive aftershave floating off him.

Jake slapped her hand away. "No, I'm not drunk.

Geez, Kacey, you're acting like I'm propositioning you for sex or something."

"That's the example you come up with? Sex? Really? Because to be honest, Jake, this is so much worse!" Her hands shook as she tried to level her breathing to a normal pace. At this rate she was going to have a full-on panic attack.

"How is this worse?" His voice rose a few octaves as other patrons of the coffee shop looked in their direction.

Kacey leaned back against the leather chair and groaned.

"I'm dead serious, Kacey. It's the only way to convince them." Jake leaned forward, his bronzed, muscular forearms flexing against his rolled-up sleeves as he rested his hands across the table.

"You do realize your parents have known me since I was three? Furthermore, I'm convinced that your mother would be able to see right through us. And don't even get me started on that grandmother of yours."

Jake's stone face cracked into a smile.

"Don't laugh! I'm serious, Jake! The woman should have worked for the FBI."

"It's her eyes." Jake shrugged. "They always get me." He shuddered. "But you're getting off topic, Kacey. I'm desperate."

"Oh, wow. Well, when you put it that way, how could I turn you down? You're desperate! Romantic man you are not. I have no idea how you managed to become the city's most eligible bachelor, and at twenty-one. Impressive." She shook her head in disbelief.

"Really, you don't know?" He leaned forward, his biceps tightening beneath his gray button-up shirt, ready to burst through at any minute. His clean-shaven face held a hint of a five-o'clock shadow, and his dark hair fell in waves across his forehead. Clear green eyes gazed back at her, and she couldn't find the strength to look away from his lips as his tongue ran across them.

Crap. She was actually sweating just looking at the guy. It didn't help matters that this was the first time she had heard from him since *the incident*. Not that this was the time to bring that up.

"Fine." Kacey told her heart to stop beating so fast and closed her eyes again. "Jake, it won't ever work. Why don't you get one of your stripper girlfriends to do it for you?" *And please, for the love of God, leave me alone*. Too many memories stared back at her through his eyes, and she wasn't sure she could stomach it. Not after hearing that the restaurant her parents had owned just opened up two new locations, one of them in Seattle. The wound seemed to open all over again. She shuddered and let Jake continue to plead his case.

"Um, because they're strippers?" Jake lifted his hands into the air and shook his head. "Do you want my grandmother to die? Because, I assure you, that will do nothing more than cause another stroke."

Kacey paused. "Another stroke? As in she's had a few?" *Is that why Grandma Nadine hasn't written me in a month?*

Jake winced. "Yes, it's been getting worse." He ran his hands through his thick hair. "Will you help me or not? I'll pay you—"

"You'll pay me?" Kacey snorted. "Just like you pay your strippers? Why do I feel like I'm getting nothing out of this?"

Jake grinned. "Wow, I hate to pull out the big guns, but you owe me."

"I owe you?" Kacey repeated. "Oh, please tell how I owe the great Jake Titus a favor. I'm dying to know, really." She raised her eyebrows and tapped her manicured nail against the cup of cold coffee.

"Fine." He leaned back and crossed his arms over his chest. "Fifth grade, you wanted a dog. Your parents said no. So I, being the good friend I am, went to the store and bought you one."

"Doesn't count," Kacey interjected. "You named him after yourself."

"He had dark hair," Jake argued. "Besides, you slept with him every night." His grin was shameless, and Kacey wanted to punch him in the face for it.

She opened her mouth to say so, but he interrupted her.

"Eighth grade—"

"Oh, Lord."

"Eighth grade," he repeated with a wink. "You had a crush on Stevenson Merrit. I, being the friend that I am, told him that you were the best kisser in the entire school. You guys went out for a year before you dumped him for greener pastures."

"Ah, so that's how you refer to yourself nowadays. Greener pastures." Kacey smiled patronizingly.

"Yeah, well, it's true."

"Not good enough." Kacey sighed. He was so close she could smell his shampoo. A spicy masculine mix of mint and cinnamon that teased her senses with visions of a man she would never have again. Scratch that. Never had in the first place.

"Fine." Jake shook his head. "I didn't want to have to do this."

Feigning boredom, Kacey merely stared back and waited.

"Your first year of college, you had a fish, named him Stuart. Ugliest fish that ever lived."

"Hey!" She glared. "He was my best friend."

"Who you also left at school for two weeks, assuming your Mother Teresa roommate would take care of it for you."

"She always did hate that fish," Kacey grumbled.

"So who took your fish in?"

Kacey looked down at her hands.

"Who took in the fish, Kacey?"

With a large sigh, she answered, "You took in the fish, Jake."

"So I win. And again, you owe me. Plus, do you really want my grandma to die? The very same grandma who helped you win homecoming queen? The one who actually wore your macaroni necklaces? It really is quite simple. Just do it for the weekend and I'll be out of your hair."

Refusing to answer him, Kacey stared at the coffee table and licked her lips. Maybe if she looked pathetic enough he'd just leave her alone. Just being in the same room with him was enough to cause her heart to clench.

"Kace." Jake groaned. "You have no idea how important my image is to me."

"Wow, so not helping your case," Kacey snapped.

"I need this." Jake reached across the table and grabbed her hand. His hands were always so large and warm, as if by holding them, he could take away all her pain. But she knew the truth. Those same hands had destroyed her, ruined her, and in the end, those selfish hands had never handed back her heart. "I'll pay off your student loans."

"How do you even know about my student—"

"I know everything." He winked. "It's my job to. Come on. You need to finish your senior year of college, Kace. It's been three months since graduation. Do you really want to be left behind while everyone else is out there making something out of themselves?"

The guy should never try to be a lawyer. Kacey would be surprised if she had any self-confidence remaining by the time she left the coffee shop. As it was she was trying to decide if it was possible to bang her head against the coffee table hard enough to cause a concussion.

"Please," Jake pleaded. His hands squeezed hers tighter. "Do this for me. Do it for Grandma. Hell, do it for you. You have to finish school, Kace, and since your parents—"

"Don't you dare bring them into this."

Jake swallowed slowly and released her hand. His fingers danced along her jaw as he turned her head so he could look directly into her eyes. "It's only for the holiday weekend. How bad could it be? We used to be best friends."

Used being the key word. He hadn't even texted her since graduation.

"Heartless billionaire...," Kacey mumbled. The guy had no shame whatsoever. What sucked was that she really did need to finish school, and she was about to default on her loans. All the money her parents left her had gone into the house and retirement, and well, it wasn't as if Seattle University was a cheap school.

"Billionaire? Not yet, babe. Heartless?" Jake reached out and touched her face with his hand. "I think we both know the answer to that."

Memories of his touch flooded her senses until

Kacey felt like she couldn't breathe. She had traveled that road one too many times with the man. First in high school and then again in college. She hadn't thought that life would get in the way of the only man she had ever given her heart to. But Jake changed, and for that she would never forgive him. Kacey looked down at her lap and closed her eyes. How did he still have so much power over her? One touch and a bribe and she was ready to do exactly as he said.

True, she had always had a weakness for his grandmother, no matter how scary she was or was not. Plus, Grandma Nadine had been the only one to help Kacey get through the time in her life when she didn't care if she died in her sleep or went on living. The dark years were just that. Dark. Kacey shuddered to think of how bad things had gotten. If Grandma Nadine was sick and Jake was really trying to help her, and if he followed through and paid for her remaining credits, it would be worth it.

"Only the weekend?" Kacey asked in a small voice. "And you say Grandma's been all sentimental and not feeling well?"

Jake nodded. "She says she wants to see you, and I need my parents off my back about this whole press fiasco with that stripper. If I bring you home with a ring on your finger, all will be forgiven. Dad won't think he needs to jump back out of retirement, and Grandma won't shoot me. It's a win-win. Besides, like I said, image is everything and I still want to have full control of my grandmother's company at the end of the month. The board won't go for it if I keep getting bad press. I need everyone on board. We'll go our separate ways and I'll fake a breakup, cry on TV, and well, then at least the board members who hate me will feel sorry for me."

He didn't wait for her to agree. Instead, he reached into his pocket. "It's for more than just me. It's for Grandma, Kace. She isn't doing well. This may be the one thing that makes her want to keep on living."

Kacey narrowed her eyes. Lying bastard. In his twenty-one years Jake hadn't learned to lie better than that? His smile was tense, his breathing a bit ragged. But he had mentioned Grandma.

Kacey suddenly felt ill. She wanted to hop on the plane right now, but Jake didn't know she and his grandma still talked. Nor did she want him to. "Fine, but Grandma can't know about the student loans. Deal?" Kacey held out her hand, hoping Jake wouldn't notice the slight tremble.

Exhaling, Jake smiled. "Thanks for doing this for me."

Kacey looked into his crystal green eyes. "For Grandma. I'm doing it for Grandma and for me." *Not for you, never again for you, Jake.* The rest of the thought hung in the air. Suddenly the coffee shop seemed a much-too-small arena for digging up past demons. Kacey gave a shaky laugh and rubbed her sweaty hands on her jeans. Worried that he was going to somehow make it worse by smiling or offering a pity hug, she took a big gulp of coffee.

Jake pushed away from the table. "Right, okay. Well, thanks for being my fake fiancée." He pulled out a three-karat ring and confidently slipped it onto her finger.

"B-but...," she stuttered. "How did you know my size?"

He smiled and rose from his seat. "A man could never forget those hands, Kacey."

"No matter how many hands the man-whore has held?" Kacey asked sweetly.

Jake chuckled. "Absolutely. I'll see you Friday morning, okay?"

Kacey sighed. "Okay."

"Thanks, Kace..."

"Don't mention it."

Kacey watched in agony as the man who still held her heart whistled, thrust his hands into his pockets, and walked out of the coffee shop. Seattle's most famous bachelor had just proposed marriage. Albeit a fake marriage, it was still a proposal. She should be thrilled.

But it was hard to be thrilled when the love of her life, the boy who used to make mud pies with her and kiss her knees when she fell, thought of her as nothing but a way out of a crappy situation.

She suddenly wished she were at a bar instead of downtown Pike Place Market.

TWO

Jake Titus thrust his hands in his pockets. Damn, she looked good. He hadn't expected his response to be so strong. After only a few months, he had expected everything to feel exactly the same. Unfortunately, it didn't. It felt damn difficult. The woman was walking sin, curvy where guys loved it the most. Her outfit had only enhanced her curves and made lust shoot straight to the wrong places for any man sitting in a coffee shop.

Kacey's long brown hair boasted honey-blond highlights, and her deep brown eyes seemed to set everything off beautifully. Add to that the cutest two dimples on God's green earth, and he was ready to throw her onto the table and have his way with her.

If anyone could take him off the market it would be Kacey—not that he would ever let her. He'd traveled that road with Kacey one too many times. They'd dated in high school, but had soon figured they were better friends. Or maybe it was that he couldn't keep it in his pants? It was probably a mixture of both, but who really dates only one person in high school?

The final nail in their relationship coffin happened after a drunken night in college. They had slept together. It had been a good night except for the fact that he would never forgive himself for the pain he caused her the next day. But what was he supposed to do? Say "thank you"? Screwing his best friend hadn't been the wisest of choices. Unfortunately, he didn't realize it until it was too late. He was her first.

Leaving Kacey had been one of the stupidest and yet most necessary things he had ever done. They were still kind to each other, but the friendship was never the same once they slept together. What had always been rumored as a way to increase the bond between two people ended up being the catalyst that ruined a lifetime of friendship.

They avoided each other as much as possible for the next few years. At his graduation, he gave her a quick hug and never looked back.

Nor had he ever apologized.

Not that it was entirely his fault, but still.

Just seeing her again haunted him, but it was a necessary evil.

The board of directors had insisted that if he didn't clean up his image, the company would suffer. According to them, it already had. But how was he supposed to know that the girl he was sleeping with just happened to be a stripper? It was Seattle, after all, and she was beautiful. He hadn't thought she would go to the media, or that photographers would be conveniently outside the W Hotel downtown after a late-night escapade that he still couldn't fully remember. The real kicker had happened when his mother called and said his grandma had suffered a stroke because of Jake's whoring around. Clearly it wasn't his fault his grandmother had a blood clot, but still.

A week later, his grandmother had called him and given him an ultimatum. Bring Kacey to see her before she died—her words, not his—and all would be forgiven. She was so insistent that Kacey come home for Labor Day weekend that Jake couldn't say no. It just happened to work out that a photographer from *The Seattle Times* would be visiting family in Portland as well. She promised to take some pictures of the two of them together in the plane, as well as some great shots of the giant rock on Kacey's finger.

Jake grinned. Sometimes he was so brilliant he scared himself. What could possibly go wrong? He was next in line to be CEO of Titus Enterprises. It was worth a pretty penny, and once he cleaned up his image, his grandmother would not only back him but would give the board the extra push they needed to make him one of the youngest CEOs in the world.

Kacey would understand. She was just that type of girl. All he needed to do was logically explain to her why it was in her best interest. After all, not only would it help business for her to be seen with him, but he was practically investing in her future.

If anything, she should thank him!

His cell phone rang and he checked his watch. Jake shook his head. He'd spent way too long convincing that gorgeous girl to be his fiancée. Now he'd have to stay at the office longer than planned.

With a shrug, he walked to his Range Rover and jumped in. Finally, he could stop stressing about his grandmother and the business.

"I'm sorry. Could you please repeat what you just said? It sounded like you said you were engaged." Char sat across from Kacey at their favorite restaurant in Belltown.

"Yup." Kacey sipped her wine, though she briefly contemplated just taking the whole bottle and downing it. "That's what I said."

"To Jake?"

"Yup."

"Jake Titus?" Char clarified, taking a healthy gulp of her wine.

"That very person." Why couldn't Kacey stop

shaking? It was one weekend. She could do one week-end. Geez, it wasn't as if she had to do anything but pretend to be in love, and attracted to him, and excited, and...

So basically she wasn't going to act at all. She just had to make sure her heart didn't get broken into a bazillion pieces by the billionaire himself.

"I can't do this."

"Of course you can't do this," Char repeated, her voice rising a few octaves. "Do you have any idea what that man did to you in college? Are the memories still fuzzy? Because I'm pretty sure he slept with you and then pretended like it didn't happen."

"I know." Kacey's voice was shaky. "But in his defense, I never tried to talk to him either..."

"Don't defend the devil, Kace. Seriously. You guys were best friends your whole lives! Remember? I was the third wheel. I saw your love drama play out quite nicely and then get run over by a truck that night. Don't do it."

Kacey knew what Char was saying made sense, but... "I already told him I would."

"Then get out of it!"

Kacey shook her head and said in a small voice, "I can't."

Char's eyes narrowed. She took three deep breaths, then motioned for the waitress.

"Yes?" the waitress asked.

"We're going to need tequila, stat."

"Char, this is hardly the time for tequila," Kacey protested.

"Really? You just got engaged to the most famous bachelor in Seattle in order to play nice and do him a favor. Again, Exhibit A: HE LEFT YOU!"

"Keep your voice down!" Kacey hushed her friend and offered apologetic smiles to the people staring at them from their booths. "It's only the weekend." Besides, Char had no idea Kacey was still in so much debt from school. She had pulled the wool over everyone's eyes about her graduation, claiming she was only a class short, not seven.

"Right." Char snorted. "If I know Jake—and I think I do—this isn't just for the weekend. He has something up his sleeve. The more handsome they are, the more manipulative. Believe me."

The tequila was placed on the table, and Char took a shot before saying anything more. "Besides, just because you agreed to this farce of an engagement, he's going to be thinking he can put his hands all over your hot body."

Kacey rolled her eyes. "He dates models and, apparently, strippers. Look at me, Char. Do I look like either? I'm not a whore. I'm not going to let him take advantage of me."

Char grunted. "*Hmph!* Haven't let *anyone* take advantage of you since that night and you know it.

You're still hung up on him and it's taken you all of college to get over it! And now you'll be back to square one."

Ignoring Char's obvious slight to her ability to get a man, Kacey looked away and huffed. Her fingers touched the edge of the tequila bottle, and thoughts of Jake poured in of their own accord.

"What the hell am I doing?"

"Now she says it." Char shook her head and took another shot.

"I mean…" Kacey looked down at her hands. "I have to be alone with him for more than three days, and even then I have to lie to his entire family!"

"And let's be honest," Char interjected, her speech slightly louder than normal. "You're, like, the worst liar on the planet."

"Am not." Travis, Jake's beast of a brother, was. But Kacey refused to think about Travis. The last time she saw him, he yelled at her for running over their mailbox during Christmas break. She cried; he yelled some more and then refused to speak to her the rest of the time she was visiting. That was three years ago.

"Are too!" Char poked her manicured finger across the table. "Remember that one time we tried to sneak out of the house and go to Jake's birthday party in high school?"

"No," Kacey lied, trying desperately to swallow the giant lump of guilt in her throat.

"Really? Out of all the times during this day that you would say no, you choose now? Seriously? What happened to no when you were talking to Jake? Or no when he was propositioning you for—"

"Totally different and you know it. Besides, I would like to point out that I didn't tell my mom a terrible lie. If the dog had stopped barking, then..."

Char threw her head back and laughed. "Let's not blame the dog. Even if the dog had stopped barking, you used that as an excuse to admit all to your mom. And later told me it was a sign from God that you were sinning."

Kacey looked away. Just because her friend was totally right didn't mean she had to actually acknowledge the fact. So what? Yeah, she was a little bit of a prude, but the one time, *the one time* she had decided in her life to go for it...

She was royally screwed.

In more ways than one.

Kacey let out a large sigh and motioned for Char to pour her a shot. "Regardless, I said yes, and you know how I am with commitment."

Char swore. "You're more loyal than my dog, and he's blind, meaning he depends on me for everything, including when and where to go pee."

"Your encouragement is astonishing." Kacey smiled sweetly and followed her shot with a large gulp of water. She needed a clear head if she was to adequately plan how the weekend was going to progress. One thing was for sure. Jake couldn't touch her—he couldn't put one of his hands on her. If he did, she wasn't sure if she would be able to say no.

"...and another thing..."

Oh gosh! Was Char still talking about her damn dog?

"If you let him touch you, or kiss you..." She slammed her fist on the table, her eyes slightly glazed over from the tequila. "If one of his perfectly manicured hands even grazes across your bare flesh, I'll castrate him."

Kacey pursed her lips together and nodded. "Thanks, Char. I don't know what I'd do without you."

"Me eisher..." Char hiccupped, and Kacey motioned for the check. Truly, it's not every day a friend gets wasted on your behalf. But Kacey knew better too. Char was the truest type of friend. When Kacey cried, Char cried. When Kacey threatened to kill Jake, Char offered to pay for a hit man, and when Kacey finally moved on and mentioned Jake only as the *man who shall not be named*, Char went ahead and nicknamed him *Bastard* for her sake.

If anything, Char was just trying to help, though her methods were a little extreme.

Kacey laid out a couple of bills on the check and helped her friend out, all the while wondering how she was going to get through the next week without dying.

THREE

"Are you out of your mind?" Travis yelled. "You blackmailed and then hired Kacey? As in the same Kacey you used to take baths with? That Kacey?"

Jake wasn't in the mood to defend himself to his brother. Seriously, why was it such a big deal? So what that he'd called in a favor? "Sorry, man, I have a lot of work tonight. Can we do this later?"

Travis was silent for a while, which really wasn't a good sign. It meant he was thinking, which meant he was probably going to get a headache and then blame Jake for it in the morning. He and Travis hadn't talked much in the past few years. That is, until their grandmother began meddling in their lives this past year. Poor Travis had been left out of it for the most part, but his number was almost up.

Out of the two brothers in the family, Travis had been the protector, the one who always played by the rules. When Jake and Kacey would set off fireworks at 2:00 a.m., Travis was always the one who took the fall. He never liked seeing Jake in trouble, or Kacey.

Which is why, when Jake messed up so horribly in college with his best friend, Travis had sworn he would never forgive him for being such an ass to the one girl who seemed to have it all. Though Jake hadn't told Travis the real reasons they had a falling out, he assumed his brother probably thought the worst. If Jake hadn't been so sure of Travis's feelings toward Kacey, he would have thought his big brother had a bit of a crush on her.

But that was impossible. If anything, Travis tortured Kacey more than Jake did, which was really saying a lot, because he had pulled his fair share of pranks when he was little.

Travis, however, took the cake. A day didn't go by where he wasn't pulling Kacey's hair, throwing rocks, or starting a Girls Are Ugly and Stupid Club and then electing Kacey as its mascot.

The silence on the other end of the phone broke. "I'm just not sure it's the best idea, man. I mean, this is the girl who saw you naked before you hit puberty. Mom's gonna know something's up."

"No." Jake cursed and ran his fingers through his

hair. "She won't know because we won't be the ones to tell her, will we, Travis?"

"You do realize that out of everyone in our family, I'm the worst liar?" Travis asked.

"No, no, you're not. Kacey is..."

"Oh well, in that case..." Travis cursed on the other line.

"It doesn't matter. It means too much to Kacey at this point. Plus, do you really want Grandma to die?"

"Um, she's going to do more than die if she finds out you're lying. Ten bucks says she has a stroke, then pleads with God to let her come back to kill you herself. Trust me, if anyone's got the *in* with God, it's Grandma. Geez, He'd probably help her plan your demise..."

"Are you done? I wasn't kidding about the work. If we're supposed to be in Portland by Friday, I have to get all this paperwork cleared."

Travis sighed on the other end again, probably cursing Jake to hell for making him swear his loyalty and silence. "Fine, but when this blows up in your face, and it will, I'm feigning ignorance."

Jake snorted. "Trust me, nobody's going to believe you were part of such a brilliant plan."

"Right, well, good luck. You're going to need it." The line went dead, leaving Jake alone with his thoughts.

Perhaps it would be best not to tell Kacey that her childhood nemesis would be present at the weekend retreat with his family. After all, if she knew Satan (her words, not his) was to make an appearance, she'd back out in a minute.

The computer hummed from the cluttered desk. He was all alone in his office with a mountain of paperwork. Paperwork he wasn't very inclined to finish since seeing Kacey that day.

When had she grown up so much? And filled out the way she had? He let out a groan. Maybe he was just exhausted. He had plenty of other women banging down his door.

Every woman but the one who got away. What the hell? Did he really think that he let her get away? He shook his head.

It didn't matter anymore. It was for the best. He knew after it happened that he wasn't good for her, that she would always be looking to him to be something that he wasn't. Kacey always had such high expectations. He was a guy, and since she had no brothers, he thought it more of a hero worship thing.

Until she gave him the look.

He was done for. The one and only time in his life he had given in to fully ruining his best friend was the same night he lost the only girl he could have ever seen himself with.

He cursed and pushed the papers off his desk.

He would have killed her spirit. She would have slowly died next to him, and he would have resented her. They would have resented each other for not being what each of them needed.

So why, in all of his brilliance, had he decided to call in a favor from her? He could have easily brought Kacey home to Grandma without this farce of an engagement. Sure, his parents wouldn't have been nearly as happy, but it would have still been fine. Maybe he was subconsciously trying to right a wrong. Being with him could only further her likability, but he could have paid anyone to spend the weekend with him. Hell, he probably wouldn't have even had to pay.

Jake's paperwork stared back at him. He left it on the floor and turned off the lights, locking his office and strolling toward the elevators.

"Why did I pick her?" Jake rubbed the back of his neck.

He pushed the button for the lobby and sighed, answering his own question. "Because she's the only one my family would believe I had fallen madly and deeply in love with."

"Ready!" Kacey threw open the door to her apartment, wearing tight-fitting running spandex, an oversize sweatshirt that fell quite nicely over her shoulder, and a messy bun.

Every man's worst nightmare. A girl who actually looks good without trying. "And don't worry. I packed really light!" She flashed a brilliant smile and pulled out two small bags.

Jake nodded his approval. "I must say I'm impressed."

Kacey did a little curtsy. "I do live for your approval."

"As you should." Jake laughed.

"Now, bring my stuff down to the car, slave. I'm your tired fiancée, so the doting must start."

"Doting?"

"Yup." She pulled her door shut and locked it. "You know, you have to actually treat me like you find me attractive, sexy, the best thing to hop into your bed since—"

Kacey froze midsentence, a look of pure horror crossing her face. Jake didn't know what to do, wasn't sure if he should hug her, ignore her, or just apologize for being a complete ass over everything that went down between them.

"Um, Kace—"

"So, we should get going!" She hit him on the shoulder and jogged past him, leaving him the tedious task of carrying her luggage down three flights of stairs.

In all honesty, it was like atonement for his many sins. Really, he would rather be stabbed than have to see that look of pain in Kacey's eyes. It was as if someone had just told her Disneyland wasn't real.

By the time he reached the car, Kacey was already waiting next to it. "Nice ride."

"I, uh..." Why was he suddenly feeling uncomfortable about his success? "It's good, I guess."

He opened the door to the new SUV and helped her in. All hints of being upset had left her face. Kacey was now jabbering on about how much she liked SUVs and why he'd made a good choice, but all he could really focus on was her lips as they moved, fast and then, suddenly, erotically slow.

"Did you get your lips plumped or something?" Jake interrupted. As the words left his mouth, he seriously wanted to rewind time so he could slap himself.

"My lips? Done?" Kacey laughed. "No, Jake. You're just confused because you date so many women who have fake lips, breasts, and hips that you forget what a real woman looks like."

Throat suddenly dry, Jake turned away. "Right, well. Okay."

Idiot, idiot, idiot. "So, you sure you can handle the forty-five-minute flight?"

Jake thought he heard Kacey mumble "bastard" under her breath but couldn't be sure.

"I'll have you know that I've flown plenty since that little incident." She crossed her arms over her chest. "I believe you're referring to the time I saved an old man's life?"

"Saved his life?" Jake burst out laughing. "Kace, you almost killed him! He had a weak heart, and you kept hitting him across the chest because of the turbulence. You were mom-arming him like crazy! I'm surprised he didn't sue you!"

"He thanked me." Kacey lifted her chin and looked out the window.

"Um, he did nothing of the sort. He thanked me, not you. And the only reason he said 'thank you' was because I put Benadryl in your soda so you'd stop freaking everyone out."

"I knew I couldn't have been that tired!" Kacey nearly shouted.

At Jake's patronizing look, she locked her eyes on the road in front of them and murmured, "I've grown up since the last time you saw me. You should know that, Jake."

Oh, he knew it all right; he just wasn't ready to admit it—or anything else for that matter. The girl had done a lot of growing up and he was very appreciative of said growing.

"Anyway…" Kacey let out a huff of air. "I'm not afraid of flying anymore."

"Swear?"

"Swear." She crossed her heart and winked.

Kacey gripped the seat so hard her fingers were numb. What the heck? Why were they taking so long getting the plane ready? If her forehead were pressed any tighter to the window, the glass would break.

"So, not afraid of flying anymore, hmm?" Jake's breath tickled her ear as he pushed his body next to hers. "Liar." His deep voice caused fluttering in her stomach. She refused to turn and look at his perfectly chiseled face. Damn him.

"How do we know they're really doing their jobs? I mean, if checking the plane is so important, why are they all smiling?"

Jake's warm hand cupped her chin forcefully, pulling her away from her stakeout. "People smile, Kacey, and a happy worker is a good worker. Maybe he's just really excited about his job."

"Or our deaths...," Kacey mumbled to herself. Seriously! Her eyes scanned the rest of the passengers. All of them reading or talking. *Why aren't they on the lookout? I mean, as Americans, it's their job—nay, their duty—to look for suspicious characters.* Her eyes darted around the small plane, landing finally on a large man who seemed to be talking into his jacket.

"Holy hell." Kacey grabbed Jake's hand. "That man is talking into his jacket. Do you know what that means?"

"He's insane?" Jake offered. "Like my fake fiancée? Seriously, Kace, if you can't calm down, I'm going to drug you again, and it's not going to be Benadryl..."

"Fine." Kacey leaned back and tried to relax, but the minute she closed her eyes, she remembered she was still holding Jake's hand and he was holding hers back.

Oh crap. It was like sixth grade skate night all over again.

Only worse, because this time the song didn't end. It was a forty-five-minute plane ride, and she had started the whole thing holding his hand. What could he possibly think of her?

Jake's thumb rubbed across her fingers delicately.

Another involuntary shiver ran down her spine. *It's not real, Kacey. Just remember it's not real. He doesn't really like you in that way. Do it for Grandma!*

The plane began to taxi and the pressure of Jake's hand increased just as her palm pushed into his. If the man had any feeling left in his arm at all, she would be shocked.

"Kacey?" he whispered, again dangerously close to her face.

"Hmm?" She refused to open her eyes.

"Let's make out."

"What!" Kacey's eyes flashed open to see the mocking grin on Jake's face. "You can't be serious."

"I'm dead serious. The way I see it, we need to have some chemistry before we get to Portland. Also, the way you're going, they're going to have to saw off my arm because of blood loss. So really, you're doing me a favor all around."

Kacey's eyes squinted. "You're too good-looking."

"Wow, nice change of subject. Thank you, but not where I was going with that."

Kacey closed her eyes again and cursed her smart best friend who had warned her of such things happening. Of course Jake had something else up his sleeve; she just didn't think it would include him making out with her on an airplane.

Not that it sounded completely horrible or anything.

"We made out in L.A.," he said, still holding her hand.

"Oh, you dirty little liar!" Kacey laughed and pushed his hand away. "You made out with me, and after a while, I participated."

"Your tongue down my throat the minute we took off wasn't participating?"

"Nope, it was an experiment."

"You realize you explain everything away with an excuse, right, Kacey? How about this? I dare you."

Kacey snorted. "To do what?"

"Make out, like we're in high school."

"I don't make out."

Jake laughed, his dimples dancing on his face. "Neither do I, sweetheart. Neither do I."

His lips came crushing down on hers with such force that she could only relent and allow him to push her back into her seat. Hot and hungry, his mouth slanted across hers with heady need. Everything was the same. From the taste of his lips to the pressure of his tongue as it pushed into her mouth.

And then, just as she was getting ready to rub her hands through his hair, just as she had made the decision to allow her tongue the luxury of tangling with his, he pulled back.

"See?" He patted her on the hand. "Don't you feel better now?"

His question was truly the type of thing that guys always say. *Are you happy now? Do you feel better now? Wasn't that great, baby?* Seriously, the man should count himself lucky that she didn't smack him across his gorgeous face.

"I've had better." She shrugged and closed her eyes, feigning sleep, knowing it would be a long shot if he believed her to be able to sleep, flying on a death-mobile through the sky.

"I know you're not sleeping." Jake's deep timbre sparked a nerve within her, making gooseflesh pop up around her arms.

"Leave me alone, man-whore. I'm trying to forget about the creepy man talking into his suit, the way-too-cheerful plane-checker people, and the fact that I'm willingly going into the lions' den with a man who pays strippers. I think I deserve some shut-eye, don't you?"

Silence ensued, making Kacey think she had won…that is, until she felt Jake brush his hand across her arm. "Why sleep when we could talk?"

"Yes," Kacey said, forcing her eyes to stay closed. *I will not look into his hypnotic eyes. I will not look into his hypnotic eyes.* "Let's talk about the fact that you're manipulating me as well as asking me to convince your entire family that I love you. As if that were possible. And seriously, how are they going to fall for this? Don't you go home, ever? Aren't they going to be suspicious when you miraculously show up with me in tow?"

Jake cleared his throat. "Not really. Say, do you need something to drink? Water? Scotch?"

Hmm, deliberate change of subject. What the hell is up Jake's sleeve? "Jake?" Kacey used her sweet voice. "What makes you think they'll fall for it? Really, I think I deserve to know."

Kacey opened her eyes to see Jake staring straight ahead, no movements, just staring. In all honesty, she wondered if he was breathing at all, he seemed so tense. The flight attendant showed up in time for Jake to motion for a drink.

He downed two shots of scotch but continued to stare, and the plane hadn't even taken off yet.

"Jake?"

"Shit..." He looked down at the floor. "They don't know...about us."

"What do you mean?" Kacey truly was concerned he was drunk at this point. What the heck was he talking about?

Jake cursed again. "Kace, they don't know we had somewhat of a falling out. Okay?"

"Okay?" Kacey repeated as she mumbled a curse underneath her breath. "So tell me, what do they know?"

Jake exhaled. "All they know is that we've grown apart, yet still managed to stay in touch over the last few years of school, okay? It's possible I've led them to assume we still hang out once a week. I update them about your life and work at the coffee shop, and that's basically it."

Kacey laughed. "But how would they know that? I mean, you didn't even—"

Jake gave her a guilty look and fidgeted with his hands.

"Jake? How do they know all that?"

Grandma Nadine had always sworn that she wouldn't update the family on Kacey's life. It was inconceivable that she would break that promise.

"I told them, all right?" Jake all but yelled. "Geez, Kace, stop with the third degree, okay? So what? I've kept tabs on you. I know all about you. Just leave it be. It would have killed them to know I screwed—"

"Your best friend," Kacey finished.

Jake refused to make eye contact, just continued to stare straight ahead. He said nothing, not that it was all that surprising. It was what he was good at.

Saying nothing when she needed him to be saying something—anything to make her feel better.

"This is your captain. We are first for takeoff, so if you'd just sit back and relax, we'll have you in Portland within the hour."

FOUR

He was a rotten bastard.

The photographer he'd hired to spy on them got a few clicks in before turning back around.

It shouldn't have been that easy to get Kacey to kiss him, and now he felt like the biggest ass on the planet. But they had to look in love! It needed to look serious! The hand-holding wasn't enough.

So he went in for the kill.

And then opened his big fat mouth again. What the hell had he been thinking? Their past history created a giant chasm between them, one that he wasn't sure he could fix.

The silence was going to kill him. He needed to think fast, but the only words that seemed to come to mind were "I'm sorry. I'm an ass. All men should burn." And truly that just seemed like he was traitor to the male population as a whole.

Plus, Kacey had plenty of opportunities to talk to him as well. The phone did work both ways. So what if he kept tabs on her? It wasn't as if she hadn't kept tabs on him.

He smirked and gave her a chilling glare. "Tell me you haven't done the exact same thing to me, and I'll let you fly back to Seattle."

Kacey shook her head and looked down at her hands.

"What?" He nudged her. "No answer?"

She shook her head one more time and sent him a seething glare. "Curse you, Jake Titus. A hex on your fancy car, your apartment, and your little dog!"

"Um, Kace, if you're going to include all my worldly possessions in your little hexing to make yourself feel better and all, well, maybe you should include my yacht, my three summer homes, my twenty-seven cars, and my goldfish, Sid."

He gave a smug wink and folded his arms across his chest.

"What the h—"

The woman was trying to kill him! Kacey pinched the underside of his arm with such force he thought he was going to lose vision in his left eye.

"Don't!"

Kacey twisted the flesh and released it.

Yes, a nasty bruise would definitely make itself known soon.

"Don't you ever throw your money in my face like that. It isn't polite, it isn't nice, and I remember you before you had it all!"

Jake shook his head. "Kace, I've always had money."

The plane began to taxi and Kacey reached for his hand. "Not as much money as you have now. Admit it. I knew you when you had zits."

He felt his face burn crimson. "I never had zits."

"Don't lie, Jake. I also remember when you used to dream of owning a chicken farm."

"I was seven!"

"You were adorable." She smirked, reaching out with her free hand and patting his head, still keeping her other hand in his. He wasn't sure if she knew that she was clenching his hand that tight, but it was obvious her fear was still ridiculously out of control.

"Also…" Her luscious mouth burst into a smile. "I was your first kiss."

Jake closed his eyes against the onslaught of memories her admission created. "Okay, yes, so I was your first kiss…"

"Before all the strippers."

"Keep your voice down, Kace!" He shushed her.

"Before you knew what French kissing was."

She laughed. *"Kacey, Kacey, what do I do with my tongue?"* she mocked.

"Hilarious." He shifted in his seat and cracked his neck.

"Is it supposed to feel funny?" She continued mocking him and burst out laughing.

FIVE

The woman was obviously insane and asking for trouble. Who holds something like that over someone's head? Of course he didn't know what to do with his tongue! He was twelve! Any guy would have been flustered, especially with Kacey as the kissing partner!

It was her braids. Lord, but she had the longest braids of any little girl he'd ever seen. Naturally, he tugged on them whenever the opportunity presented itself and then in a fit of desperation threw rocks at her when she wouldn't chase him anymore.

Obviously in need of attention, he went in for a kiss and was pleasantly surprised when her mouth opened in a scream for him to stop, and his tongue slipped in.

He'd like to think it was purely instinctual, but

Kacey ruined that thought the minute she started making fun of him.

As if she could point fingers, the girl was literally cutting off all the circulation to his left arm.

"Kacey, do you think you can make it?" he asked, trying to pry her death grip away from his arm. He still held her other hand and knew it would be stupid to let it go.

Mainly because holding her hand felt good.

And he wasn't lying about her having nice hands.

He'd be a fool to let her go.

Again.

Damn, he needed to get laid. At the rate he was going, they would be married by the end of the weekend. The sappy sentimental Jake needed to be punched in the face.

"Forty-five minutes," Kacey chanted. "Just forty-five minutes!" Maniacal laughter came from her lips. "I mean, I can do anything for forty-five minutes, right? Right?"

Apparently it wasn't a rhetorical question. "Er, right. I'm sure you can handle it, Kace."

"If he orders a drink, I'll calm down." She nodded her head as the plane began to take off.

Saying good-bye to not only his sanity but all the blood that Kacey was currently draining from his arm, Jake winced and tried to gather what nonsense she was spouting off this time.

"If who orders a drink?"

"The guy talking into his jacket. If he orders a drink, he's not a terrorist, and if he doesn't, you have to save the plane if it goes down."

"There are so very many things wrong with that sentence. First off, how does his drinking alcohol prove anything? Second, why would I have to save the plane?"

Kacey rolled her eyes, finally relinquishing her grip on his arm. *Thank God.* "The way I see it, he's going to want a clear head if he has to wave a gun around." Oh great. Not only had Kacey just said *terrorist* on a plane, but the word *gun*. Crap. If there were air marshals on the plane, he was throwing her under the bus. No hesitation.

"And what about my saving everyone?" Jake prayed for the flight attendant to hurry with the beverage service. At the rate he was going, he'd be totally wasted by the time they landed.

Kacey gave him a look of pure stupidity. "You're a guy. It's what guys do."

"Save complete strangers?" He waved at the flight attendant. Seriously, what the hell was taking her so long?

"Yes, well, no. I mean…" Kacey let go of his arm completely. "It's what you do. You fix things."

"Not all things." The phrase hung in the air, making Jake feel tenser, if that were even possible.

After a few minutes of silence, in which Jake contemplated taking over the plane himself if it would make Kacey talk again, the flight attendant brought the cart down the aisle.

"What would you two like?" She handed Jake napkins and gave them each a packet of pretzels.

Kacey opened her mouth to speak, but Jake clapped a hand over it before she got a word in. "We'd like two mini bottles of vodka." Kacey bit his hand. "Make that four, thanks."

Kacey rolled her eyes after he set the cup of ice in front of her and poured her two of the bottles. "Drink this."

"I don't need alcohol. I'm fine!"

"Says the girl who just accused a clergyman of being a terrorist." Jake pointed to the man she had just been accusing. Jacket now removed, a very visible clerical collar peeked through, showing his profession.

Kacey cursed.

"Hey, now!" Jake elbowed her. "We're in the presence of God, now drink up."

"You do realize you used *God* and *drink* in the same sentence, right?" Kacey grumbled, throwing back the clear liquid. "Holy crap! That tastes like sh—"

"Sugar!" Jake interrupted with a laugh and cough. The clergyman turned around and gave them a peculiar look before glancing back at his magazine.

"I don't think I believe you anymore." Jake drank his vodka as fast as humanly possible.

"What do you mean?" Kacey croaked.

"You can't do anything for forty-five minutes. It's been ten and I'm ready to parachute out of this thing."

"Just be thankful you're not really engaged to me." Kacey winked and laid her head back against the seat.

"Oh, believe me, I am." Jake's tone was slightly nasty, but it was the only way to keep ideas out of her head. He needed to stay as far away from Kacey as possible, and the only way he could do it was to be a complete ass. At least then his heart wouldn't be in danger of getting lost for the second time, and he could hopefully keep hers intact.

SIX

Liar," Kacey mumbled a half hour later.

"Excuse me?" Jake looked up from his laptop and squinted. The idiot had spent the entire flight using the Wi-Fi on the plane, sending business emails like they were going out of style.

Meanwhile, Kacey was checking out every single shady character on the plane and studying the diagram in front of her just in case she had to make an escape.

Well, the joke would be on Jake when the plane crashed. She would know at least seven different ways to exit the plane as well as the quickest way to get to any door, while he would probably save his laptop and every other worldly possession he owned.

Perhaps she had built him up in her mind too much? As a friend he had been great. And yes, every other kiss had paled in comparison to his. But if things were different, if they had stayed friends or maybe even gotten married, would her life be so wonderful?

Or would she be flying around with him, watching, while he paid more attention to his laptop than he did to the fact that she was having a major panic attack?

"Fifteen minutes," she mumbled to herself, forgetting that she had actually just accused Jake of lying.

"First you accuse me of lying, and now you're giving me a countdown? You okay, Kace?"

"Fine." She clenched and ground her teeth as she watched him shrug and look back at his computer.

The temptation to smash his computer with her bare hands was strong, but it would accomplish nothing other than ruining her nails, which she had worked hard to perfect hours before. Not that Jake would notice.

"It's only fifteen more minutes," she chanted more to herself than to the idiot next to her. "Plus? It's not as if things are going to get any worse, right? I mean, it's not as if Travis is going to be there." Kacey suddenly felt so much better.

Jake's brother, Travis, had been the bane of her existence. While Jake chased and played with her, Travis wouldn't give her any attention at all. Well, that wasn't entirely true. When she was really little he was relentless. And then he suddenly stopped. It was simply like she didn't exist. And she wasn't sure why it bothered her so much, but he always seemed to be irritated with her when she was young. Kacey was his little brother's best friend. She could count on one hand the number of times he had actually spoken to her, and each time she ended up crying and running away, while Travis continued to taunt her.

Outwardly shuddering, Kacey managed to stay silent the rest of the flight.

He knew he was being rude, but he had business to finish up, and well, Kacey needed to understand that some things were just more important. It wasn't as if he didn't care that she was hyperventilating next to him, but he couldn't just drop everything in order to cater to her every fear.

Geez, he'd be catering to her all night, and he had a few things he needed to finish up. Because she looked so good in what she was wearing, it was taking him three times as long to even finish his emails, let alone put together sentences that would make sense to his colleagues.

Jake had never been so happy for a plane to land. He pulled out his cell to text his mom that they had arrived.

His phone beeped immediately; he looked down and felt the blood drain from his face.

"Shit."

"What? What is it? Is it Grandma? Oh my gosh, Jake, I have to see her. Is she okay?" Kacey was gripping that same arm she had pinched earlier. He was going to have to have plastic surgery to remove the imprints of her fingers on his arm.

"No, not Grandma." Wanting nothing more than to slam his phone against the seat or crush it in his hand, he managed a tight smile. "Mom can't pick us up. Her nail appointment ran late and she had to run home to put dinner in, so someone else has to get us."

"Oh." Kacey shrugged and reached for her purse.

Oh God. He looked up and sent a prayer heavenward. "So yeah, um, and Dad is helping grocery shop and Grandma's most likely sleeping, so um, Travis is gonna come get us."

Kacey froze. "Your brother, Travis?" People began shuffling into the aisle. Maybe he could make a run for it. Or jump off the plane and break something so she'd feel sorry for him. He looked at her face, not even a hint of a smile.

"Come on, Kace, it's not that bad. Travis is a grown man. Get over it." *Oh wow, that was sensitive.*

Apparently Kacey thought so too. Her nostrils flared. She nudged past him, nearly knocking an old man to his knees. Great, maybe Kacey would get him sued for assault.

"Excuse her," Jake mumbled as Kacey continued to move toward the exit. Luckily, it wasn't a very full flight, so she was able to make it without causing any more physical harm to the other passengers.

He cursed and grabbed his carry-on, then followed her out.

SEVEN

She couldn't believe it! What the hell? Travis had to pick them up? Wasn't Jake rich enough to get them a car or something? Curse his family and their closeness. Mr. Titus wouldn't allow it—that much she knew. For as much money as they had, they sure reminded her of *Father Knows Best*. Grinding her teeth, she walked to the baggage claim and cringed when she heard the voice that still haunted her every waking nightmare.

"Well, well, well. Look what we have here." Travis's smooth voice seemed to rumble in her chest.

Stupid man.

Dear God, please have mercy and let him be bald and fat.

Slowly, she turned and faced her nemesis.

Hell.

Would it have been too much to ask for him to at least not have grown into his perfect nose?

"Kacey." He nodded.

"Satan."

"Your hair's different."

Kacey flinched. "You've grown into your nose."

Jake walked up and stood between them. "Can you guys at least pretend to play nice?"

"No," they said in unison.

"Look…" Jake glanced at his phone. "This is work. I've gotta take this. Travis, can you drop me off at the Portland office and then take Kacey to the house?"

"Pretty sure Mom's going to be upset if you don't make it home for dinner. Not that I'm scared to be alone with this one." He pointed to Kacey. "But last time we were alone in the car, she nearly killed me."

"Don't be a drama queen," Kacey huffed.

"Drama queen?" Travis raised an eyebrow. "There was a cliff, snow, and I'm pretty sure Benadryl was involved."

"Always is." Jake shook his head.

"Anyway, she's really looking forward to seeing you, and Grandma refuses to take a nap until she sets eyes on you."

Jake shrugged. "I won't be long. Now, let's grab our stuff so we can get a move on."

Kacey was suddenly exhausted, and the fight left

her. She mumbled *bastard* under her breath, not really caring who took offense, considering both Titus brothers deserved the title, and hauled her bag over her shoulder.

They hadn't checked any bags, so she followed the men to the waiting car. A limo! That was more like it! Visions of seltzer and leather seats danced in her head. That is, until Travis bypassed the limo and went to the driver's seat of a Ford truck with a lift kit.

She'd have to beam herself up in order to even reach the door.

"Hey, Travis, can you help Kacey? I've got another email I need to answer really quick." Without even glancing in her direction, Jake hauled himself into the truck and slammed the door, leaving Kacey very much ticked off.

"We're so in love." Kacey sighed to herself as Travis walked around the truck to help her in.

God alive, he was ridiculously gorgeous. Since when had his looks surpassed his brother's? No doubt, he was the most eligible bachelor in Portland. With his curly golden brown hair and hazel eyes, he looked dangerous and brooding. Not to mention the way his hair fell over his forehead or the biceps that bulged out of his T-shirt. Must. Stop. Looking.

"Kace?" Travis leaned in, his breath hot on her neck. What the heck was he doing? "Don't move, Kace."

Don't move? How about stop breathing? She couldn't think, couldn't respond, as Travis reached around and grabbed something off her back and threw it to the ground. "No biggie. Just a spider."

"It was huge!" Kacey gasped and grabbed at whatever was in front of her, which just so happened to be Travis's biceps.

"Hmm." His eyelashes fanned across his cheekbones, his very chiseled, cursed cheekbones. "If I knew you would react this way, I'd have put spiders in your bed."

"You and your spiders are not welcome in my bed. Ever."

"I wasn't offering myself, just the spiders." He winked. "Besides, what makes you think I'd find you appealing? I have seen you naked, twice."

"I was ten and you were an evil little boy with a stutter!" Kacey pushed past him, then realized she still had to be lifted into his giant truck. "Would it be too much to ask for you to at least drive a normal car in the city?"

"I don't live in the city." He smoldered. *Wait. Do guys smolder?* She looked again. Apparently they did.

"Where do you live?"

"On my ranch." *Merciful Lord above.* That explained the biceps and tight jeans and truck and… where was the Benadryl when she needed it?

"So you're a ranch hand?"

Travis chuckled. "Sure, I'm a ranch hand. Now get in." His touch was quick, too quick, as he eased her into the truck. "Don't forget to buckle up, princess. I drive like I ride."

Disgusting.

Kacey forced her cheeks to stay pale instead of burnt crimson. She pulled out her cell phone as the truck door slammed. Soon Travis was in the driver's seat and they were taking off.

Jake turned around. "So, I know we've gone over specifics on the plane, and I think the kissing really did help set the mood, don't you?" He winked.

The truck swerved.

Jake swore. "Been driving long?"

"Sorry," Travis muttered.

"So what I think we need to do is stay in the same room. You know, really sell the whole thing. Thoughts?"

Memories of their one night together came flooding back. Was he really trying to do what was best or was he seducing her? She had no idea. Besides, why was it so important for him to show his parents that he could be in a committed relationship? It's not as if they lived under a rock. They read the newspapers. His mom would probably laugh in their faces the minute she saw the ring.

Travis cleared his throat. "Actually, Mom would never go for that. She's real protective of Kacey. You know that, Jake. She'll have to stay in my old room. I'll stay in the new part of the house."

"Oh." Jake shrugged. "Okay. Now remember, Kacey, we're in love, we're getting married, and you have to make it believable. Think you can do that?"

Why was he talking to her like she was a five-year-old? "Yeah, I think I can handle acting like a normal human being in front of your family. They won't suspect a thing."

Jake turned around and gave her a brilliant smile as he reached for her hand. She felt his lingering kiss and suddenly was repulsed by his haughty attitude. She really did feel like a stripper, and a poorly paid whore.

EIGHT

Travis couldn't remember a time when he had been so frustrated. Nothing sounded better than pulling over the truck and giving his little brother a piece of his mind, or his fist.

What the hell had he been thinking? To kiss Kacey? After everything that rat bastard had put her through? What was more sickening was that Kacey seemed fine with the whole ordeal. It was as if she were selling her soul to the devil.

But in her defense, she had always looked at Jake through rose-colored glasses, whereas Travis with his stutter was the evil big brother set out to ruin the world, one ponytail tug at a time.

How was it that one look from the girl could put him back in high school, when she'd chosen his brother over him? Not that she knew of his ridiculous crush. And his stutter hadn't helped matters. If anything, it had made it worse. She took his silence as hatred, when instead he was afraid to open his mouth because his stutter worsened when he put pressure on himself to talk smoothly.

It had been much easier to chase the girl and taunt her than give her the pretty words Jake so often did.

But that didn't mean his heart wasn't involved.

Stifling a curse, he pulled into downtown. Luckily, the office was only a few minutes from his parents' house.

The tall high-rise sparkled through the dreary rain, the booming name of Titus Enterprises blaring above the cityscape. Fighting the urge to scowl at the obvious money the building represented, he shook his head slightly. He hadn't wanted a part in the family business. Nope, that job had gone to his little brother, and he could keep it.

Travis had used the trust fund in his name to open his own ranch and breed horses. It also doubled as a bed-and-breakfast. A beautiful twenty acres overlooking the Columbia River. It was living, whereas being in the city was stifling. He pulled at his shirt.

Travis pulled the truck to a stop and Jake hopped out. "I'll call for a car when I'm done. I shouldn't be more than an hour. See ya, and, Kacey, try not to kill Travis while I'm gone, okay?"

"Can't make any promises!" Kacey waved him off and turned hate-filled eyes toward Travis. "So, you have any immediate plans to kill me and bury the body?"

"Under a tree, I think." Travis put the truck into gear and moved into traffic. "Or maybe under the swing set. They'd never look for you there."

"Ha-ha, you're hilarious."

"I like to think so. Now, what's this I hear about Jake kissing you? I mean, I know it's none of my business, but shouldn't you be keeping this strictly professional? After all, he is paying you—"

"Like one of his prostitutes. I know," Kacey finished. "But technically he's not paying me. I mean he is. He's paying off my school loans. Besides, I'm doing this for Grandma. And somehow I've found that inside my chest beats a very large heart. I do kind of owe Jake. Or at least he made me feel like I did."

"I wasn't going to say that you were a prostitute." Travis coughed. "So he really does have strippers as girlfriends?" Travis shook his head with disapproval. "Maybe we should leave that little tidbit out this weekend. My grandma's health and all."

"Agreed." Kacey snorted. "She'd have a stroke if she knew how egotistical our young little Jake has gotten. But I love him regardless." Kacey sighed.

"Apparently, otherwise you wouldn't be here. But then again...things aren't always what they seem, are they, Kace?" Travis cleared his throat.

"Just drive the truck, Travis. I'm hungry and my stomach is in knots from that stupid plane ride."

Travis put the truck into gear. "Still afraid of flying?"

"I thought I was over it, but then I accused a clergy-man of being a terrorist."

Travis laughed. "Out loud? Damn, woman, maybe you should take the train back."

Kacey's eyes lit up. "Brilliant plan, but it takes three hours."

"They have a bar."

"Where do you buy tickets?"

Travis chuckled as he pulled into traffic. "I'll take care of it, all right? Just stop saying *terrorist* in planes for your own sanity and safety, little girl."

"I'm not a little girl," Kacey snapped.

The truck stopped at a red light. Travis turned to look at Kacey, every bit the woman she was. From her pouty lips to her tight little body. "Yeah, I know, Kace. I'd have to be dead not to notice." His body flared to life the longer he stared at her. Well, that was uncomfortable.

"Wow, a compliment from the little boy who used to pee his pants when he saw clowns. I'm touched, really." Kacey fluttered her eyelashes and tilted her head.

"It was only o-once!" The light turned green and Travis pumped the accelerator with ferocity. "And the clown knew my name, Kace. Come on. Any little boy would be freaked out a bit. Thanks for that, by the way."

"Whatever do you mean, Travis?"

"You told the clown my name. Admit it. Admit it or I'm dropping you off by the ice skating rink."

"You wouldn't!"

"I would, and I am. Tell me, how many accidental deaths are there a year by ice skating incidents?"

"You're the devil!"

Travis grinned. "So you've said."

"Fine, I told the clown your name, but only after you tripped me."

"Ah, victory at last." Travis sighed, stealing a glance in the rearview mirror to see Kacey scowl and cross her arms. "Kace, can't we at least try to get along while you're here? After all, according to my entire family, you're about to be the new daughter-in-law. I would hate to give them the impression that I'm going to kill you in your sleep."

Kacey groaned. "You're right. And don't you dare gloat! This is for Grandma, right? I'm doing this for Grandma." She chanted *grandma* five times before pausing. "Trav?"

It was the first time she had actually said his name instead of an expletive or her favorite nickname of *the devil*. "Yeah, Kace?"

"Is she going to be okay?"

"Who? Grandma?" He chuckled as he pulled into

the large estate also known as Titus Abbey. "Kace, I think Grandma could walk away from a nuclear holocaust and still be fine. Don't worry too much, all right? Besides, seeing you will make all the difference. She's getting all sappy in her old age."

"But..." Kacey sighed.

Travis pulled down the driveway, shut off the car, and turned to see Kacey chewing on her fingernails.

"But what?" he asked.

Fingernails still in her mouth, she answered, "What if she finds out? I mean, I doubt Jake even told Grandma it wasn't real. So she's going to think we're together, and..."

Travis gulped at the knot rising in his throat. Naturally, it had been one of his first concerns as well. If Grandma found out...well, Travis would gladly point at Jake and shake his head, throwing him under the bus. But the point was his grandma loved Kacey. If she knew they were tricking her to get her to feel better and to make her believe that Jake was more responsible than she gave him credit for...

Then, well, he wasn't sure it would be a pretty sight. After all, Grandma had once done a stint with the CIA, though he was the only family member who had actually pried that information from the old bat.

"She won't find out," Travis confirmed. *Because if she does, I'd hate to be my brother.*

NINE

Kacey hopped out of the truck and looked up at the giant house. It was exactly as she remembered. A colonial-style home set very neatly across a few acres overlooking the Columbia River. Nothing had really changed, other than the paint seemed fresher than she remembered. A dark blue outlined the windows, and a pristine white shone off the bulk of the house. Attached was a seven-car garage, a pool house, and a playhouse that was bigger than Kacey's entire apartment.

"Ready?" Travis asked, coming up beside her.

Taking a deep breath, she looked at the house one more time before nodding. "Off to war we go."

"Keep your gun in your pants," Travis mumbled, setting Kacey to laughter just as the door swung open.

"As I live and breathe! Kacey! Oh sweet girl, you

take my breath away!" Wescott Titus wrapped her in his giant arms and kissed her across the forehead. At a towering six feet four inches, it was like getting wrapped in a hug rather than receiving one.

"Kacey? Is that Kacey?" a feminine voice shouted from behind Wescott.

"Hey, Mrs. Titus!" Kacey reached for a hug from the lady but was scolded.

"Now, you know I've told you to call me Bets!"

Bets was Jake's mom's nickname. When Kacey was young she'd had a hard time pronouncing Betsey for some reason, so she just called her Bets. But at the ripe old age of twenty-two, she wasn't sure if that was still allowed.

With a warm smile, Kacey embraced Bets. "I've missed you."

And she had. Desperately.

Bets's warm hand enclosed Kacey's. She led her to the couch and began chattering about Jake.

"We just knew you two would end up together one day! Didn't I tell you, Wescott?" She giggled and reached for her iced tea, her long red fingernails clanging against the cool glass. "Now, honey, we know that you and Jake are trying to be private about things, but... well, we would love it if you got married here!"

Kacey felt panic tighten her chest. "We would love to!" She looked to Travis for help, but his eyes had taken on that darkened hue that said he'd murder anyone who breathed in his direction. "But, you see, the thing is…We aren't sure we're going to get married locally. We both work so hard, and we thought maybe of just going to Vegas or something."

"Vegas?" both parents asked. They shook their heads in unison and laughed.

"Oh, honey, I forgot about your sense of humor! Why the rush? Why get married in Vegas, that is unless…" Bets looked at Kacey, her eyes squinting. *Oh God. Oh no, is she thinking…?*

"You're pregnant!" she shouted, nearly dropping her tea to the floor. "Oh my heavens! Oh dear me. Oh, Grandma's going to be so delighted!"

"I'm not—" Kacey argued.

"She's not telling anyone yet," Travis interrupted with a devilish smirk. "You know, the media and all that."

"Oh, oh, oh!" Bets scurried around the room until she finally stopped in front of a few shelves. "Oh, honey, don't you remember when you and Jake used to play house? And, Travis…" Bets looked at Travis and pointed. "Didn't you play with them? Because they needed an extra person to stand in for the…"

"Dog." Kacey smiled at Travis and stifled a giggle. "He was our dog when we played house."

"Oh, how nice." Bets winked at Travis and returned to digging out scrapbooks. "I'm sure I have some pictures we can use for the wedding."

Kacey, still trying to gain control of her panic, swallowed before asking, "Why do we need pictures?"

"You know." Bets waved her hand in the air. "For the video montage! You have to have a video montage! They're all the rage. You know, baby pictures, prom pictures, that sort of thing. Guests love it!"

"But what about Vegas?" Kacey asked in a hopeful voice.

"Posh." Bets shook her head vigorously. "We'll pay for the entire thing. And you'll get married here, at Titus Abbey."

"Swell," Kacey mumbled, then glared in Travis's direction. He was gone. She leaned across the sofa and noticed him in the kitchen opening a beer. Oh, nectar of the gods! Just when she needed something strong the most, and Jake's family thought she was pregnant.

Oh God. She was going to have to be a closet drinker. She would have to sneak down to the kitchen just to snag some tequila to numb the guilt and pain. His parents were going to kill her, and they would hate her forever. Which meant she actually had to marry Jake and then turn a blind eye to his inability to keep his pecker in his pants. And then she'd start hoarding and buying cats in order to fill the void in her life.

The drinking would get worse. Jake would hate her, and in a final desperate attempt to regain her youth, she'd die on the table trying to get plastic surgery.

This. Could. Not. Happen!

"I, uh, I'm going to see what Travis is up to!" Kacey bolted from her chair and ran into the kitchen.

TEN

Travis watched in amusement as Kacey continued to schmooze the family as if she'd never left.

His own father, traitor that he was, just smiled and patted her hand continuously, like she was some sort of puppy.

Mother was even worse. At one point, he was convinced she was going to throw an actual party in honor of Kacey's return. In a fit of pure joy, his mother had gone to the scrapbooks and pulled out every single picture of their childhood together and laid them all across the table.

Of course Jake was in every picture.

And, naturally, Travis was in the background sulking.

Damn his brother. Always taking the limelight.

Kacey had been his and never Travis's. With a growl that was unfortunately out loud, Travis walked into the kitchen and grabbed an ice-cold beer from the fridge. His parents, anticipating their arrival, had stocked the house with snacks—and enough alcohol to get wasted for a year.

Which actually sounded like quite the idea after all. He was stuck at this godforsaken house until the whole escapade was over. And with the way things looked, Jake wasn't going to be hanging out much, not with all that was going on at work.

Travis, being the responsible one that he was, had given the ranch hand a bonus to hire some extra high schoolers over the course of the summer, giving him more time with his parents and his grandmother—who, at this very minute, looked the peak of health.

"Grandma? Should you be out of bed?" Travis squinted at his tiny grandmother. Color had returned to her face, and she looked ready to go golfing. According to the doctor, she was supposed to be taking it easy. After all, a mini-stroke was still a stroke.

"Where is she? Where is my sweet girl?" Grandma Nadine clapped her hands in front of her and sighed. Bright red lipstick stained her lips and an ungodly amount of eye shadow was beautifully brushed across her eyelids. Grandma had always been a knockout, and at eighty-five she was still breaking hearts.

The latest conquest just so happened to be their

next-door neighbor, Mr. Casbon. The poor man walked his dog by their property at least three times a day. Travis used to worry the man would get overheated and have a stroke in the driveway, but he was relentless and never stopped his pilgrimage to wave at Grandma.

"Travis! I'm going to kill you! Give me that!" Kacey stormed into the kitchen and grabbed the beer out of his hand, throwing back the entire can before slamming it down on the counter and accidently letting out a loud burp. She slapped her hands over her mouth, and her face turned red.

In that moment, Travis fell a little more in love with her, if that was even possible.

Grandma Nadine let out a hearty laugh. "Oh my, honey girl, still chugging beer in the kitchen away from the watchful eyes of this one's parents, huh?" Grandma reached for Kacey and pulled her into a tight hug. "Mum's the word. I think a margarita is just what this one needs here, Travis. Now, why don't you two run along and have some drinks out on the porch. I'll take care of things in here. You just leave those two to me." Grandma straightened her tight-fitting jacket and strutted into the living room.

Kacey gaped after her. "I swear she could have been the first female president."

Travis didn't think it was the most appropriate time to let Kacey in on the family secret that Grandma had, in fact, enjoyed an affair with one of the presidents.

Instead, he grunted and grabbed the tequila from the pantry. "Get some cups with ice and I'll grab the mix. This should be enough to get you good and drunk before Mom starts planning your wedding." Travis winked and ignored the pain in his chest when he thought of Kacey in a wedding dress, standing opposite his brother.

The bastard didn't deserve her. He dated strippers, for crying out loud! Real strippers! He paid for sex. He lived the life of a true bachelor. He didn't even know how to do laundry! He would be the death of Kacey. Travis knew his brother was just sneaky enough to manipulate his way into Kacey's life. Most likely, he'd deliver the line of *doing it for Grandma* and say they could divorce when she kicked the bucket.

And then Travis would have to feel guilty every time Grandma woke up with a smile on her face. Oh, he'd love for Grandma to live another day, but it meant another day that Kacey and Jake would spend in holy matrimony. Her lips pressed against his. Jake's hands running along Kacey's hips...

"Travis? Travis? Hello, anyone home? We gonna drink margaritas in the tree house, or are you going to stand there with your mouth open all day?"

"Tree house," he grumbled and walked out of the kitchen to the backyard. The tree house sat on the edge of the property, far enough away that his parents wouldn't be able to see them through the tiny windows.

He pulled the ladder down and balanced the tequila and mix in his left arm as he hauled himself up. Travis set the drink stuff inside the door of the tree house and, still grasping the top rung, turned around to grab the glasses from Kacey below.

Her eyes were glued to his ass.

He would have been flattered had she gasped or sighed or done anything except scream.

"Crap! Crap! Crap!"

"Kace, what the hell is wrong with you?"

"G-g-giant spider! On your ass!"

"GET IT OFF!" he shouted in a not-so-masculine voice.

Kacey moved away from him, slowly dropping down the ladder to the bottom rung. "I can't! You know I'm afraid of spiders! What if it lunges at me!"

"Better it lunge at you than take a chunk out of my ass! Now, scare it!"

"If I scare it, it's going to eat you, and I can't have that on my conscience." Kacey's eyes widened again. "Oh gosh, it's moving! It's so gross! Can't you just, like, flex your butt or something?"

"Why, yes." Travis clenched his teeth. "Why don't I just clench my butt muscles in hopes that it will shock the spider enough to crawl back into the hellhole it came out of?"

"You don't have to be mean!" Kacey argued. "Okay, um. I'm going to grab a stick. Do you think that will work?"

Did he think a stick in his ass would work? Well, so much for impressing her. "Just kill it!" His muscles tightened as he kept himself positioned on the ladder.

"Found one!" Kacey announced. "Okay, now don't move. I'm just going to smack it against your jeans."

Travis laughed. He couldn't help it. It was one of those moments that he wished he would have caught on camera, so that others could enjoy the ridiculousness. And then…searing pain.

He cursed, loud, dropping in a few inappropriate words that would cause his mom to smack him. What the hell kind of stick had she grabbed?

"I did it! I did it!" Kacey squealed.

Travis turned and glared.

"I killed the spider!"

"You almost killed the man too! What did you use? A baseball bat?"

Kacey blushed. "It was all I could find." She lifted a wooden bat in her hands as if sacrificing it on the altar before him.

After a few more curses, Travis wordlessly reached for the tequila, opened the bottle, and took two gulps. "I'm going to have a giant mark on my ass for months."

"But I killed my first spider in a year, so that should

at least make it worth it, right?" Kacey's grin was beautiful. White teeth peeked out from her pink lips.

"Fine. Good job, Kacey. We'll do a toast to your victory. You're such a hunter."

"Thank you, good sir." Kacey did a little curtsy and followed him up into the tree house.

It was absolute torture watching her lips close around the tequila bottle. Thankfully, they brought actual glasses to make the drinks on ice. If she was going to drink out of the bottle each time, he would lose his sanity, not that he wasn't already dangerously close, what with being beaten senseless all within an hour of bringing her into the house.

"So…" He needed to change the subject or he was going to make a complete ass of himself. "Jake? Married here? Think he's going to flip?"

Kacey groaned and placed the bottle on the wooden floor of the tree house. "What are we going to do? Your parents don't know. They think it's our childhood fantasies come true!"

Travis shook his head. "Um, no, they think it's your childhood fantasies coming true. Mine, however, had nothing to do with playing dog while watching you guys kiss and have se—"

"What the heck kind of house playing are you referring to, Trav? We did not pretend to have any sort of"—she waved into the air—"relations, and frankly, I'm a little concerned for your childhood if those were the thoughts going through your head while playing dog."

"In my defense, I really didn't have anything else to do but watch." Oh God, that made it sound so much worse, as if he were daydreaming or something.

Kacey leaned in. "Are you already drunk?"

"Nope, just beaten. Thanks, by the way, for that lovely bruise. I've always wondered what it would be like to be on the opposite end of your scorn."

"That's not true." Kacey lifted the bottle to her lips again and took a staggering drink before pouring tequila into the iced cups.

"What's that supposed to mean?" Travis poured the mixer and waited.

"I tortured you just as much as you tortured me in high school. Admit it." She smirked.

Did she know? Impossible. There was no way she knew he had a crush on her. He attempted to play it calmly. "I don't think I know what you're talking about. I blocked out at least half of high school. According to you, I was a eunuch. You can understand my reasoning."

"Please." She rolled her eyes. "Every time the cheerleaders did a pep rally and needed volunteers, I paid them to pick you."

"You lie!" He closed his eyes to keep himself from doing something he'd regret, like attempting to strangle her and kiss her senseless instead.

"Nope." She grinned and winked. "Thought it was luck of the draw, huh?"

It was Travis's turn to laugh. "No, I just thought Jake hated me that much. He always did have those cheerleaders deep in his pockets." *Among other things. Cheerleaders, strippers? Truly he's moved up in the world. Bastard.*

"What are you gonna tell Mom? She's going to want to know what's up with you two when Jake gets here."

"What do you mean?" An irritating male voice interrupted their private discussion and then Jake's head poked through the bottom of the floor as he lifted himself up into the tree house. "Sweet! I forgot this was out here." *Probably just like he forgot Kacey was here. Idiot.*

"Hey, Jake, work okay?" Kacey held out her hand and Jake took it. Immediately Travis wanted to cut off his brother's hand. *When did I turn into such a raging lunatic?*

And then Jake winked at him, and the rage came back full force. Oh yes, that's how, because his brother was a selfish ass who deserved to get the crap beaten out of him. And suddenly Travis was taken back to the time when Jake and he had fought over Kacey and made that stupid bet. They were just little kids, but Travis's competitive nature burned through his veins as he watched Jake reach out and touch Kacey's hand.

Travis needed to remember that her hand wasn't his to touch. It never was. He swallowed another gulp of the margarita and looked away.

Kacey watched the tense exchange between the brothers. It was like being in one of those twisted melodramatic TV shows or something. One minute she and Travis were laughing, and the next he looked ready to burn a hole through his brother's face.

Tequila did weird things to people.

Jake lifted the bottle to his lips and smiled. "So, Kace, how goes it with the parents?" His smile was devastating, perfect, and ridiculous. Why didn't he just go to Hollywood and get it over with?

"Great!" she lied. "Although, they did talk about our upcoming wedding and it's possible I told them we were thinking Vegas; then things got a little fuzzy. All in all, we just have to convince your parents not to have the wedding next weekend, and we'll be good to go."

Kacey nodded her head enthusiastically, trying to get Jake not to panic—which he didn't. *He probably didn't even hear a word I said. He was actually texting when I made that speech.* Just to test her theory, Kacey added, "Oh, and they think I'm pregnant."

"That's great news, Kace," he said, his eyes never leaving his phone.

"And," she added, "when Travis played house with

us when we were twelve, he pretended we were having sex."

That got his attention. Jake's head shot up. "Dude, that's gross. Why would you do that? What's wrong with you?"

"I did nothing of the sort...eunuch's honor." Travis snorted, and then the man crossed his heart and winked at Kacey. If Jake was devastating, then Travis was mind-numbing. From here on out, both men shouldn't be allowed to smile, ever. It wasn't fair to the female population, or the oxygen levels in that cursed tree house.

"So, babe..." Jake played with a piece of her hair, fumbling it between his fingers. "There's this thing tomorrow. You probably don't wanna go, but..."

Travis shook his head in Kacey's direction, warning her of something.

"What is it?" Kacey asked.

"It's kind of our four-year high school reunion tomorrow night. Remember how the senior class decided to do get-togethers every year instead of every five years? Last year's was a blast."

If it's possible for a person's heart to stop from fear and dread, she was a goner. All of a sudden she felt like she couldn't breathe, like the air was being sucked out of that tiny tree house at rapidly increasing speeds. She always ignored those stupid Facebook class updates, wanting absolutely nothing to do with those crazy people.

"So you'll go?" Jake dropped her hair and gave her *that look*. The one that many a woman lost their virginity to, no doubt.

"I, uh . . ."

"Please, Kace." He moved closer and lifted her hands into his. "It will be just like old times. I promise."

Old times? Old times? Obviously he was clueless about how awful it was to go to the same high school with him. As his best friend, at times it was awesome, but most of the time it was like wearing a T-shirt that said, "Not his girlfriend, so please, all girls, hate me, despise me. I welcome it."

Most of the girls were so jealous of their status that they started nasty rumors about her; she nearly had to transfer schools. It got worse when they finally did date. Death threat worse.

Travis, Satan himself, had been tame compared to those rumors and threats.

"Please?" Jake asked again. "It's only a brunch on the water. Please?"

What the heck. People grow up, right? They aren't that immature to still hold grudges or cause rumors at the ripe old age of twenty-two, right? That would be ridiculous!

"Fine." Kacey rolled her eyes when Jake pulled her into a tight hug and kissed her cheek.

"Good, and don't worry, babe. Mum's the word. They won't know a thing about our little deal."

The way he said it made her feel dirty and in great need of a shower.

"Kids!" Bets called from the ladder. "Time for dinner! Wash up!"

They groaned in unison, and suddenly she had a strange sense of déjà vu, as if she were back in high school having dinner at Jake's house. Travis had always hung out with them but had been silent most of the time, thinking of new ways to torture her. But tonight, things had shifted. Jake was the ridiculous one she prayed would fall out of the tree house, and Travis, well . . . She looked up into his eyes again. They were warm, kind, with a hint of something else, but Kacey wasn't stupid enough to think it was desire. She hadn't had that much tequila. She shook it off and took Travis's hand as he helped her down.

Jake had already run into the house, leaving them behind. Someday he would make one woman a very, very happy trophy wife—that is, if she didn't mind being ignored and compared to what he thought of his own beauty on a daily basis.

"Kace, you don't have to go." Travis wrapped his arm around her shoulder and walked beside her slowly. "Plus, it's not that important. I mean, I still haven't made it to any of my reunions for anything."

She laughed. "What? You afraid to face those cheerleaders again?"

He threw his head back and laughed. "Yes, twenty-three years old and cheerleaders still frighten me. All that pep, all that joy, it's not normal."

Kacey looked back at the house, memories of them playing in the yard before dinner bombarding her every sense. "It's fine, Travis. I mean, what's the worst that can happen? If anything, it's going to be a handful of people, and none of them will even remember me."

Travis squinted at her for a long while before turning his focus back toward the house. "If you say so."

"I do." Kacey hooked her arm with his. "Now, let's go face the parents again."

"Yes, and be sure to eat something before you kiss Mom on the cheek. Don't want her thinking you're pregnant and drinking."

"Ugh!"

Travis laughed and reached for the sliding glass door.

"Hurry up!" Bets clapped her hands. "I keep telling Grandma to hurry, but she's across the street still! Imagine that."

"Across the street?" Kacey whispered so only Travis could hear her.

"Yeah, Grandma's got a…*fling.*" He made air quotes with his fingers and rolled his eyes.

Kacey could not imagine why *Grandma* and

fling should be used in the same sentence. Who flings at eighty-five? "Who is she . . . having this fling with?"

Travis shuddered and mouthed, "You don't want to know," before disappearing into the bathroom.

ELEVEN

Jake couldn't help but feel suspicious as his glance went from Travis to Kacey and back again. Naturally, he wasn't the suspicious or jealous type, at least not typically. But he felt a little on edge. And it had nothing to do with the fact that Kacey was wearing such tight spandex, he was finding it hard to walk and talk at the same time.

It was his stupid brother, Travis. Travis of all people! He was looking at Kacey like he was attracted to her—which was ridiculous because, well, he'd always despised her, and she him. Jake couldn't even count on his fingers the ways they'd proven that.

It's just that he knew Travis. At least he'd like to think he was intelligent enough to know his own flesh and blood. But by the looks of things, well, it seemed like Travis was staring at Kacey, like...like a man. Hell. He was losing his damn mind. Everyone knew Travis hated her with a passion. He'd been nothing but cruel to her since they met in elementary school. If anything, Jake had always needed to protect her from his brother more than he had from the other kids at school.

Who had carried her to the house when Travis had pushed her and she'd scraped her knee? Um, Jake had.

Who had asked her to prom when every other guy would have been blacklisted if they had so much as set foot near her, as per order of the girls at the school? Again, the younger of the two brothers.

And who, in the middle of the gymnasium, when crowned homecoming king, had gotten down on one knee his senior year and asked Kacey to be his girlfriend? Jake hated to boast, but yes, that had been him, while Travis had just sat there like a fool. Granted, he was in college and only visiting for the weekend. But still. It was always Jake. It had always been Jake.

So the thought that Travis was currently looking at her like...well, like guys look at girls, was actually quite alarming.

After all, the rumor at school had been that Travis was gay or something, not that Jake had ever asked him. He hadn't wanted to embark on such an uncomfortable conversation and all that.

Jake pushed the thought from his mind. *Honestly, I am just too tired.* He had been working endlessly to make sure everything was in order at work, and to make matters worse, Samantha, his on-again, off-again girlfriend, had declared she was going to go to the papers to report the little engagement was a ruse.

Naturally, he'd threatened to sue her.

Which she'd found extremely hot.

Needless to say he'd flown her down for the weekend as well.

It's not as if Kacey was really going to be that realistic in this role, not that Jake would let her. After everything that had happened between them, it was safe to say that they needed to stay friends, lest he ruin both their lives for the second time.

"Jake?" Dad reached for the potatoes once everyone was seated. "How's the office? Everything going well?"

No, he wanted to yell. Everything was not going well since Dad had retired, but it was imperative that Jake appear in control. He shrugged and answered, "Not a problem."

Grandma chose to make a grand entrance, complete with lipstick smeared on her face, and he couldn't help but smell some sort of man-scent coming off of her in waves.

Always nice to know Grandma's getting play while faking your own engagement.

"What's this about the business?" Grandma could destroy a man with one harsh look.

"Nothing," Jake said, diverting attention away from himself. "But you can ask about Kacey and my plans to wed."

In that moment, Jake's heart stopped as Grandma clutched her chest, wheezed, and then literally toppled out of her chair.

"Grandma!" everyone yelled on key, as if to somehow revive her.

Jake fell to his knees and grasped her hand. She opened her eyes on cue. "I was playing the shocked grandmother. Did I do well?"

"Damn it, Grandma! Don't ever do that again!" Jake swore fluently. Mom glared from her side of the table, but he was sure she was thinking the same thing, if not worse.

"I was an actress once," Grandma announced when she was back in her chair.

Jake guessed that nobody really knew what to do except the obvious. Kacey gave him the *help a girl out* look and began to clap.

He followed, and soon the entire table erupted in applause.

Note to self: Media should never sit in on family dinner night. Under no circumstances should that ever happen.

"So..." Grandma tossed the napkin on her lap. "You're finally tying the knot, hmm? You kids always were so close to each other. Can't say I'm surprised.

And you know what this means for your business, right?" Grandma elbowed him.

Jake dropped his fork, making a huge clattering noise in the silence.

"It means I'm growing up." He faked a smile and shoveled more food into his mouth.

She knew. His conniving grandmother knew about the board members' ultimatum. Shit. Kacey couldn't find out that Grandma knew or she'd kill him and then tell all to Grandma, who would then ruin his chances with the board, considering she still had pull with those old geezers. Hell, it wouldn't surprise him if his grandmother was behind the board's ultimatum for Jake to clean up his act.

Manipulative family members.

Well, at least he'd brought Kacey down for the weekend as he'd promised. What Grandma did with that was her issue. Not his. Whatever. At least now he could spend time doing what he wanted to do rather than worrying about Kacey at the house. Sooner or later his parents would catch on, but he'd be sure to get plenty of pictures with Kacey around town. Maybe he could sneak in the photographer to their reunion brunch. That would be the perfect setting for a photo shoot. He grinned.

Jake looked over at Kacey. She was smiling warmly at his mother. Is this what life would be like if they got married? It wasn't as if it would be difficult, by any stretch of the imagination. In fact, it would be quite pleasant. A nice wife at home and then a mistress in town. The American dream come true. Speaking of mistresses . . . his cell phone went off.

"So . . ." Kacey reached across the table and grabbed Grandma's free hand. "Where were you earlier? I looked for you."

Jake swore he felt Travis kick him under the table and silently mouth "Sorry." Kacey jumped out of her seat as if she was the next target.

"Oh, honey." Grandma swirled the wine in her glass, while Kacey longingly looked at the red liquid. "I was merely helping out our neighbor."

Mother spewed the contents of her wine onto Dad's lap.

Travis began to choke on the chicken.

And Jake was left wondering what the hell kind of aliens replaced the family he thought he had been sitting with.

"Oh." Kacey blushed. "That's nice. What exactly did he need help with?"

Travis's eyes bugged out of his head.

Grandmother played with the stem of her wineglass. "Oh, some of this, some of that."

And suddenly Jake had a nightmare of what his grandma meant by some of this and some of that. As well as the inkling that he would never again look at his neighbor the same.

Where was Samantha when he needed her? If his grandmother was getting action, no way was he going to stay home tonight. He remembered that the earlier text had been a notification of an email.

As if answering his plea for help, Jake's phone went off again. "I should take this." He quickly left the table.

"Hey, baby," Samantha crooned. "How about drinks downtown in a half hour?"

He should say no; he really should. After all, he had a fake fiancée now. He couldn't be seen downtown with another woman this early into his plan. His mind made up, he was just getting ready to turn her down when she began talking about how badly she wanted and missed him.

"I'm wearing a new dress, baby. It's tight in all the places you like. Come on! Just for a few hours, Jakey. I'll make it worth your time."

"Be there as soon as I can." He ended the call and went back into the dining room. "Sorry, guys, work emergency. One of the faxes didn't go through, and I have an early-morning call from overseas. I'm going to have to run back to the office and make sure everything's ready to go."

The lie flew so easily from his lips even he was surprised—and slightly alarmed that he could be so devious to his own family.

Kacey tilted her head, her eyes narrowing. "Can't you fax from here?"

All eyes turned to him.

He began to sweat. "I wish I could, but I don't have the number, and the papers are at the office."

Kacey still didn't look convinced. What had he ever done to her to earn her mistrust?

Slept with her? Abandoned her afterward? Yes, there was that. "Kace, I'm sorry, babe. You know how I was looking forward to spending time with you tonight. But we're still on for brunch, right?" He gave her his most devastating smile, hoping it would work.

She looked down at her plate. "Okay, well, drive safe."

Free at last! He tried to keep himself from running out of there. Bestowing a kiss on Grandma's cheek first, he made the rounds and bolted out of the house, ready for drinks and a much-needed night full of sex.

TWELVE

Travis knew his brother was lying. What kind of fool falls for that type of crap? But sure enough his father, upon Jake's exit, sighed and said, "I just wish I wouldn't have retired. He seems so stressed."

"Must be the strippers," Kacey mumbled under her breath so only Travis could hear. He choked on his chicken for the second time that night.

"Travis, honey, be careful to chew your food before you swallow!" his mother scolded. Kacey took his mother's scolding as a hint that he needed help cutting his chicken. Smiling sweetly, she reached across his plate, her arm brushing his, and cut his chicken into tiny manageable pieces, then poked the fork into one of the pieces and lifted it to his lips.

"Here comes the choo-choo train!"

Obviously, Kacey wasn't frightened by Travis's murderous glare. The rest of his family looked on as if it were completely normal for her to be feeding him like a small child.

Then again, he had played the dog when they were little.

And he did have headgear when he was fourteen.

It was also possible that his mother knew he'd named his bunny after Kacey.

She looked up, her eyes shining with humor.

Damn. Travis opened his mouth, and a small bite of chicken swooped in. Kacey giggled. "You're welcome."

He shook his head but ended up grinning like a fool when she picked up a second piece. It was still hot, and she blew on it to cool it off. He found himself so damn distracted by the way her lips pouted over his chicken that it took every ounce of willpower he possessed not to take her on his family's dinner table.

Ah, lust by chicken. How humiliating.

Travis looked longingly at the table again. Maybe if he just pushed all the dishes to the ground. Too bad she wasn't wearing a skirt. What was wrong with him? Was he really weighing his options here on where best to screw his brother's fiancée?

His parents would be livid.

Grandma, however, would probably applaud, then take pictures for the scrapbook. Though he wasn't so

sure that scrapbook would be legal, considering its por-
nographic nature.

Grandmothers made grandsons so proud at times.

Travis sighed and quickly grabbed the fork from
Kacey's hand. He couldn't take much more.

"So, Kacey…" His mother shoveled more food
into her mouth, chewed, swallowed, and winked. He
groaned. She didn't know how to converse over dinner
and eat at the same time. It made for very long dinner
conversation and even more torture for everyone around
them.

"I was just wondering…" She took another sip of
wine.

He eyed his dad, trying to give him a private message of stealing his mother's plate and wine so she
would spit it out faster.

"Are you guys going to move into Jake's place once
the wedding is over, or buy something new?"

His dad elbowed his mom.

What were they getting at?

Kacey looked to Travis for help. He gave a slow
shake of his head.

"Uh," Kacey said as she pushed food around her
plate. "The thing is, I have a really small apartment,
so Jake's would be best, but I kinda don't want to live
downtown."

"Perfect!" His mother clapped her hands and

nudged his father. He jumped out of his seat, grabbed an envelope, then brought it over to Kacey.

"Just consider it an early wedding present."

It was like *Leave It to Beaver* threw up at the table. His father stood behind his mother, holding her shoulders, and both their heads were tilted with frozen smiles on their faces.

Travis glanced at Grandma. At least she was acting normal, drinking her fourth glass of wine, bless her heart.

Kacey's hands were shaking. No doubt they were giving her something ridiculously expensive. Travis leaned over and nearly choked. He really shouldn't eat in front of these people ever again.

A house.

They'd bought a house.

And it wasn't just any house. It was nestled quite nicely on Lake Washington, in prime real estate.

"We thought you might want something close to downtown but not too close that you can't enjoy everything Seattle has to offer." His mother squeezed his dad's hand, and they sighed simultaneously.

Wescott patted Kacey's hand. "It's been in the family for years. Lots of homes, lots of investments, but it's yours if you want it."

Kacey still hadn't looked up from the deed.

Travis didn't know what to do, so he changed the

subject. "Hey, is it cool if Kacey and I go start cutting the pie for dessert?"

His mom and dad nodded in unison.

He practically had to drag Kacey out of her chair. Once they were in the kitchen, he very gently pulled the deed from her hands and made her sit in a chair.

She promptly burst into tears.

Kacey felt like such an idiot for crying. But since her parents had died a few years back, she'd always wanted to have a home. A real home.

A home like the one Jake's parents had just given them.

And it was all a lie. She felt violently ill in that moment and placed her head between her knees, trying to take large gasps of air.

"Hey, hey, it's fine. It's okay." Travis rubbed her back. "Just breathe. You're just having a panic attack. You'll be fine. There's my girl. Just breathe." He rubbed slow circles around her neck until she finally calmed down and laid her head on his lap.

"Wanna talk about it, Kace?"

She shrugged. She didn't really want to talk about it to anyone, least of all Travis. She still wasn't sure what alien species had taken over his body to make him both gorgeous and nice, but part of her felt like she couldn't completely trust him.

After all, he had thrown rocks when he was little.

Kacey shook her head as another sob escaped her mouth. This house was full of so many memories. How many family dinners had they shared together? The food was always catered by her parents' restaurant. Her mom and dad would drink wine with Jake's parents, and then all the kids would watch Disney movies in the living room. And now that she was back, it was as if a huge chunk was missing. She sat in the same chair, talked with the same family she adored, but a giant piece was missing. She wasn't sure it would ever be okay. Not after repressing the pain for so long.

She shrugged. "I feel horrible. Your poor parents think it's real, and then to make everything worse, they give us this." She hit the packet on the table next to her. "And it's tempting, so tempting that I hate myself for it." It was partially the truth. She did want it, but more than that, she wanted her parents to be alive.

Travis sighed next to her. "You don't need a man like Jake to give you what you want. Believe me. When you have the perfect house and tons of money, you still won't be complete if the man you share it with is out paying whores to do things you would never do."

"Oh, I don't know about that," Kacey joked.

"Kace! Jake isn't worth it!"

"No." She laughed. "I meant things that strippers do. Pretty sure I know how to please my man. I could drive circles around those girls. I just need the right guy."

Travis tensed next to her. He cleared his throat and pushed away from the chair. He walked over to the counter and began cutting the pie.

What was his deal lately?

"Let me guess." Kacey leaned over the counter. "Raspberry pie?"

"How'd you know?" He smirked. His voice was hoarse.

"It was the only pie your grandma taught you how to make, and if I remember correctly, you made it for your senior prom date."

"Ugh." Travis carefully cut it into eighths. "If I remember correctly, she spilled it on her dress and blamed me for making raspberries red."

"She always was such a charmer. What was her name again?"

Travis chuckled. "Oh no you don't. That's just what I need. You digging up my past girlfriends and making fun of them. Besides, I don't date girls anymore. I date women." He eyed her up and down before slowly licking the fork.

Kacey averted her eyes, mainly because the picture of him licking that fork was so erotic she nearly jumped across the table and assaulted him. Apparently, this is what happens when you don't have boyfriends and the closest relationship you've had in the past year has been with your e-reader and a fictional duke named Henry.

"So…" Kacey nudged him a bit with her arm. "Women, hmm? What women are you dating? I don't see any of them here for family dinner night."

"There are no women."

Kacey's heart hammered in her chest.

"If you must know, there is one woman. *One* being the key word."

She clenched her fist and cursed herself for bringing the subject up. "What's her name?"

"Oh no you don't!" Travis placed the knife on the plate and grabbed Kacey by the shoulders. "That's just what I need, you stalking the one woman I'm interested in."

Did he say he was interested in only one? Damn the man. *Be unattractive!* She wanted to yell. "C'mon, Trav, you know me. What harm could I possibly cause?"

"Junior year—" he began.

"Forget I asked."

"Junior year." He held his finger in the air as he was making his point. "Somehow you discovered I had a crush on Ashley Willis. I still don't know how, considering I'm a guy and I don't keep a diary."

"No." Kacey dipped a fork into the pie and licked the tangy berries off it. "But you did moan her name one time in your sleep. But carry on."

He glared. "You told her."

"Okay, Trav, come on. I did nothing of the sort. I merely hinted that you had a tiny bit of a crush on her."

"Kace, making a poster with my face on it and heart stickers is a hell of a lot more than hinting. God, I don't even think you know the meaning of the word *discreet*."

"Do too!" she argued.

He walked around the table and pulled her into a tight headlock. "Do not!" She fought against him but was helpless. "Do you give?" he whispered into her hair.

His hard-muscled chest was heaving behind her. Did she give? Oh God, what she wouldn't give for something, anything.

Ah! Red alert! What was she thinking? It's Travis, Travis!

"Travis!" she screamed, totally unintentionally. He released her and winked.

"Come on. Let's take the pie in before they think you stabbed me or something."

"Close," Kacey grumbled, though stabbing wasn't necessarily what she had in mind. Rubbing his body down with berries and licking it off? Yes. Violence? Only that of a sexual nature.

She needed to trip and hit her head or something to shake Travis's smile and scent out of it before she lost her mind.

"There you two are!" Grandma winked as they

rejoined the family and began to enjoy the pie. "I thought maybe Travis was having an encounter in there with you, little girl." Grandma winked again. Unfortunately, at that exact moment, Kacey, having taken a ginormous bite of pie, began to choke.

It worsened when Travis lifted his hands in the air and said, "I was trying to be discreet."

Kacey glared.

His entire family laughed, and she kicked at him again under the table. He moved his foot in time and then stuck out his tongue like a two-year-old.

And really, maybe it was the sexual frustration, but she lunged for him, his chair tipped backward, and she straddled him, shoving pie into his beautiful face all the while screaming, "I'll get you!"

In her mind, the family was cheering, when really everyone was completely silent.

Except Travis, who was yelling and cursing and spitting pie back out at her. Luckily, they had hardwood floors instead of carpeting.

Finally, when the pie was done, she wiped a berry off his face and licked her fingers. His eyes darkened, and for a minute it looked like he was going to kiss her.

He leaned forward and reached up behind her. And suddenly she had hot pie all over her face.

"I win, Kace," he whispered huskily into her ear.

Yes, yes, you do.

THIRTEEN

Kacey checked her phone for the tenth time that night. Nothing, not even a text from Jake.

What the heck was wrong with him? She was here helping him! And he had to work? She didn't buy it. She wasn't stupid. But it did make her feel awkward when his parents kept giving her concerned looks.

They finally went to bed shortly after the pie incident, which she decided was one of those freak moments when you lose control of bodily function as well as logic and make bad choices. Kind of like when you're drunk, which she wasn't, because according to Jake's parents she was carrying his love child.

Damn Jake Titus.

"Kace!" Travis strolled into the room, absolutely shirtless and wearing nothing but pajama pants. Was her tongue hanging out of her mouth? Oh God, she was beginning to sweat. Geez, at least turn the air on in this place.

Averting her eyes, she managed an awkward laugh. "What's up?"

"Movie night." He threw a pillow at her and went to the DVDs.

"Um, is it naked movie night? I'm not sure I got that memo." She looked him up and down when he turned around.

"I'm sorry. Does my masculinity frighten your prudish nature?"

She snorted. "Please. I just don't want to get last night's skank on me. I hear diseases travel through too much skin contact."

He rolled his eyes. "I'll put on a shirt if you take off yours."

How tempting that was... "Take off my shirt? So you can finally see my boobs? Oh gosh, Travis. Let me think. Give you the fantasy you've been dreaming of for years or keep my pride? Yeah, I think I'll keep my pride."

He shrugged. "Suit yourself, but it really isn't a slumber party if you're not naked."

"What the hell kind of slumber parties were you subjected to as a child?" Kacey asked.

Travis grinned shamelessly. "Only the good ones. Now seriously, go change into sweats. I'll wait."

"Fine." She hopped off, her heart beating erratically out of her chest. This witty banter had to stop. For crying out loud, they were adults! Not teenagers! She grabbed some short Victoria's Secret shorts and a black tank and put on her slippers to make it look less... seductive. Not that she was seducing him. Her stupid skin betrayed her in the mirror as it turned a very nice crimson color.

She really needed to start dating more.

Taking the stairs two at a time, she went back down to the living room and saw Travis opening a bottle of wine; thankfully he had put a shirt on. She wasn't sure she could handle any more of his glistening muscles that evening. "Thought you could use this, even though it's not good for the baby." He winked.

"I would drink that whole bottle if I knew it wouldn't get me completely drunk. I miss wine."

"Um, you haven't had it for one night, and you miss it?"

"Clearly, you underestimate my relationship with wine and what I do on the weekends when I'm by myself reading."

"You wild thing, you." Travis nudged her and filled her glass to the brim. He should be sainted, immediately.

Their fingers brushed slightly as he handed the wine over. His eyes flickered to her shorts, and he cleared his throat. "Those are nice."

"Thanks." She inwardly smiled.

"Are they shorts or underwear?"

Was he being serious? "Shorts, you ass. Now, what movie are we watching?"

"Guess."

"Not in the mood, not near enough wine in my system for me to embark on such a strenuous activity."

"Ah, pregnancy brain, it does it to ya; it really does." Travis got up and turned off the lights, then pressed Play. "I thought you might want to watch a horror movie."

"Horror movie?"

A cartoon popped up on the screen. Kacey blinked as the music came on, then nearly fell out of her seat. "Oh my gosh, we can't watch this, Travis. I can't watch this. It's been forever and…"

"Conquer your fears, Kace."

Kacey scooted a little closer to him, just in case some of the cartoons did in fact decide to pop out and devour her.

He pressed Pause and laughed. "Kace, really? I thought you'd be over this fear by now."

"It's not a fear." Kacey drank her wine faster. "It's a scary movie!"

"It's *Alice in Wonderland*."

Kacey shook her head a few times and drank some more wine. "Damn that Cheshire cat."

Travis held up his wine. "To conquering old fears?"

Something shifted between them then. His eyes, though it was dark, seemed to be hiding something, as if he were talking about more than her stupid phobia. She leaned in, now completely relaxed from downing half her wine already, and whispered, "To conquering old fears."

Travis knew it had a double meaning for him. He really did need to conquer his old fear and actually kiss the girl and, once and for all, get it out of his system. Great. Now he had that damn crab singing "Kiss the Girl" in his head. Swell.

He sighed; surely that would make this blinding attraction go away. God, it was hard enough watching the movie sitting next to her, breathing in her scent, let alone viewing her shapely legs.

He wanted to run his tongue up and down her thigh until…

Stop! He needed to stop, or he was going to have a serious problem staying comfortable during the stupid cartoon. And then she'd probably assume cartoons somehow turned him on. That's just what he needed, for her to think *Alice in Wonderland* made him horny.

He reached for the wine bottle twenty minutes into the movie, only to find they had nearly finished it. He blamed Kacey. She was drinking it like water, not that he could blame her. One dinner with his family was likely to do that to a person, especially when Grandma had a tendency to flaunt her liaisons.

He still couldn't figure out why Grandma seemed to be doing so well. She was supposed to be bedridden, ill! Instead she was sneaking across the street to see the neighbor.

Oh, that mental picture did wonders for his aroused state. Consider him officially turned off.

The music started up, and it was the part where the Cheshire cat appears for the first time.

He looked at Kacey to gauge her reaction.

She closed her eyes.

"Kace," he whispered. "Open your eyes. The cat isn't going to magically float into the living room."

She peeked behind her hands, then reached for the last bit of her wine, downing its contents and handing him her glass. "More."

Far be it from him to deny her anything. He went in search of another bottle.

The minute the cork was out, Kacey held out her glass, still not taking her eyes off the TV. She really did have a weird fear when it came to that dang cat. To her credit, she didn't scream like the last time, which would have been when she was fifteen, but she did inch closer and closer to him until her thigh was touching his.

Sweet torture.

He began drinking to keep his hands and lips

occupied, and as the credits flashed, he realized they had finished two bottles of wine.

Kacey, however, looked wired. "We have to watch something happy to get rid of those mental images."

Travis shook his head, feeling way more relaxed than he should, his arm draped around her, pulling her closer. "What do you want, then?"

What he meant to say was, *Well, what do you want to watch, then?* But he was slightly drunk and a little loose-lipped.

She shrugged, snuggling closer into his body. His arm, once on her shoulders, caressed her back, moving lower and lower until it grazed her butt.

"Kace?" he asked again. She hadn't moved, and the room was spinning, partially from the wine and partially from his lust-filled state.

"Hmm?" She looked up. God, she was beautiful, and so damn close to him he could nearly taste the wine on her lips.

"Your call," he said, lowering his head to hers.

"This means nothing," she whispered against his lips. "We're drunk, and it means nothing," she repeated as her hands tangled in his hair.

With a moan, he shook his head.

"Right, nothing." He licked her lower lip, tasting the red wine, then running his tongue along the bottom of her jaw.

She arched her back, and he pulled her closer. His control was hanging on by a single thread.

When his lips grazed hers, she opened her mouth to him. All hell broke loose. He hadn't expected her to taste so good, to feel so ripe, to feel perfect in his arms, to moan his name.

His tongue tangled with hers. Kacey ran her fingers up and down his biceps, then tucked her hands underneath his shirt, peeling it off his body.

"Told you naked slumber parties were more fun," he said between kisses.

She giggled and reached for her own shirt. No way in hell he was going to miss watching this. He leaned back, mesmerized, as she began to strip, and then... the lights flipped on.

"Grandma!"

"Travis! Kacey!" She put a hand over her heart.

Oh God, this was it. His grandma had just seen him getting ready to screw his brother's fiancée. He was going to be the reason for her death. He just knew it.

She tilted her head. "Kacey, that brassiere is quite charming. Pink. Now, why don't I have any pink lingerie?"

Travis hid his head in his hands, praying to disappear.

Grandma shrugged. "You kids be sure to clean up

now. Don't want Jake coming home and seeing remnants of your lovemaking."

There was something so wrong about his grandma saying *lovemaking* as a woman was straddling him.

She waved good-bye and turned the lights back off.

But the mood was officially gone.

"Do you think she was drunk?" Travis asked pleadingly.

"Either that or high." Kacey pushed herself away from his chest and pulled her shirt back on. Sadly, he wanted to shed a tear of selfishness that their little party was over.

"I should, uh, go to bed..." Kacey got up, a little unsteady on her feet.

Travis grabbed her arm. "Let me help you. I'll just throw away the evidence and help get you to your room, okay?"

She nodded and stretched her arms above her head.

He quickly tossed the wine bottles in the trash, put the glasses in the sink, folded the blanket, and turned off the TV.

"Ready?" he asked.

"Yes." She didn't look him in the eye.

He walked with her up the stairs and led her to the guest room. She began to protest when he walked in, turned on the lights, and made sure the windows were open. He knew she liked fresh air when she slept, something he was sure she probably never got tired of.

"Off to bed." His gut clenched. It should be him in that bed, not the damn teddy bear or even the other pillow. *I'm jealous of her pillow?* He needed to take a cold shower.

"So…" She shrugged and looked at the floor. "About tonight."

"Kace, don't. We're drunk."

"I'm not that drunk," she whispered.

He chuckled. "Me neither."

"I still hate you."

He smiled. He couldn't help it. "Kace, don't worry. I still wouldn't sleep with you if you were the last girl on the planet." *Lies, all lies.*

"Fine!" she yelled. "I don't even like you anyways!"

"Well, don't worry, Kace. My brother's sloppy seconds aren't really my type anyway." *Where the hell did that come from?*

Her hand came crashing across his face. He totally deserved that.

"Kace, I'm sorry. I didn't mean…"

"It's safe to say I know exactly what you meant, Travis. Good night." She slammed the door in his face.

He was a complete ass.

FOURTEEN

Samantha was ruining everything.

First she'd asked for Jake's promise that he wouldn't really marry that whore he was engaged to, and then when he'd said he was actually thinking about it, she'd slapped him. Incredible.

It wasn't as if he was going to kick her to the curb or anything. He was perfectly happy having a wife with a mistress on the side.

Once he explained things, Samantha calmed down a bit, but it ruined what would have been a perfectly great evening of mind-numbing sex and drinking.

He ended up driving back to the house around 1:00 a.m. It wasn't worth staying over with her if she was going to be such a snatch.

He fumbled with the lock and let himself quietly in the house. Where exactly was Kacey staying? He forgot to ask. He took the stairs two at a time and bumped right into Travis, who was exiting one of the guest rooms.

"What are you doing?" they asked in unison.

Travis scratched his head and looked back at the room he'd just come out of. "Uh, Kacey had too much wine, so I wanted to make sure she made it to her room."

Jake wasn't buying that. He wasn't an idiot.

"So you gallantly helped her up the stairs and fought off the monsters and dragons in order to protect her honor?"

Travis rolled his eyes. "You done? I'm tired. I need to go to bed. Just don't bother her, okay?"

"She isn't your concern, Travis. I'll bother her if I want. I'll jump right into that bed and screw her senseless, and it still wouldn't be your problem. This isn't about you."

Travis hurled Jake against the wall. "If you dare touch her again, I swear I'll kill you."

"Touch her?" Since when had Travis turned into such a prude? "I'll touch her if I want, and again, it's none of your business."

"What the hell is wrong with you!" Travis released him and cursed.

"Nothing." Jake straightened his leather jacket.

"Just lighten up, okay? I'm over it. She's over it. We're both over it. Seems the only person still hanging on to the past, big brother, is you."

That ought to show him. Jake sneered and knocked on Kacey's door, then quietly let himself in, leaving Travis glaring from the hallway.

"Hey, sweetie. I'm back." Jake kissed her forehead. She didn't look drunk or confused. If anything, she was flushed, her lips swollen. God, he had forgotten how beautiful she was. Her hair was splayed across the pillow. She sighed and tilted her head toward him.

"Work okay?" she mumbled.

"Yeah." His voice cracked, and he couldn't focus on anything but the feel of her skin when he caressed her face again. "It was fine."

And then he couldn't help himself. He'd promised himself he wouldn't actually touch her, but he was a guy and allowed stupidity to rule his common sense. His lips grazed hers, tentatively, and then harder as he pushed her into the bed.

Travis burst into the room like a freaking knight in shining armor, then cursed when he saw Jake hovering over Kacey.

"Bro, can I help you? We're kind of busy."

Travis's eyes flickered to Kacey, who seemed to disappear under the covers, and then back at Jake. "You're right. It's none of my business what you two do. I don't give a damn. Good night." He slammed the door.

Geez, his brother needed some sort of anger management. What the hell did he care if Kacey and Jake had something between them still?

Kacey nudged him. "You should go." Her face was wet with tears. Was she crying?

"Why are you crying? Is everything okay? What's wrong?" All the questions came out in a rush.

"N-nothing," Kacey stuttered. "I'm sorry, Jake. I had way too much wine. I didn't mean to kiss you." She turned her head and closed her eyes.

"It's fine." But it wasn't. In fact, everything would have been going in an entirely different direction if Travis hadn't barged in on them.

Maybe it was for the best. After all, he knew it would only lead to him hurting her again. He wasn't really a one-girl kind of a guy. But she provided something so tempting he had trouble pulling away. Maybe it was memories of their friendship together. Or the way she smiled and teased. He shook his head. He really should have gotten laid tonight. Things would have been so much easier.

He kissed her one last time on the forehead and let himself out of the room, grinning smugly as he passed his brother in the hall. Apparently his older brother was going to play chaperone. Fine with him.

He stopped before going into his room. "She's

sleeping. I'm sure she's tuckered out after all that excitement." With a wink, Jake stepped into his room and slammed the door, enjoying immensely the sound of his brother's curses all the way down the hall.

FIFTEEN

Kacey wished she could disappear into the covers when her cell alarm went off at 8:00 a.m. What in the world had she been thinking last night?

Obviously, she wasn't thinking, just drinking and grabbing the first guy next to her. Well, not the first guy, the only guy. The hottest damn guy she'd ever seen in her life.

All Titus men should be shot; that much was clear.

He kissed her first, didn't he? No, she leaned in first, but what did he expect her to do? With all that wine in her system? And the way he was looking at her? His eyes piercing through her, his scent floating off him. It would have taken extreme self-control to push the man away, and she'd been running on fumes by the end of the night.

Two more days.

She had only two full days, and then she could return to her boring life and forget about Travis. Even the idea of it made her heart clench a little, but that was silly.

She hurried through her morning routine, grabbed her running shoes and sunglasses, and ran toward the front door.

"Where do you think you're going?" Travis called from behind her. Crap.

"If you must know, I'm going running."

She refused to turn around. It was too early to deal with his perfect face.

"I'll join you."

"No!" Kacey yelled before she could stop herself. "I mean, you don't have to. I'll be perfectly safe."

Travis cursed. "Believe me, I couldn't care less if some homeless man picked you up off the street. I just have to talk to you. Hold up. Let me grab my shoes."

She nodded, still not making eye contact, and ran out the door to stretch.

"Ready?" Travis called five minutes later. She turned and nearly stumbled.

"Sure, yeah, let's go. Fine." Snapping her mouth shut, she closed her eyes and imagined a world where perfect male specimens weren't looking at her the way Travis was. Though his eyes looked more angry than anything else.

"Hope you can keep up," she called behind her as she set the pace.

Travis laughed. "Please, I ran a marathon last week. Pretty sure I can keep up."

She clamped her mouth shut and scowled.

"So..." He ran up next to her, not even breathing heavily, even though he was keeping quite a fast pace. "...you and Jake."

Crap, crap, crap, crap.

"Yeah?" She glanced at him nonchalantly.

"Don't do it."

"Do what?" Kacey asked.

"With him, don't let him in, Kacey."

"What, did you nominate yourself my protector?"

"Somebody has to protect you!" He grabbed her arm, pulling them both to a stop.

"Oh, really? Is that what you were doing last night? Protecting me? Because it sure as hell felt like something else. Thanks for clearing that up." Kacey pushed him away, but he grasped her wrists.

"You know that's not true—not that it matters, considering you kissed my brother in the same hour."

"Believe what you want, and for the record, Travis..."

His head popped up.

"It was a drunken mistake. It never happened, okay?"

His nostrils flared as he cursed and looked at the

ground. "Right, so what happened between you and Jake was another accident?"

"Again, none of your business. Just leave me alone, Travis. Go find someone else to torture, all right? I need to get my run in before I go to the stupid brunch."

"If that's what you want." He looked back down at the ground, then cursed, running a hand through his thick hair. "You're going to get hurt. You know that, right?"

Kacey sighed. "I'll get hurt either way, Travis. Just depends on which brother I decide to give that opportunity to, don't you think?"

He was silent.

It was all the answer she needed.

Nodding her head, she turned in the opposite direction and began to run. Tears threatened to pour down her face. But over what? Over Travis? Over Jake? She didn't even have feelings for Jake! He was a selfish bastard, but Travis? Travis could be real. Or could he? The trust wasn't there, but it had seemed lately they were two different people, and then...

Then he said something that made her heart turn to ice. He knew about Jake and Kacey, about them going separate ways in college, of course, but the fact that he would throw that back in her face, as if she were some sort of whore and only afterthought material made her want to shoot him. How dare he say that? Even in anger, it wasn't acceptable.

She wiped a stray tear and focused on the pavement. All she needed to do was get through today and tomorrow. And then she could go back to Seattle, back to her job at Starbucks and to finishing school. She just needed to remember everything else she had waiting for her and forget Travis ever existed.

Five miles later, she returned to the house totally spent. Only to find Grandma Nadine strolling out the front door as if she were going on some hot date.

Was she really as ill as Jake said? She looked completely fine.

"Oh, doll! How are you this morning?" She winked. Oh gosh, she was referring to catching her and Travis last night.

"Um, Grandma, there's something you need to know—"

"Oh posh, don't you dare excuse your behavior, young lady. If anyone understands, it's your dear old grandmother. Goodness, if I had your legs, I'd be doing much worse. Now, you just have your fun and be safe, dear."

"But Travis and I aren't, and Jake and I are, and..."

Grandma Nadine winked. "Our little secret, dear. I didn't see anything. I know you love both those boys, in different ways, of course. I think it's about time you stop following in Jake's shadow and break out as your own woman and all that."

Kacey swallowed the lump in her throat. "We aren't engaged." She didn't mean to blurt it out.

"Honey, I'm not stupid." Grandma Nadine pulled her into a hug even though she was sweaty. "I'm also not sick," she whispered. "Oh, I had one of those silly scares old people get when things stop working properly, but I'm right as rain."

"But?" Kacey was torn between feeling happy and confused. "Why did you tell everyone that you were?"

Grandma Nadine's eyes turned very serious. "Honey, it's at the end of one's life when a person realizes past mistakes made. One of my greatest mistakes was not forcing you to return home, to face your demons, to conquer your past." Grandma lifted Kacey's chin with her wrinkly hand. "Did Travis drive you by the restaurant?"

Kacey wanted to pull away, but instead she bit down hard on her lip to keep from crying. "No. No, he didn't. I don't think I can see that place now, Grandma. Not after all those memories. And then when they died, I just wanted to sell the place, to leave everything."

Grandma sighed. "I understand, honey, but don't you think it's time to return?"

"Return?"

Grandma pulled her into a tight hug. "Home, honey girl. Time to return to where you belong."

Kacey hugged Grandma as tightly as she could,

allowing herself to relax as the smell of Grandma's French perfume washed over her.

"I know my bastard of a grandson ruined things. I may have threatened him to get you down here, but don't for a second think that this little visit has anything to do with him. This visit—it's for you."

"I don't understand." Kacey looked down at her hands; everything seemed so confusing all of a sudden.

"You will." Grandma Nadine pinched her cheek. "My dear, very soon you will understand why it's important. Why all of this"—she pulled away and lifted her hands into the air—"is important. This is life, and, honey, you need to start living."

Kacey nodded.

"Now…" Grandma Nadine straightened her suit jacket. "I have a date."

"Grandma, it's nine in the morning."

"Who says you have to date only at night?" She pulled out a mangled tube of lipstick and formed an O as she coated it across her lips. "The way I see it…" She smacked her lips together. "Is if you date a person in the morning, that gives you all day to play."

Too much information.

Way too much.

Was it possible to rewind conversations and forget they ever happened?

"I'm off." Grandma winked and strolled across the street in six-inch heels.

Something was seriously wrong when your adopted grandmother had better clothes than you. *Note to self: Raid her closet later.*

Fascinated, Kacey watched as Grandma knocked on Mr. Casbon's door. It swung open wide and she was pulled in.

The drapes were closed. Thank God for small favors.

Kacey entered the house more in a daze than anything. Grandma wasn't sick. She knew Kacey and Jake weren't engaged, and she was encouraging Kacey to do what? Find herself? Why did she have to come to the one place packed with all her childhood memories to do so?

The one house, the one family, who was almost closer to her than her own.

When she and Jake had broken up, it was as if her world had shifted. She went from spending every holiday at his house to making excuses about work obligations. All because of one stupid night. One careless night when she'd imagined she could be more to him than just his friend.

Oh, she'd been his girlfriend for a year before they had ever done anything, but it was more of an agreement. It had been a way for him to protect her from creepy guys, from the senior year of high school into their first year of college.

It had never meant anything.

They hadn't ever acted on anything.

She swallowed back more tears, remembering the smell of the dorm room when they'd gotten back from the party that night.

Jake had been laughing about some guy who had fallen into the pool, and Kacey had been drinking water like there was no tomorrow. They'd never gone to parties without each other and had always made sure to hydrate and stay out of trouble. They'd gone for social reasons, that was it.

But when Jake had dropped her off that night at her apartment, he'd asked if he could crash on the couch. He'd stayed, and after a while they'd started kissing.

She wasn't even sure what had started the kissing. Had she leaned in first? Had he? Did it matter now? Then the clothes had come off, and all she could remember was thinking that she was finally going to be with the man she loved. The man who'd stood by her side her whole life.

In her innocent mind, she'd thought giving herself to him meant . . . forever.

In his mind, it had meant . . . a moment.

One crappy non-mind-blowing moment that ended with tears of frustration.

It had been awkward to say the least. Jake had sat on the edge of the bed, his head in his hands, repeating over and over again, "Oh God, what did we do? What did we just do?"

And she'd sat there, vulnerable, no longer a virgin, and had fought to keep the tears from pouring down her face. If it had been any other guy, she would have kicked him out and called Jake to come take care of her.

But who do you call when you screw your best friend? When the one person who understands you is the one who can't even look at you?

"I have to go," he had said, not bothering to say good-bye, ask if she was okay, or anything. The door slamming had felt like a hammer hitting her body.

She had sat in the silence, trying to even her breathing. Not really understanding why the experience hadn't been as magical as she had heard it would be, and not knowing if she should tell someone or just lie there.

Her parents had been away on vacation, but little did she know that if she'd have called them, they wouldn't have answered anyway. It had been the same night they'd died in a car accident on the way back from the airport.

A week later, Jake had mumbled an apology, then said he was going to be really busy with classes for a while.

He'd begun calling only once a week, then once a month, until finally she'd received cards from him and his family only on the holidays.

The pain washed over her anew. She hadn't realized until now that she'd lost every loved one she had ever had in her life that fateful night.

Her parents, Jake, Grandma Nadine, and his family. Everyone, taken from her in an instant. And she suddenly wondered how she had made it so far without having a nervous breakdown.

With a shuddering breath, she ran up the stairs. There would be time for self-pity and reflection later, but now, now she needed to get ready to hang on Jake's arm, even though it was the last place she wanted to be.

SIXTEEN

Travis kept telling himself it wasn't creepy or weird or even slightly strange that he was tailing Kacey and Jake to the brunch.

He had it all worked out. He'd hang out in the background, mingle, have a mimosa, and once he saw that Jake wasn't making a complete ass of himself and actually paying attention to Kacey, he'd leave.

Despite the hurtful things said between them, he still felt this raw possession for her. It was intense and strange, but he couldn't fight it any more than he could tell his body to stop breathing. He needed to know she was going to survive the brunch. Even he wasn't deluded enough to think people change that much after high school.

They boasted about their maturity, yet still gossiped on Facebook.

They said they're above the drama, yet held grudges against one another when one became more successful. In fact, adulthood was almost worse than high school because for some reason it was suddenly okay to be manipulative. *"Oh, I'm so concerned about so-and-so. Did you hear what happened?"*

How was that not gossip?

Or when his mother's friends came over and asked about Jake because some of their daughters were still single. He'd never mentioned to Kacey what people said behind her back once she and Jake were no longer talking as much.

It was awful, to say the least.

Rumors ran rampant through their little social circle that Kacey had cheated on Jake, gotten pregnant by some other guy, and the worst of it was that he had downright rejected her and she was institutionalized.

That one was fun.

His poor mother nearly had a stroke, but managed to set everyone straight, because according to her, Jake and Kacey were just busy with work but still constantly in touch, though nobody ever saw her car at the house anymore.

People talked.

And Travis hated them for it.

So, yeah, he was following them, playing the crazy

stalker, but if it meant that he could somehow jump in and save the day, he was okay with it. He didn't want to see her hurt again. He wasn't sure he could handle it. Jealousy aside, he truly just wanted her to be happy.

Even if it meant she was going to end up with Jake, the lucky bastard.

The family BMW pulled into the driveway for the River Walk restaurant. Travis pulled onto the opposite side of the street and turned off his truck.

He contemplated ducking in his seat, then realized his truck was already a dead giveaway, so it didn't really matter much.

Kacey emerged from the BMW in a form-fitting white dress. It was completely open-backed except for a line of fabric by her neck, and had capped sleeves and a scoop neckline. His throat went dry when she turned to Jake, her body perfect.

Obviously Jake noticed, if his smug grin was any indication. Travis clenched his fist and watched as Kacey threw back her head and laughed. Her purse clutched tightly against her, she walked up ahead of Jake as he placed his hand on the bare skin of her back.

If Travis could have growled or roared, or maybe even run into something with his fist, he would have felt a hell of a lot better. Instead he tortured himself by watching and imagining what it would be like if the roles were reversed. What if it was his hand? What if she laughed at his joke?

"Don't go there," he said aloud and cleared his throat.

Finally, after endless minutes of torture, they disappeared into the restaurant and Travis was able to relax, at least a bit.

He glanced in the mirror to make sure he looked all right. He hadn't dressed up for the occasion much. But his style was different from his brother's. It would be like comparing the finest champagne against an expensive whiskey.

Jake's suits cost more than most people's house payments. He screamed money, from the Rolex watch to the perfectly pressed pants, the jacket, and the button-up, carelessly unbuttoned to show his tan skin. His glow-in-the-dark smile paired well with his short dark hair. Not to mention the fact that he had somehow perfected the art of smooth shaving.

In a word, Jake was like a girl.

Whereas Travis, well, he took off his sunglasses and threw them on the seat. He was more of a jeans and T-shirt type of guy. Yes, he liked good fits and name brands, but he wasn't as feminine in his choices as Jake.

In fact, he found it quite funny that today Jake wore a khaki suit, while Travis sported Rock & Republic jeans with a tight black Armani shirt.

He wanted to show off his best assets if need be.

And he was vain enough to know his arms and chest did wonders for women.

All women except the one he wanted the most.

"Stop," he told himself again. With a curse, he jumped out of the truck and slammed the door shut.

Now was as good a time as any to walk straight into hell. He pasted a smile on his face and walked across the street.

What he saw when the doors opened should have shocked him, perhaps repulsed him, but he was so damn used to it, it almost didn't faze him.

Jake was standing in the middle of the open bar to the right with about twelve girls all standing around him asking for his autograph.

Please, he did one shoot for *GQ*.

The girls around him giggled in unison, each of them leaning over so Jake's eyes could easily blaze a trail across each and every one of their chests.

He seemed to be enjoying himself immensely.

And then he heard a different type of laughter. It wasn't fake. It was hearty, rich. He whipped his head around just in time to see Kacey sitting at a table of women.

Most of them looked old. Not the type of women that would be at a four-year high school reunion, but as he inched closer the faces became more recognizable. Funny how a few years does things to people. Lots of them had gained weight, some were pregnant, and a few had dyed their hair different colors and acquired face piercings.

She looked fine, absolutely fine, but where were all the men?

He looked around again and noticed a group of guys sitting directly behind Jake, drinking beer, belching, and laughing heartily.

They looked like death.

What the hell kind of reunion was this? How depressing.

Some of them had wedding rings, some were starting to get thinner hair, and a great majority of them were acting like they were still teenagers, making catcalls and drinking at noon. Travis suddenly wondered what had happened to the world.

With a shake of his head, he made a quick exit toward the restrooms to rethink his strategy.

A young woman came barreling out of the bathroom and ran directly into him. "Oh, I'm so sorry, si—" Her eyes widened as she slowly lifted her head in appreciation. A wide smile broke out on her face. "I'm not sorry."

Travis laughed. "Why the sudden change in attitude?"

"Honey, you just let me stare at you for a few more minutes, and I'll change more than my attitude." She raised an eyebrow and ran a hand down his biceps. Was he being molested in the restroom hallway?

"You gonna be here a while?" She purred.

"Um, I'm not sure yet."

"What can I do to convince you, sugar?" She patted his biceps with her left hand, and he noticed a large sparkling ring.

"Honey," he drawled, reaching for her hand and bestowing a kiss on it. "I don't need convincing when a pretty lady asks me to stay. Now, you go on and have yourself a good brunch." He winked.

She nodded her head and giggled, this time gaining attention from the table of women. He glanced up to see all of their jaws drop, all except Kacey's, who had chosen that exact moment to dig for something in her purse.

He nodded once and walked into the men's bathroom.

Where was her cell phone when she needed it? Crap, it was in Jake's car! She needed to get out of there before she lost her mind! It was all about Jake today. People asking if they'd stayed in touch over the years. Oh, aren't they so excited to be married after all this time? Oh, no one believed for one second that Kacey had been institutionalized! What the hell?

A classmate she vaguely remembered came rushing to the table. Her name was Joy, and Kacey thought it fit.

"I'm officially in love." She plopped into her chair and downed her entire mimosa. Wow, Kacey wished her bathroom experiences were that exciting.

"Did you see him?" Sandy, a friend from senior year, nudged her in the ribs. "He is hands down the hottest piece of man candy I've ever seen in my entire life."

"I want to lick him," another girl piped up.

"I'll lick him all day," a guy shouted from across the room.

Good to know this guy, whoever he was, could bat for both teams. He probably was gay. All the good ones were gay.

"No offense, Kacey." Joy reached across the table and patted her hand. "But he's even hotter than Jake!"

Gasps were heard all around. "No! Are you kidding me? You don't say?" people kept saying over and over again. Absolute silence took over as a man in a tight black T-shirt walked out of the restroom and made a beeline straight for their table.

His eyes focused only on Kacey.

Her heart nearly stopped in those few seconds.

His bright smile was for her, and only her.

Damn him.

"Kacey, why is he looking at you? Kacey?" Sandy nudged her, but Kacey kept her eyes focused on Travis, her smile getting wider and wider.

When he reached her side, he hunched on his knees in order to be face-to-face with her. He reached in to kiss her cheek, lingering an extra second before pulling back.

"I figured you might need rescuing."

Sandy cursed next to her.

Joy giggled.

Another woman said, "How does she do it? Jake *and* the mystery man?"

"Thank you." Kacey swallowed her pride and took his offer for what it was, a way to get out of that place, away from Jake's admirers.

"Sorry, ladies." Kacey pushed out of her seat and gathered her purse and sunglasses. "I forgot that Travis and I were going to go to…"

"The park," he finished for her. "I hope I'm not stealing you away too soon."

"No," Kacey answered, while everyone else at the table said, "Yes!"

"Wait," Sandy interjected. "Travis? Travis, you look kind of familiar."

"Bro!" Jake shouted. "Get over here!"

Kacey rolled her eyes.

Gasps were again heard around the table.

"You're Travis Titus! Oh my word! Oh my word! Look at them both!" If Sandy didn't watch it, she was going to have a heart attack.

Just then her husband came around the corner, his pudgy stomach all the more evident next to Travis's perfect physique. "Hey, baby." He tried to kiss her on the cheek, but Sandy pushed him away.

Kacey pressed her lips together to keep from laughing.

"Hey, Kace, where you going? Travis, what are you doing here?" Jake tried to act happy. Kacey could tell because his lips were twitching like he wanted to scowl and then punch his brother in the face.

"Grandma wanted me to take Kacey to the park, something about the wedding or something."

Well, that was a lie. On both accounts, but Kacey wasn't going to argue.

"Oh, well, um, I guess I'll go too."

"No!" the girls all but yelled. "Jakey, stay with us." A girl came up to his side and pouted. "She'll be fine. We haven't seen you in years!" She rolled her eyes.

Kacey wanted to pull her hair out.

Jake opened his mouth to speak, but another girl looped her arm with his. "Please, Jake, you still haven't told us about your trip to Africa to help the nomads."

Seriously? They were buying this? Really? Kacey wanted to scream. He chuckled and nodded his head. "Sure, I'll stay, but only for a little bit." His eyes turned back to Kacey. "I hate to be away from my love for too long."

Kacey wondered if slapping him or choking him would be more satisfying.

Jake leaned in and kissed her cheek. "See you soon."

"Yup." Kacey gave him a lame side hug and attached herself to Travis's person like a leech.

Once they were outside she mumbled, "I'm still mad, but thank you."

"Of course." He put on his sunglasses.

"And I didn't need saving."

"I know."

"Okay, I just want you to know that I was handling things fine and—"

"Kace, I know. Now, do you want to go have fun or sit here and argue?"

"Fun," she mumbled.

He laughed. "Right. Well, let's see what I can come up with."

SEVENTEEN

Jake watched their disappearing forms. Well, actually he watched Kacey's. His brother could go to hell for all he cared.

What was he doing here anyway? It wasn't *his* high school reunion.

Just as he was ready to go after them, a hot blonde tugged at his shirt and smiled up at him as if to change his mind. "Are the rumors true, then?"

"Rumors?" He gave her a dazzling smile.

"That girls cry when you leave them in bed because they want you so badly." She was trying to be sexy, but honestly, the minute she said *cry* and *bed* together, he lost all his sexual appetite in one giant rush.

Kacey.

God, he was stupid.

He should have apologized.

Or at least done something, anything other than just sit there with his head in his hands, ready to burst into tears over ruining the most important friendship in his existence.

It had destroyed him.

Most people talk about straying, how choices eventually led them to be the people they were, how it was a slow fade into what was now their lives.

But with Jake it was different. He knew the exact time. Three o'clock in the morning. He knew the exact date. February third. He knew everything.

The way the room smelled like coconut from one of Kacey's ridiculous candles from Bath & Body Works. The feel of her jersey sheets across his legs.

Her smooth skin under his hand.

Yes, he knew the exact moment when he gambled and lost everything dear to him.

It was the very same day he decided he couldn't be her friend anymore. A crossroads had appeared that day. He could have chosen to be the good guy going after the girl and apologizing, living a safe life with 2.5 children and a house with a picket fence.

Or he could have chosen to be an ass.

The choice he'd made was obvious, but he'd felt trapped and alone, and it wasn't any help that his friends had told him the easiest way to get over a girl was to get with a new one. So he had, again and again, until he was so numb and disgusted with himself he hadn't even wanted to live anymore.

Eventually the pain faded when Kacey started her own life.

It was easier for him to forget it ever happened. To pretend it didn't really matter. But it did. Oh, how it did.

Kacey didn't know.

How could she?

It had been his first time as well as hers. He'd never told a soul that he'd stayed a virgin through high school. It was easy to keep the secret though; girls had wanted him so bad that they lied about his skills in the bedroom. Granted, he'd never been an angel, but he'd always known he wanted his first time to be with someone special, with a girl he truly cared for. He'd thought he loved Kacey, but she'd had a way of making a man feel like more than he was, and for Jake that was difficult. He'd known he wanted more than he could give Kacey. He'd wanted to sow his wild oats, make mistakes, get crazy, be famous. Kacey would have been happy dropping out of school and having kids right away.

Nothing makes a guy run faster than knowing he could have it all, and lose it all, with one woman.

To be frank, it had scared the hell out of him.

What if? What if he had apologized? Loved her as she deserved? In his mind he would have still destroyed her. It was so much easier being who he was.

Which is why, when the hot blonde stuck her hand into his belt loop and whispered something naughty in his ear, he left with her. Not caring if people whispered behind his back that he was cheating and not caring as she took off her top in the car that what he was doing was stupidity at its finest.

He just wanted to be free, to live. To separate himself from the boy he was so long ago.

EIGHTEEN

Travis tried not to look at her legs. Really he did. It was a gargantuan effort on behalf of men everywhere. In fact, several times he wished someone were documenting the extreme self-control he was exhibiting by biting his lip, breathing in and out, and keeping the truck between the yellow and white lines of the road.

"So, where to?" Kacey asked.

He still didn't look. He knew if he looked at her, even glanced, his eyes would stray and he would be responsible for a twelve-car pileup.

His nerves were already shot with the way her perfume was floating across the truck, tickling his nose, teasing his senses, and arousing him more than should be allowed.

Taking a shuddering breath, he responded, "It's a surprise."

"Oh, I love surprises," she said dryly.

"Cut the crap, Kacey. Are you forgetting who you're with? I know how much you love surprises. Crap, you cried when we threw you a sixteenth birthday party."

She crossed her arms.

"Remember." Travis fought the urge to nudge her out of her bad mood. "You were so happy because Mom and Dad paid for everyone to go to that Backstreet Boys concert. You went backstage and met Brian and announced you were going to marry him."

She let out a snort, then a laugh. "Gosh, how I loved those Backstreet Boys."

"Every girl did. I, however, wanted to set fire to their trailer and watch them die very slow agonizing deaths."

"You and every other guy out there," she teased.

"So, admit it." He turned down the side street. "You like surprises."

"Travis Titus, are you taking me to see the Backstreet Boys?"

"No." He shuddered. "Thank God. I'm taking you someplace that will make you feel happy, not resort back to the high-pitched screams of sixteen."

"Happy?" She played with the radio. "Hmm, what would you know about making me happy? You threw rocks, taunted me, teased me, and chased me, and you think you know the one place in this town that's going to make me happy?"

In that moment he did look at her legs, her face, her eyes, her lips, and answered with confidence, "Yes, yes I do."

Kacey squinted in confusion, then looked back out her window. It was for the best that they didn't talk. He was getting more attached by the minute, and she was leaving in a matter of days. Two to be exact.

His heart clenched. He'd get over it. *Just like I got over her in high school?* His memory reminded him that it wasn't likely.

Taking a deep breath, he turned onto the correct street. The entire drive was quiet, up until he saw the sign and pulled into the parking lot.

"The zoo," Kacey stated. "You're taking me to the zoo?"

"Don't sound so impressed," Travis teased. "Maybe we can find an ass that looks exactly like my brother! Perhaps I'm being too hopeful." He sighed and parked in the first available spot and turned off the car.

"What makes you think this is going to make me happy?" Kacey didn't budge; her seat belt was still fastened, her arms crossed.

Travis unbuckled his seat belt and leaned over. "Get out of the car and find out."

Never one to back down from a challenge, Kacey

glared at him as she unbuckled her seat belt and threw open the door.

Geez, the reunion must have been worse than he thought.

They walked side by side to the entrance. Travis paid for the tickets and flinched when he noticed her walk ahead of him. He wanted to put his hand on her back, to touch the smooth skin peeking out from her dress. He hated his brother all over again for having the honor of touching something so sacred.

"So, where to, oh, happy-maker?" Kacey had her hands on her hips.

"Are you going to be like this the whole time?"

"Like what?" Her lip jutted out. Adorable. She was trying too hard to be angry and hold a grudge.

"Look, I'm just trying to repair the damage done by my blood relation. You can participate or not. Your choice."

Kacey broke eye contact and sighed. "You can't fix that damage. It's already been done."

Honestly, he had no idea what kind of damage had already been done; he just knew they'd broken up and parted on bad terms, and to be frank, it wasn't any of his business.

"I mean, what he did today," Travis clarified. "Flirting with anything in a tight skirt and making you sit next to lustful women." He winked. "Not to mention springing a ridiculous reunion brunch on you, when we both know how much you hated high school."

"Key word is *hate*," Kacey chimed in.

"Ah, there's my girl. Now, how about a smile?"

Her nostrils flared.

"A tiny one?" he asked, getting closer.

Her lips parted.

And suddenly a smile was the last thing on his mind. Crap, he needed to stop doing this to them. Slowly he backed off and grabbed her hand. "Follow me."

With reluctance, Kacey trudged behind him, but he knew her better sometimes than she knew herself, a thought that often scared him, and again he was back to stalker status.

He cleared his throat when they reached their destination.

Kacey slowly approached the small glass container, then looked up at him with confusion.

"Just watch," he said, then looked around to make sure nobody was looking and gently tapped the glass.

Kacey cursed, a small child began to cry, and a mom gave them a dirty glare. All in all, it was the perfect surprise.

"You son of a—"

"Kace," he interrupted. "Tell me you're not smiling."

She burst out laughing. "You creepy, weird man!

Why the hell would you take me to the tarantula exhibit!"

"Because you hate spiders."

She threw her head back and laughed. "How is that supposed to cheer me up?"

"It's working." He pulled her into a hug, purely instinctual, but she hugged him back. "Isn't it?"

"Yes, you idiot. It's working only because I'm too shocked and upset to do anything but laugh."

"Ah, and she gets to the bottom of it."

"Huh?"

Travis released her and looked back at the spider. "Sometimes, when life gets hard and people make you angry or even when you're scared, the best response is laughter. Laugh in the face of fear, in the face of what scares you the most. It's the only way to get you through the things that bring you to tears."

Kacey was silent and then said, "You've been drinking Grandma Nadine's Kool-Aid, haven't you?"

"I do love grape," he joked.

Kacey looked back at the spider and made a face. "Thanks. Oddly enough, this did work. I'm more worried about that stupid spider breaking out of its container than my horrible morning. By the way, when was I institutionalized?"

"Oh, that was after the pregnancy."

"Which was before?"

"The cheating," he confirmed.

"That explains it. I'm such a hussy."

Travis nodded. "So, ready to go look for the asses?"

"You didn't tell me Jake was here!" She slapped him playfully.

"Oh, there's a whole cage of them. Just follow me!"

Travis took her hand and led her to the monkeys. The minute they stopped in front of the exhibit, one of them began pooping by a tree, another scratched its butt, and the other began licking a body part that shouldn't be mentioned.

Travis sighed. "It's like watching little Jakey grow up all over again." He put a hand over his heart and sighed longingly.

Kacey covered her mouth in laughter. "Poor guy."

"Don't feel sorry for the child prodigy. He brings everything on himself and then some."

"You guys still talk?"

Travis looked away. "Me and Jake? That would be a resounding *no*. This weekend is the first time we've spent more than a day together in years."

"Why?"

Because of you.

Because I love you.

Because he's an ass.

"Let's just say we had a falling out. I didn't exactly agree with the path he took in his life, and he thought I was too uptight. End of story." Travis held out his hand. Kacey took it.

He led her to the next exhibit.

"Do you miss him?" Kacey asked.

"I miss who he was. I miss who he could be." He laughed bitterly. "Is that terrible? To wish someone was different just because you don't agree with the person he is?"

Tears welled in Kacey's eyes. "No, I don't think that's terrible. If it makes you feel better, I miss him too."

"You live in Seattle."

"I miss who he was. Besides, the first time I talked to Jake in two years was last week."

Travis wasn't sure if he was relieved or upset that his brother had been proven a liar yet again. So he hadn't kept tabs on Kacey like he'd told everyone? Interesting. Though his heart still had trouble with the thought that she had any sort of tender feelings toward Jake, regardless of if it was for her old version of him or the new one. "Well, you guys were best friends. So I understand."

"He never held my hand." Kacey laughed. "Isn't that ridiculous? We never held hands."

"What?" Travis's head snapped up. "But you guys dated, and you were together all the time. I mean"—he nudged her a bit—"you held hands at sixth grade skate night. That has to count."

Kacey laughed and shook her head. "Yes, let's bring up skate night, because that's not totally forced! I swear they encourage it! Playing Savage Garden while telling the girls to pick a cute boy. That's probably how Jake's gold diggers first learned how to hit on men."

"Skate night," they said in unison.

"Doesn't count, though," Kacey interjected. "Like I said, it was forced. I mean he kissed me when we dated…"

Travis hoped his cringe wasn't too obvious.

"I remember the one time I reached for his hand in high school when we were dating. He pulled it away and shook his head. Later he told me he didn't want to appear like we were too exclusive."

"What an ass."

"Yes, I think that was the beginning of the end." Kacey sighed. "Look! The bear's out!"

"Crap, are you serious?" Travis grabbed her and pushed her into the brick wall lining the far side of the exhibit. Adrenaline coursed through him.

"Um…" Kacey shook his flexed arms. "What are you doing?"

"You said…" Travis's breathing was ragged from fear. "You said the bear was out."

Kacey bit her lip, then burst into laughter. Her head rested against his chest as her shoulders shook. "I meant that he wasn't sleeping behind the little alcove.

Maybe I should have yelled that he was visible? Then you wouldn't have had a heart attack." Kacey leaned in and gave him a mocking smile. "Well, at least I know you're still afraid of bears."

He hated damn bears. Even the gummy ones. "I was just trying to protect you."

"And yourself." Kacey nudged him, then grabbed his hand. "Admit it. Your heart was beating like crazy. You were sweating."

"I hate bears." Travis felt like he was ten all over again. Kacey had asked him why he was crying, and he'd told her it was because Care Bears were on TV again.

That Christmas she'd bought him a Care Bear.

He'd cried.

Again.

He blamed his parents for taking him camping too often as a child. When he was three, a bear wandered into their campground and he never got over it. His mom said he'd cried for the entire day when he found out the bear ate his graham crackers.

"Look." Kacey pointed at the large, menacing bear. "He's just playing."

What she probably saw was the bear happily playing with a piece of wood. What Travis saw was a bear ripping things apart with its ten-inch claws.

"Do you still have Mr. Happy?"

"I hate you just a little bit right now. How did this go from me cheering you up to discussing my phobias?"

"Do you?" she teased.

"No, Mr. Happy, my Care Bear, suffered a very tragic accident the same year you got him for me. Something about the bonfire and no firewood."

"See if I ever get you a present again."

He'd probably accept a damn bear from her at this point if she just kept holding his hand.

Travis looked at his watch. "Well, as much as I loved our quick one-hour trip, we've got to head back. Grandma really did say something about wedding plans, but I'm pretty sure that was code for *Go rescue Kacey so I don't have to drive without a license.*"

"Really?" Kacey squinted her eyes in disbelief.

"Yes, she does believe you're getting married, and my parents are literally planning the ceremony as we speak. You better hope Grandma reins them in. Otherwise you're getting married Sunday."

"Very funny." Kacey shivered. She knew Grandma was just pulling the wool over everyone's eyes, but it was still irritating that his parents didn't know. "And we are not getting married. It was an arrangement, though . . ." She trailed off.

"What?" His heart dropped to his stomach. "Though what?"

Was she having second thoughts? Did she really want to marry him?

"Though it seems weird that all of a sudden Grandma's doing great, don't you think?" She hoped the hint would be enough.

"I guess." Travis scratched his head. "I haven't really been by the house much. It was weird, because one day she seemed totally fine, and the next it was as if she were taking her last breath or something. She was putting in all sorts of weird orders. Arranging her funeral, figuring out where the shares in the company went, wanting to marry all of us off."

He stopped and looked up. "You don't think Grandma's faking her illness, do you?"

"Now, why would she have any reason to do that? Maybe she's just trying to act healthy since I'm around?" Kacey broke eye contact and began playing with her purse.

"Right." Travis waited for her to say something else, but she quickly changed the subject.

"So, wedding plans. I hope this means I get to look at more scrapbooks." She nudged him.

"Yes, remind me to burn those later. I want no paper trail leading to my role as a dog."

"You were a cute dog."

"I had no tail."

Kacey closed her eyes and laughed. "But you did have a really cute patch right here." She touched his stomach, her hand lingering, then pressed against his abs. His breath hitched, and he looked at her lips. The pull was incredible.

Kacey's tongue peeked out to wet her lips as she stretched on her toes and whispered in his ear, her lips nipping at the edges. "For the record, I like the dog better than the ass."

"Was that a compliment, Kacey Jacobs?"

"Why, yes, yes, it was, Travis Titus."

They laughed and fell into easy conversation the entire way to the truck. If only that moment could last forever.

NINETEEN

Kacey was sweating.

Stupid Travis and his stupid ideas about cheering her up, and his damn smile with his ridiculous dimples. She sighed. His tight ass and ridiculous jokes about Jake didn't help matters.

So many words screamed through her head, most of them curse words. They brought out the worst in her, those boys.

Whatever was going on between her and Travis, she had to fight it. First of all, his parents still blissfully thought that she and Jake were engaged.

Grandma had other plans, though Kacey was still waiting to hear why Grandma was trying to pull one over on the family.

And Travis, well, Travis thought it was all a hoax

and was still worried that his grandma would keel over at any minute.

As if she didn't have enough stress in her life, when they arrived home Jake pulled up and hopped out of his car, looking far too pleased to be coming away from such a boring brunch.

"Hey, baby." He pulled her into his arms and kissed her across the mouth.

Immediately, she slapped him. "You kiss your whores with that mouth!"

Seriously, she hadn't meant to say it out loud.

Travis gave a low whistle behind her.

"What the hell, Kacey? Is that the kind of greeting you want to give your fiancé?" He gave her an innocent smile.

"You bastard!" She raised her hand again, but Travis pulled her away before she could do any damage to his face.

"What the hell kind of lines has he been feeding you?" Jake lunged toward Travis, but Kacey stood between them.

"Nothing. He said nothing. You, however, have said everything that needs to be said without opening your sorry mouth."

"I'm confused." Jake held up his hands in defeat.

"You reek of skank. Geez, you promised, Jake. You said this was for Grandma, that you could do anything for a weekend. Really? What are your parents going to say when you march into that house smelling like a cheap Dolce and Gabbana knock-off? Hmm?"

"It *was* D and G. I would know," he corrected, pulling off his jacket and swinging it over his shoulder. Kacey lunged again.

Travis grabbed her. She turned around and gave him a glare that said *Just let me kill him!*

Jake stopped in his tracks. "I don't see what the big deal is anyway. I have my fun; you two have your fun. Everyone wins. My parents think we're getting married. Grandma finally has you home, though it's ridiculous that you'd be that important. I mean, it's been years and now she wants to see you? Look, all that matters is that by all appearances, I'm grown up, you're reunited, and we'll be engaged in marital bliss soon." He shrugged and walked off.

"Selfish bastard," Travis mumbled under his breath.

"I want to scratch his eyes out." Kacey felt herself flush with anger.

"Yeah, you and every girl he's ever slept with."

Kacey felt herself tense and then blush, the heat spreading across her face and down her neck until finally she couldn't take it anymore. Her lip trembled just slightly, and she began walking purposefully toward the house, but Travis pulled her arm back and pushed her through the doorway nearest the garage.

"What's wrong?"

"I'm fine." Kacey's legs suddenly felt weak.

"You're not fine, Kace. You're shaking. What aren't you telling me?"

Oh, just about everything, she wanted to say.

Defeated, she just hung her head and remained silent.

Travis cursed. "Fine, don't tell me, but I'm here, if you ever want to talk." He began walking away, then turned around. "Listen, Kace, I don't know what happened between you two. I know it's none of my business, but it had to have been bad for you guys to have had such a falling out. Promise me you'll talk to someone, even if it's not me."

She would do no such thing, but she nodded her head anyway. Nobody knew. Well, except her one girlfriend, but her parents died thinking Kacey was eventually going to be marrying into the Titus family.

God, it felt like the ultimate letdown.

Her parents were so proud of her going to school, and they loved Jake like a son. They always joked about taking family vacations together and spending all the holidays baking cookies.

What do you do when the life you thought you were supposed to have is stolen from you? What do you do when it's your fault and you can't even tell anyone the reason why? What do you do when the one person that caused you the most pain in your entire life is suddenly offering you everything you've ever wanted on a silver platter? She was facing the ultimate in golden handcuffs, because she knew Jake possibly better than anyone. It wouldn't take much to convince him to truly marry her. His parents would see to that, especially if he broke things off.

What was she doing? Did she really want to be with a guy who couldn't keep it in his pants?

Her hands were still shaking from the encounter.

It was too real. Smelling a foreign perfume on him had successfully transferred her into the past. When she'd seen him the first time after their night together.

He'd been wearing a worn Abercrombie sweatshirt and tattered jeans. He'd looked gorgeous.

When their eyes met, he'd smiled and walked up to her. Within minutes they'd hugged, but he hadn't smelled like Jake.

He'd smelled like another girl, and then someone had appeared at his side and asked if he was ready to go. Another girl, a beautiful girl. She'd squeezed his butt and they'd walked off.

So started the first day of the rest of her life.

Lost in thought, she walked into the house where the family was, no doubt, planning her future marital bliss and nearly tripped over Jake, who was lying on the floor yelling.

"What happened?"

Jake was cursing up a storm, his mother was fighting a losing battle with the wine cork—no doubt trying to drown her sorrows—and his dad was trying to put ice on Jake's eye.

Grandma Nadine was smirking, and Travis was clenching his fist.

All in all, a normal scene for the Titus house.

"He ran into the wall," Travis said simply.

"A wall did that?" Kacey pointed at Jake's eye. It was puffy and already starting to change colors.

"It was a big wall." Jake moaned from the floor. "Damn wall. I hate walls."

Travis smirked, and Grandma Nadine began to choke and fan her face.

"Okay." Kacey wasn't really sure what to do next, so she crouched down at eye level with Jake. Taking the ice from his father, she slapped it onto his eye as hard as possible.

Bets gasped while Grandma Nadine burst into laughter.

"Sorry," Kacey said sweetly. "It slipped."

Jake glared, but said nothing.

"Can we have a minute alone?" she asked.

Slowly the family trickled out of the room, leaving them alone. Kacey leaned in, wanting to whisper so nobody could hear her, just in case they were waiting to hear fighting from the kitchen.

"Never again, Jake."

He opened his mouth to speak.

"No." Kacey shook her head. "No, you don't get to talk. You get to listen. Difficult task for you I'm sure, but try."

He nodded once.

"If I'm here doing this giant favor for you, then you better learn some self-control. You can't run around sleeping with your skanks and expect not to get caught. Cameras are everywhere, and one of these days you're going to get careless. Do you honestly think those girls care for you anyway? I guarantee they want nothing but your money, status, and hot body. If you don't stop grinning, I'm going to slap you."

He swallowed convulsively and stopped smiling.

"I know it's important to you to have your parents' approval. And I can even respect that underneath all that selfishness you want what's best for the company. I think I, of all people, understand that, but you can do all those things without manipulating people you love. After this weekend, I'm done. Just know that I'm done."

Shaking, she rose to her feet.

Jake reached out and grasped her wrist. "Kace." His eyes were uncertain, and he cursed under his breath. "I messed up."

"Story of your life."

He gave a half smile. "Only when it comes to women I care about."

Kacey believed that. She shook her head and began to walk away.

"I loved you, you know."

She stopped in her tracks, her heart pounding out of her chest. Kacey took a few soothing breaths, then turned to face him, the man she had loved for so many years. No longer her childhood friend, but a selfish man who thought only of pleasure. "I loved you too, Jake. But this, the man you are now, not so much."

With that, she walked out of the kitchen, directly into Travis, who actually had been eavesdropping.

Funny, she expected it of Grandma, not her nemesis.

"So, that was a special moment." He tensed and ran his fingers through his hair.

"You punched him."

He stuffed his hands in his pockets, and his curly hair fell across his forehead. "I did."

"How'd it feel?" Kacey wanted to know.

"Not as good as I thought it would."

Kacey laughed and slapped him playfully on the shoulder. "Maybe next time let me fight my own battles?"

"No."

"Excuse me?"

Panic crossed Travis's face, as he looked out the window and then back at her. "I said no. Why do you get to have all the fun anyway? I think I have just as many reasons for wanting to punch my brother."

"Like what?"

Travis froze. Should he tell her? Should he say it? Golden opportunities don't always present themselves. He opened his mouth to speak just as Grandma came sauntering in.

"Oh, honey girl, don't you know?"

Oh no. Oh God. No, no, no.

"Travis, here"—she pinched his cheek; kill him now—"had the biggest crush on you when you were little! Why do you think he was so insistent on playing house even if he had to be the dog? Why, it was precious. I remember when you had your sixteenth birthday party and your date didn't show, he—"

"Grandma!" Travis shrieked. "Really, let's not exaggerate my boyhood crush. Plus, I'm guessing Kacey already knew, what with the ponytail pulling and rock throwing."

He hoped she at least suspected.

Kacey's mouth was slightly ajar, her eyes focused on the two of them as if inspecting them. "You're telling me..."

Oh God.

She approached both of them, still squinting. "That he put me through hell because he liked me?"

He gulped. Somehow he saw this happening differently in his head. He would confess his love, and they'd laugh about how silly it was and make love on the kitchen floor.

One by one he watched his daydreams shatter as Kacey advanced toward him. "You told the entire fifth grade class that I peed my pants during recess!"

Yes, yes, he had.

"You hid a spider in my lunch box, and when I cried you told everyone the reason I was crying was because my mom left the crust on my sandwich."

"It wasn't that bad. Come on, Kace—"

"I was in high school. And yes, it was that bad. People thought I had some weird crust fetish until I graduated. I found crusts in my locker for an entire year."

Travis backed up against the counter.

"Oh, look at the time!" Grandma chuckled. "See you later, you two. Now, don't go fighting over things you can't change!"

Travis mentally pleaded with his grandma to stay. Really, he was on his knees, tears pouring down from his face. He began to sweat. And then when she disappeared, he resorted to praying for God's intervention.

Kacey looked ready to explode.

Not good.

"You cut my hair." Her tone was clipped, as if that were the final straw in her book.

"I did," he confirmed, slowly inching farther down the counter toward the door. "But in my defense, I was trying to get the gum out."

"THE GUM YOU PUT THERE!"

"You can't prove that!" Why was he yelling? "Besides! You told everyone my junior year that I only pretended to stutter to get extra help from the teachers!"

"You did!"

"One time!"

"That's nothing compared to what you put me through." She pushed his chest. Travis reached behind him. A carton of eggs was on the counter. His mom must have been getting dinner ready.

Slowly, he reached inside and grabbed two. "Well, I guess I just like to be one step ahead of you, Kacey." With that, he plopped the eggs onto her head.

And tried to take off in the other direction.

Kacey tripped him. He went sailing to the floor.

Cursing, she grabbed for his arms, pinning him to the floor. "I'm going to murder you!"

"Kacey, I was kidding. I'm sorry, I—"

Her eyes were blazing as if possessed. She frantically looked around the room, and a smile erupted across her face. "So . . . you want to do this here? Now? Get all that childhood angst out? Fine, let's go."

"Go?" Oh God, he could feel the stutter coming on, as his tongue felt thick in his mouth.

"Yeah, go." She reached onto the counter and grabbed two eggs, then skillfully, while he was still frozen in fear, pulled at his jeans and stuffed the eggs into the front, straddling him as they cracked and oozed down his legs.

He closed his eyes. Never had he been so angry or aroused. Really? What was with him and food? First, chicken at the dinner table, and now eggs. He'd probably never eat a normal meal again without getting painfully turned on.

"That's it." He knew he was stronger, bigger, tougher. He grabbed her arms and flipped her onto her back, egg staining his pants. Damn, that was uncomfortable.

She squealed and tossed her head from side to side. He pinned her arms on either side of her head. Egg was beginning to dry on her face.

"Say you're sorry and I'll let you go."

"Never." She smiled.

"Fine." Arms still pinned, he leaned over her and gathered some spit in his mouth.

"No, no, Travis, don't you dare." She struggled underneath him. Damn she felt good.

"All you have to do is say you're sorry."

Her eyes flashed.

"Fine." He let the spit fall from his mouth just slightly. She screamed.

And suddenly he was getting pulled off her.

"What the hell is wrong with you two?" Jake yelled.

His parents came running into the room.

And he could only imagine what they thought. Travis with wet stains on the front of his pants as if he'd had an accident, Kacey with egg in her hair, and Jake with a black eye.

As if on cue, Kacey and Jake both pointed to Travis. He cursed.

His mother clenched her fists at her sides. "Travis Titus!"

"Uh-oh, she used his full name," Jake interjected.

"He's dead now," Kacey added.

Travis wanted to roar.

His mother shook her head. "Really, Travis, it isn't like you to be so immature! Oh heavens, Kacey, is that egg on your head?"

Kacey nodded solemnly.

Travis clenched his teeth.

His mother inspected him more closely. "Honey, did you have an accident?"

Jake chuckled and began coughing wildly next to him. He looked to Kacey, and she bit her lip and looked away.

"Yes, I'm twenty-three, and I had an accident. Really, Mom?"

"Well, honey, I'm sorry. It just looks like—" She

pointed, then blushed. "And then I know how you were when you were little." Oh no.

"How exactly was he?" Kacey asked, suddenly intrigued.

"Oh, he used to have little accidents and nightmares, nothing serious."

Kacey beamed. "Really? Well, I'm sure the bunny he slept with was a huge comfort during those difficult times."

"Bunny?" Jake and his dad said in unison.

The only people who knew about the stupid bunny were Kacey and his mother. It had been a gift from his grandpa before he died, but he had named it after Kacey, not that he'd ever told her that.

After one careless night of sleeping with the damn thing in junior high, Kacey had wandered into his room and found it.

It was the only time they had been civil.

Now all bets were off. "Really, Kacey, I doubt it's any worse than that stupid lamb you used to sleep with. You know, the one you refused to let anyone wash?"

"It wasn't dirty!" she argued.

"It was gray."

"So?"

"Its original color was white."

Kacey's mouth went into a firm line, and she raised her hand.

Travis's mom clapped. "Children, really. Goodness. Everyone go wash up and be down here in the next hour. We're going to have an early supper and go over wedding plans, and then have family game night, a normal family game night."

"Fine," they all snapped and walked in different directions.

TWENTY

Jake had tried to appear unaffected by Kacey's little speech, but after going to his room and feeling sorry for himself, he'd realized he needed to give her a real apology.

He'd gotten to thinking. What if? What if he could change? What if he could be the man Kacey needed? What would life really be like with her? Would he be bored out of his mind? Or did he owe it to both of them to at least try?

Confused, he had run downstairs only to see his older brother straddling Kacey and attempting to spit on her face.

Their immaturity knew no bounds, but at least now he knew there was absolutely nothing romantic going on between the two.

Travis was twenty-three, and at that age, if he used violence to attract girls, well, then no wonder he was still single. And a girl like Kacey wouldn't fall prostrate for a guy who still resorted to childhood pranks in order to win her favor.

Geez, if Jake were a nicer guy he'd actually give some tips to his brother. He desperately needed them.

Maybe everyone would be safer if he just kept Kacey and Travis away from each other. It seemed they brought out the worst in each other.

By the time they had all returned to the dining room, his mother had actually put name cards on the table.

Classy.

Kacey was sitting between him and Grandma. Good choice.

Travis was sitting on the opposite end of the table with—Wait! Why was there another place setting?

"Company tonight?" Really? Did his mother think that safe after the escapade in the kitchen? Not to mention his brother punching him in the face for no reason.

Okay, so he punched him because he was upset with Jake for not paying attention to Kacey. It's possible he kind of deserved it, but only slightly.

"Oh, Grandma invited Mr. Casbon."

Jake choked on his laugh. "Our neighbor Mr. Casbon? The one who lives for Grandma's smiles? Well, this should be interesting."

"That's an understatement," Travis muttered, entering the kitchen.

"Good to see you changed your pants, bro."

Travis glared. "At least I can change my clothes. You, on the other hand, are stuck with that wonderful personality."

Jake clenched his fist. His brother smiled.

Kacey entered. "Well, I think my hair looks the shiniest it's ever looked. Thanks, Trav. I owe it all to you." She winked.

Travis rolled his eyes. "Yes, and my balls are—"

"Travis!" Bets almost screamed. "We're going to have company any minute. Could you all at least try to act your age? Goodness, Jake, you've been groomed to take over the company. Act like it! Travis, you've owned that ranch of yours for a few years. By all that is holy, be mature!"

"You own a ranch?" Kacey asked. Jake watched the exchange. Travis shifted his feet as if uncomfortable, then cleared his throat.

"Yes, a small one. No big deal."

"Oh, that's rich." Bets laughed. "You own one of the largest ranches on the West Coast, but if you want to pretend it's small, I guess that's your prerogative."

It was a new feeling, being ignored, but Jake was interested to see how Kacey would respond. He crossed his arms and leaned against the counter.

"But you said you were a ranch hand."

Jake laughed. "Him? A ranch hand? Babe, he's no more a ranch hand than I'm a janitor."

"But…" Kacey's brow furrowed.

"It's no big deal." Travis shrugged and began filling the glasses with water.

Kacey turned to Jake. "Any other family secrets?"

Probably not the best time to tell her that his grandmother was manipulating all of them.

"Um…" Jake shoved his hands in his pockets. "Travis used to have a crush on you? At least that's what I assumed, considering he stuttered every time he was around any female."

Travis froze. "Yeah, rewind to about an hour ago, and you'll see how she reacted to that certain piece of information."

Jake chuckled. "So that's what started the fight. I see…"

Kacey looked angry all over again, so Jake decided to make it better. Slowly he walked to where she stood. "Kace, I'm sure it upset you, but what you don't know is that even though he did some awful things…emphasis on awful—"

"Thanks, Jake."

"No problem." He smirked. "He's also the reason that your sixteenth birthday party was a success."

"What do you mean?" Her shoulders relaxed.

"Well…" Jake put his arm around her tiny frame. "This one over here, the one with the stutter, was so angry that your boyfriend at the time didn't show up, that he begged Dad to call in a favor."

"What favor?"

Travis glanced at them nervously and shook his head. "It doesn't matter, Jake. It was a long time ago."

"Hey, I'm just trying to help. But yeah, Travis was the one who convinced Dad to get that local band to come play at your party. You know, the one everyone was so obsessed with?"

Kacey nodded. "Everyone heard they were playing exclusively at my party, so they came, even when my idiot boyfriend Tanner told everyone to blacklist me because I wouldn't sleep with him."

"Yeah, well…" Jake shrugged. "Travis also took care of that guy." Why the heck was he being so nice to his brother? If he'd had any suspicions that they were physically attracted to each other he wouldn't be helping at all, but he didn't like it when they were fighting so much. It stressed him out. And he didn't want to get wrinkles before his time, or gray hair.

"Jake!" Travis waved him off. "Don't."

"He beat him up, threatened him, and then told everyone he had an obsession with vampires."

"That's why people kept bringing garlic to school?" Kacey laughed. "Aw! Travis, why didn't you tell me any of this? I might not have stuffed eggs down your pants."

"Gee, thanks," Travis muttered.

Jake used this golden opportunity to pull Kacey into a hug. "Well, can't I have a reward for sharing good information about my brother?"

Her eyes darted between the two of them. She nodded and returned his hug.

And in that moment he remembered exactly why he had fallen for her in the first place.

She fit.

Perfectly in his arms.

As if made for him. Her scent, the way her hair tickled his nose, everything about her screamed comfort and home. He didn't want to let her go.

Travis cleared his throat.

"Sorry." Jake pulled back. "I must have spaced out."

"It's okay." Kacey blushed and walked over to the counter.

Oh, hell no.

Not this time.

Not this time.

Travis was ready to unleash whatever tricks he could to get Kacey to stay away from Jake.

He would kidnap her and take her to Mexico before he let his brother sink his claws into her all over again.

"Kace." Travis stacked the napkins in her hands. "Wanna help set the rest of the table?"

"Sure." She went around the table putting napkins

on the plates, while Travis whistled. Jake eventually got bored, as Jake often did, and made up some excuse about seeing what was on TV.

Finally.

"So, vampires, huh?"

"It was the best I could come up with. I did have a stutter, you know, and my only social interaction was that of my family and the drama club."

"Ah yes, the lovely drama club. Tell me, what part did you play again?"

He smiled. "Not the dog, thank you very much."

Kacey raised an eyebrow, pausing with the napkins midair.

Travis burst out laughing. "Fine, it was the cat, but in my defense it was the musical *Cats*, so you can't make fun of me."

"I suppose not." Kacey jutted her bottom lip out as if pouting. "Do you remember the song?"

"Not gonna happen, Kace, so don't get your hopes up. You'd have to get me very, very drunk to ever hear that song from my lips again."

"It would be totally worth it."

He laughed. "Maybe for you."

"Aw, come on, one tiny little phrase. I won't tell a soul." Kacey put her hands on her hips as she moved closer to him. Damn, if he didn't feel like a cat as he watched those hips sway. Truthfully, he was nearly happy enough to break out in song.

He opened his mouth to possibly sing or perhaps curse—he wasn't sure which—when he heard the door slam.

"We're here!" Grandma announced as she strolled into the kitchen, Mr. Casbon in tow.

The man was wearing a silly grin and a Hawaiian shirt tucked into khaki pants. All in all, the perfect man for Grandma. She did love Hawaii.

And men.

Lucky Mr. Casbon.

"So, are we having *pupu* first?"

Kacey's eyes widened in horror.

Travis whispered in her ear, "She means appetizers. That's what they call them in Hawaii."

"And she's suddenly Hawaiian?"

At that moment Grandma began to hula dance in front of Mr. Casbon.

Travis exhaled. "Apparently."

Jake walked into the room, took one look at Grandma dancing, and turned around. Good to know Travis wasn't the only one alarmed at Grandma's behavior.

Mr. Casbon grinned and joined in.

Kacey laughed and patted Travis on the shoulder. "Should we show them how it's done?"

Bewildered, he watched her slowly move her hips. His brain told his mouth to close. He also told himself that if he kept lusting after her he was going to be damned uncomfortable in front of his grandmother.

"C'mon, Trav." Kacey winked and lifted her arms above her head.

He pulled her close and began a rhythm that was anything but hula dancing. It was slow, fluid, sensual. His hands rubbed slowly down her sides until they fell to her hips, staying there, unable to move as he closed his eyes.

Travis didn't care.

He was beyond caring.

So what if he was embarrassing himself? He was over it, done. He just wanted to touch her, to hold her close.

"Travis?" He opened his eyes, and Kacey was inches from his face. "I think we have a little audience." Her blush told him he should look, but he was too embarrassed. Quickly he jerked away from her and then looked.

Grandma and Mr. Casbon stood watching them, each of their heads tilted at an angle. "Well, that was romantic." Grandma winked.

"I was just..." Travis scratched the back of his head. What? Lusting? Having graphic daydreams of what it would feel like to hold Kacey naked in his arms?

"Dancing," Kacey interjected.

"Back in my day"—Mr. Casbon cleared his throat—"when fellas danced like that they got them girls pregnant."

Travis felt his face burn.

"You're not gonna get her pregnant, are you, son?"

Was this guy for real?

"Umm…" No, just *say no*. Why wouldn't his mouth work?

"Not unless you can get pregnant from dancing too close, Mr. Casbon." Kacey patted Travis on the shoulder, shocking him out of his paralyzed state.

"I'm sure it's possible." The old man pointed his finger into the air, then turned toward Grandma and pulled her flush against him. "I'm just glad we're old enough not to care."

"Oh merciful Lord above," Kacey muttered.

Travis elbowed her.

They continued to stare as Grandma laughed while in Mr. Casbon's arms.

"She's kind of a hussy," Kacey whispered.

"Kind of?" Grandma wasn't just flirting. She was… Well, the word was not something Travis wanted to use in the same sentence as *Grandma*.

"Time to eat!" his mother announced, strolling into the room. "Oh, heavens." She placed a hand over her heart when her eyes caught Grandma and Mr. Casbon embracing. "Let's, er, just take our seats then! Jake! Jake, get in here. It's time to eat!"

Everyone sat around the table. "Wescott!" Bets yelled. "Wescott, it's time, honey. Stop messing with the computer and get in here."

Travis's dad rushed into the room and took a seat. "Why do we have place cards?"

Bets glared. "I thought it best, considering..." She eyed Travis, then Kacey, and finally Jake, who felt the need to act innocent and shrugged his shoulders, then winked in Travis's direction.

Idiot.

"So," Mr. Casbon said as he began dishing heaping amounts of meat loaf onto his plate, "do I understand that we're going to have a rousing game of Monopoly tonight?"

Grandma tittered and blushed.

He said *rousing*, not *arousing*. They weren't playing strip Monopoly. Images he never wanted to see started pounding through his head, and then he looked at Kacey. Immediately, the images were replaced with visions of tasting her pouting lips, running his hands through her hair, kissing down her body until...

"Travis? Did you hear what Grandma asked?"

Caught, he looked around the dinner table; every eye was on him, which was somewhat of a blessing, considering he'd most likely be embarrassed beyond words if they were to look at the state he was in *under* the table.

"Sorry. What did you say, Grandma?"

"I said"—she gave him a pointed stare—"that last time I played Monopoly with you, you had the audacity to win."

"That is the point."

"I'm older. You should let the elderly win."

"Grandma, if I remember correctly, you not only tried to get me drunk by spiking my soda, but you crushed half a Benadryl in my drink when I wasn't looking. We're lucky I was breathing by the time the game ended."

Grandma sniffed. "Nothing wrong with a little stiff competition or some manipulating to make things more interesting. Besides, the Benadryl idea was completely Kacey's. It's her answer for everything. Just like that Greek wedding movie and Windex."

"Pardon?" Travis leaned forward.

"Oh, you know." Grandma waved her jeweled hand into the air. "Have a mosquito bite? Take a Benadryl. Can't sleep? Take a Benadryl. Can't perform in the bedroom—"

"I highly doubt Benadryl will help in that situation," Travis interrupted.

"Oh, I don't know about that," Mr. Casbon added, a wicked gleam in his eye as he picked up Grandma's hand and kissed it.

Travis jerked his head in his mother's direction, willing her to change the subject.

She was flushed and playing with her food; his father was trying to stifle a laugh. Was he the only sane one at the table?

"So, you never answered me." Grandma stabbed her salad with her fork.

"What was the question? Sorry I was distracted by the talk of extracurricular activities brought on by drugs."

"Will you be Kacey's partner? She always cheated as a child, and I need someone with a firm hand to spank her if she gets out of line."

The water that should have, by all means, gone down Travis's throat, spewed out of his mouth, landing directly in Jake's face.

"Thanks, man."

"S-sorry." Travis choked, glaring at his grandmother. She gave him a saucy wink and sipped her wine. She knew exactly what she had said. If she didn't watch it, he really was going to drug her, and it would be a hell of a lot stronger than Benadryl. She could count on that.

"I would love to." Travis wiped his mouth with his napkin and smiled at his grandmother. "After all, I doubt Kacey will get out of line. She already knows it's a losing battle when she tries to go up against me."

"Oh, but, Travis," Kacey cooed across the table. "That's exactly where I want to be."

She was teasing. He knew she was teasing, but he still couldn't force his heart not to leap, or his breathing to return to normal. Unable to speak, he merely lifted his water glass in her direction and prayed nobody would notice how jerky his movements were.

As the conversation grew quieter and people began to eat, Travis suddenly had a feeling of dread wash over him, as if something was about to go terribly wrong. He looked at each individual at the table, trying to figure out why he felt so skittish. And just when he was getting ready to laugh it off, his eyes focused on his mother.

She had the look.

The same one small children fear.

The look that every mom has when she has something she needs to say but would rather freak the crap out of you before opening her mouth. It's the silent look, the one that brings a man back to his childhood within seconds.

With dinner finished, everyone left to change into more comfortable clothes for the Monopoly game, but Travis stayed.

His mother cleared her throat and leaned forward, placing her elbows on the table. "What's going on, Travis?"

"Nothing," he lied, and looked away, an obvious tell.

"She's not yours," his mother said softly.

"What?" His head jerked up.

"Kacey." She shook her head and pushed away from the table, slowly rounding it and taking a seat next to Travis. "Honey, she's your brother's *fiancée*."

"I know that." He also knew that Jake was a lying, manipulative bastard, but he kept silent.

"It's just a crush."

She was talking to him like he was fifteen, and suddenly he was angry. Hadn't he grown up? He was a man, a man able to make his own decisions.

"Mom, I'm twenty-three."

"You're acting like you're in high school, Travis. You're constantly at each other's throats, and I swear if you keep looking at her the way you were over dinner, Jake's going to find out. He'll be heartbroken."

Travis snorted. "He'd have to have a heart in the first place."

"Travis Titus!"

"Sorry," he mumbled, feeling ancient and immature all at once. "It's not a big deal. She means nothing to me. You know that. We're just having fun."

A dish dropped behind him. He whipped around to see Kacey standing in the kitchen. "Sorry." Her smile was forced as she knelt down and picked up the dropped dish. "I don't know what happened. It just slipped. I hope I wasn't interrupting anything. I found this dish in the living room and wanted to make sure it got washed with the rest of them." Kacey rambled only when she was really angry or nervous.

Bets quickly helped her clean up the mess. "You're still planning on playing the game later, right?"

"Of course." Kacey smiled sweetly, then glared at Travis. "I have a partner to carry, after all."

Angry. She was definitely angry.

TWENTY-ONE

By the time everyone had gathered in the living room, Kacey was fuming.

She took a seat at the large card table and sighed. Travis was an idiot, so she refused to look at him. And Jake was staring at his reflection in his spoon. Seriously?

Things had changed between Travis and her, or so she had thought.

But her world had shifted tremendously all within the span of five minutes. She had been cleaning up the living room area, literally picking up after Jake's snacking session, when she'd heard Travis and his mom talking in hushed tones.

Not thinking anything of it, she'd walked into the room, and then had heard the topic of the conversation. It was her.

And Travis was denying having any sort of affection for her at all. If anything, he'd basically told his mother that he hated Kacey.

She means nothing to me. Why had that simple sentence made her heart clench? It wasn't as if she liked Travis.

She gulped.

It was a minor attraction, an inconvenient little pain in her heart. Maybe it was just because he was giving her attention and he was gorgeous. Either way, it was ending. Now.

And she knew exactly how to get revenge.

Rubbing her hands together, she smirked.

"I know that look," Jake said, sitting across from her. "And I'm man enough to admit that I'm a little afraid right now."

"Please." Kacey snorted. "When have I ever done anything remotely cruel to you?"

"You mean other than breaking my heart in the ninth grade when I saw you kissing Tom Williams behind the gym?"

The others at the table ignored them, all but Travis, who was now shifting restlessly by her side.

"I didn't even like him. I was merely experimenting," Kacey argued. "Besides, we all know who the best kisser I've ever had is."

Travis cleared his throat.

"Oh yeah, and who is that?" Jake leaned forward.

"I'm not telling." She bit her lip as she examined each game piece, trying to decide what she wanted to be.

"I bet I know." Jake folded his hands behind his head. "I mean other than myself." He winked. "Was it John Davis?"

"John Davis?" Kacey wrinkled her nose. "No, not John."

"Kevin Tate?"

Kacey shook her head. Maybe she should be the shoe. And then when she passed Travis on the game board, she could step on his game piece.

"Sean Halverson?"

Kacey rolled her eyes. "Please, that boy was at the bottom of the list and I think you know why."

"Wandering hands, that one." Jake shook his head. "I've got it!" He snapped his fingers. "Cooper Reynolds! It has to be him. Girls used to cry as if someone were dying or something when he broke up with them. I guarantee you it's him. Did you know that he's single now and—"

Travis slammed his fist on the table, silencing the conversation. "Sorry, thought I saw a bug."

Kacey looked at him and raised her eyebrow. "Really? I didn't see anything."

"It was there." He pointed, teeth clenched.

"You sure you're not imagining things?" she said tightly. "After all, we both know how much you like imaginary things. Take for example, your little bunny. Granted it was real, but you were convinced it was your friend. Do you still sleep with it?"

Travis smiled tightly. "I don't know, Kace. Do you still suck your thumb?"

Her eyes narrowed. "*Ooh*, mature, Travis. Tell me, do you have to plan conversations in your head so you don't stutter, or are you beyond that now?"

She knew she'd hit a nerve. He murmured a curse word. "Can we just play the damn game?"

Grandma laughed. "Oh, kids, you've always been such teasers. Yes, let's play. Now, Kacey, remember not to cheat."

"I don't cheat." Kacey crossed her heart. "I'm not the cheating kind."

Jake's eyes flickered to her before he looked down and cleared his throat.

Kacey was glad nobody noticed the exchange, but then looked to her right. Travis was staring at the two of them, his head looking back and forth. She forced a smile and shrugged.

"Kace, you want some tea or something? You know, to calm you down."

"I'm calm." She was by no stretch of the imagination calm; just sitting next to Travis and his perceptive eyes made her want to scream. On top of that, his cologne decided to float off of him very near her nose, making her mouth go dry and her tongue feel thick in her mouth.

"I'll be right back, regardless of how much we despise each other. I still need you to be a good partner so I can beat Jake."

"In your dreams." Jake laughed, then looked at his money. "Okay, guys, it's time. Let's roll to see who goes first!"

Travis left the room but quickly returned with tea and handed it to Kacey.

"Is it poisoned?"

"No. You should be proud. I didn't even put any Benadryl in there."

"Pity," Grandma said from the other side of the table.

"Let's do this." Wescott pumped his fist in the air.

All in all, the Titus family was way too excited for family game night.

She had forgotten how intense it usually was.

She soon remembered when Grandma began screaming that Wescott was embezzling money from the bank.

"Um…" Kacey raised her hand. "How does one embezzle in Monopoly?"

Wescott shrugged.

Grandma glared.

Bets laughed and patted her husband on the knee.

Kacey watched the exchange, then noticed that yes, money had been left on his leg.

"Cheaters!" She pushed her chair back. "Both of you, cheaters!"

Suddenly she felt very, very wired, as if someone had given her a double shot of espresso. Caffeine pushed her over the top. She did not have a good reaction when given too much.

"I have no idea what you are speaking of, dear." Bets shook her head innocently.

"Lies!" Jake pointed at both of them and turned to Mr. Casbon, who was also nominated as game referee. "I request an investigation, sir."

"On what grounds?"

"Cheating, money changing hands under the table. If you look at the evidence, you'll see as clearly as I do. Mother is hiding something and Father is sweating."

Mr. Casbon rose from his seat and began walking in circles around the table.

Everyone was silent.

"Wescott, what say you?"

"Not guilty."

"Hmm." Mr. Casbon stopped behind Bets and looked over her shoulder. "And you, what have you to say for yourself, miss?"

"N-not guilty." She swallowed.

"Then you won't mind if I look under your chair?"

"Um, well, I'm not sure that's . . ."

"Ah-hah!" Mr. Casbon waved a few pieces of paper money in the air, then stood to his full height. "My ruling." He cleared his throat. "Disqualified!"

Bets and Wescott burst out laughing, then kissed. "We tried, honey," Wescott crooned in Bets's ear. "We had a good run."

"Well, that ends our night." Bets rose. "Kacey, I expect you and Travis to pull through."

"What about me?" Jake looked hurt, but everyone knew he was just joking.

"You, my dear, win every time. So I never root for you, only the underdogs."

"Fine." He pouted, then began counting his money in a very irritating voice.

It was just the five of them left.

Kacey felt like her eyes were going to fall out of her head; they seemed to be too open, as if she couldn't relax and too much air was hitting them, making them dry.

"Do you have any more tea?" she whispered to Travis.

He smiled and nodded. "Sure, I'll be right back."

Within minutes he had another steaming mug of tea. "This should help."

She drank it down fast, fully expecting it to do the trick.

An hour later, Jake had also been disqualified; apparently embezzlement ran in the family—that and cheating. He left the room in a huff, leaving a paper trail of stuffed money falling from his pockets. Classy.

It was nearing midnight and Grandma seemed to be winning despite Kacey's attempt to put a hotel on every property she owned.

"This could go on forever," Mr. Casbon sulked. "I say we have a tiebreaker."

"Deal." Kacey wasn't tired, but she figured the old people wanted to . . . socialize.

"The first person to roll a double six wins the game."

"Easy enough." Travis grabbed the dice and rolled. "A two and a four."

Grandma rolled. "One and a five."

Mr. Casbon cursed when his roll ended up on double ones.

"Your turn." Grandma handed over the dice to Kacey. "Why don't you have Travis blow on them for good luck?"

Travis stiffened next to her.

The jerk. He could at least pretend not to be so offended by her presence.

Rolling her eyes, she turned to him and opened up her hand. "Blow."

Travis's eyes darkened, his lips parted, and for a second he looked as if he were going to kiss her. Slowly, his head descended, and he blew softly across her hands, sending shivers all the way down to her toes.

The dice flew across the board.

"You win! You win!" Grandma clapped her hands. "Well done, kids!"

But Kacey didn't look at the board. She didn't look at Grandma. Her eyes were still trained on Travis's lips. Damn him.

To his credit, he didn't smirk, nor did he pull his gaze away. They simply sat staring at each other, breathing raggedly.

"We'll just be going then," Grandma announced.

Kacey snapped out of her haze. "Going? But Grandma you live here."

"I do," Grandma confirmed, helping Mr. Casbon to his feet. "But my lover is the boy next door, so I'll just be walking over there with him."

"What are your intentions with my grandmother?" Travis asked, entering into the conversation.

Mr. Casbon smirked. "I'm gonna make an honest woman out of her."

Travis laughed. "That's all I ask." He threw his hands up in the air in surrender.

They disappeared out the door, leaving Kacey and Travis and the board game.

The silence was deafening.

TWENTY-TWO

Would they never get along?

As if answering that question, Kacey blew the hair away from her face and glared at him. "You gonna help me clean up the mess or what?"

"Hmm, let me think." He leaned back in his chair. "Help you clean up the game or watch you bend over and do it yourself. Tough decision."

"You. Are. An. A—"

"Hey now." Travis slowly rose from the chair and sauntered over to the card table. "Do you think we can go an entire conversation without calling each other names?"

"Yes," she said tightly.

She was horrible at masking her emotions, and she was obviously upset. "What's up, Kace? You're not yourself."

She snorted. "How would you know?"

"I've spent more time with you than Jake this weekend. I think I can tell when you're pissed, especially considering you've been straightening that stack of money for the past five minutes."

Her hand froze over the money. She collapsed in the chair.

He wasn't sure if he should scoop her up in his arms and kiss away her anger or just have it out right then and there.

"I want to punch you," she said lightly, as if she were commenting on the color of the carpet.

"Okay..." he drawled. "Now?"

"Now's good."

She made a lunge for him and slugged him in the shoulder. His balance was off, making him fall to the floor with a loud grunt.

Kacey stayed on top of him, clearly unaware of how much he wanted to rip her clothes from her body and have his way with her on the card table.

"You were an ugly bully when I was little." She punched him in the arm again. "And then you have the audacity to grow up handsome?"

Oh God, she was finally losing her mind. He had successfully pushed her over the edge.

"How dare you be anything but unattractive!" She pinched his arm.

He howled with pain. "What do you want me to do?"

"Apologize," she ground out.

"For what?"

"For—" She looked down at her hands and whispered, "For saying I don't matter."

Travis groaned and put his hands over his face. "You heard that?"

Kacey nodded, still straddling him. She looked down and flashed him a smile. "It's not a big deal. I just wanted you to suffer a bit."

"Kace, look." He grabbed her arms. "You matter. You know you do. If you didn't matter..."

He couldn't do it.

What was stopping him?

"If you didn't matter," he repeated, "then why would I waste all this time picking on you?"

Her eyes narrowed. "I guess that's the closest I'm going to get to an apology, isn't it?"

"Absolutely." He grinned.

"At least I got a few swings in," she muttered, peeling herself away from him, even though his body begged her to stay.

"Yes, you did." He got to his feet. "And who knows? Maybe I'll wake up with a few bruises you can push tomorrow morning."

"One can only hope." She held out her hand. "Truce?"

Hell no. *No truce*, his body screamed at him; instead, like an idiot, he shook her hand. Friends. He could do friends. He was an adult after all.

Kacey smiled and bent over to grab the paper money off the floor.

His eyes focused on her butt.

So maybe he was a fifteen-year-old stuck in an adult's body. It was alarming how fast he was turned on just by looking at her.

"Um, Kace? Why don't you go to bed? I'll clean up. I probably deserve it after saying you don't matter."

"True." She winked, then dropped the money back onto the floor, allowing it to scatter so he'd have to gather it again.

"Mature." He nodded his head.

"Always." She bounced off.

Geez, she had a lot of energy for . . .

Oh crap. He forgot.

He'd been so mad that she was flirting with Jake and not paying attention to him he'd made her tea caffeinated. And then she had driven him so insane the next pot he'd made was the same.

He had a very sneaking suspicion that the truce was about to be over.

"Well, that was short-lived," he muttered as he gathered the game pieces and began throwing them in the box.

By the time the game was cleaned up, it was nearing 1:00 a.m. Tired, he sluggishly walked to the new wing of the house and entered the master bedroom.

Everything seemed unfamiliar. Kacey was in his

room, which was technically the guest room, and he was in this monstrous master suite with nothing but the crickets chirping outside to keep him company.

How, in two days, had he made such a mess of things?

His mind was a swirl of confusion. First Kacey, then Grandma acting as if she hadn't had any mini-strokes in the past few months, and now Jake acting nice. He could handle Jake being an ass, but when he was nice it seemed so forced and fake. He didn't want Kacey falling for it.

But how couldn't she?

Jake was too damn good at being charismatic.

Travis sat on the bed and groaned into his hands. Kacey was an obsession, one he couldn't seem to get over no matter how many years passed between seeing each other.

One minute she seemed irritated with him; the next, he could almost swear she wanted him to kiss her.

Which probably meant his mind was playing tricks on him. The last time they kissed she admitted to being semi-drunk, which didn't bode well for his confidence that she wanted to repeat the act.

Cursing, he went to the bathroom and brushed his teeth, then peeled off his clothes and jumped into bed.

TWENTY-THREE

Rat bastard!" Kacey punched the pillow with her fist. "Of course the tea wasn't decaf, you idiot." She cursed herself and threw her legs over the bed.

With a grunt she opened the door to the room and padded down the hall to the new wing of the house.

I will not allow myself to get creeped out by the weird sculptures, she chanted over and over again as she got farther into the new wing. Travis was the only one staying in this section of the house. Which, on one end of things, was good; it meant she didn't have to see him as often, considering he had separate entrances to and from the giant estate. Not that it mattered. She had spent nearly every waking moment with the man.

On the other hand, it also meant that when she had

to go searching for him at 2:00 a.m., she had to bypass an actual gallery of masks that, in her opinion, could suddenly burst to life at any minute.

She finally reached the end of the hallway where two double doors resided. The master suite.

I'm going to castrate him. "Travis!" She pounded the door. "I know you're in there! Come out here and fight me like a man!"

No answer.

"Son of a—"

"What the hell, Kace? Do you know what time it is?" Travis opened the door just as she was about to curse him into the fiery hole he crawled out of.

Words, however, would not flow out of her slack-jawed mouth. The man was naked—well, not entirely. He was wearing short boxer briefs that did nothing to hide the strong muscles plunging into his—

Truly he was sin incarnate. Big shock there.

"You!" She pushed his chiseled chest and backed him up into the room, slamming the door behind her. "You and your trickery are not welcome, Travis Thomas Titus!"

"Whoa, easy now. Don't go dropping my full name like that. Things can't be that bad." He pushed his curly golden-brown hair away from his face and yawned. "Now, can you please tell me what I did so I can go back to sleep? Some of us don't stay up all hours of the night contemplating ways to torture others."

"The tea"—Kacey pushed him again—"was not decaf!"

A grin broke out on Travis's face. "Oh?"

Kacey reached for his shoulders, but he was too fast, throwing her on her back on his very comfortable bed and hovering over her. Not good. Oh God above, he was warm and—*Don't look, Kacey. Just don't look.*

"Kace, why are your eyes closed? Come on. Open them, and fight me like a man." He winked and leaned in close enough to brush a kiss across her lips.

To her ultimate shame, she leaned forward expectantly.

"Sorry about the tea, but I do have a reputation to protect. And you did promise never to tell anyone about the bunny I used to sleep with, as well as everything else you laid out on the table tonight."

"It slipped!"

"We took a blood oath!" he argued, his warm breath sending chills down her neck. "And I wanted revenge."

"Fine!" Her teeth clenched together in annoyance. "But now you will have to suffer the consequences."

"I tremble with fear." Travis pushed away from her and dove under the covers. "Hey, can you grab the lights when you leave?"

Maniacal laughter erupted from her lips. Yup, definitely running on no sleep. "I'm not leaving."

"Normally, when a scantily clad woman says that, and she's this close to my bed, it means I'm about to get laid. But judging by the look on your face, I'm going to guess you're not offering."

"I'm going to sleep with you."

Travis's eyes bugged out of his head. He looked from right to left and then carefully pulled the blankets back and leaned close to her, both hands up as if she were a dangerous animal ready to snap.

"And you're not going to get laid. You're going to sleep too. So move over, bed buddy. You've just acquired a roomie!"

Travis glared, then nervously looked around the room. "I'm a bed hog. Trust me. You're better off sleeping on the floor."

"No, I think I'll take the bed." Kacey grinned. "Oh, and I snore, and sometimes I have night terrors. So if I start screaming, just shake me, but make sure it's gentle. If you wake someone up from a night terror and freak them out . . . well, let's just say that's when they turn homicidal."

It looked like Travis wanted to say something, but instead he marched over to the light and turned it off. Then crawled back into bed.

"If you ask me to spoon you, I'm going to smother you with my pillow," he grumbled.

"Please, like I want your favorite appendage anywhere near my body."

"Keep telling yourself that, Kace."

"Night, Satan."

"Night, sweetie."

Oh God, it felt so good. So damn good. What the hell did he do in his past to deserve such punishment as to have the one girl he'd had a crush on for practically his whole life sleeping in his bed?

He fought for control of his lust, knowing it was a losing battle. But what would she think if he suddenly attacked her? No doubt he would get stabbed.

So, after two restless hours, Travis finally fell asleep with dreams of Kacey in her nightgown dancing in his head.

What the…? Travis jolted awake as Kacey punched him in the gut. He recoiled and brought his knees to his chest in an effort to protect his manhood. "What are you doing!"

"Oh, sorry," Kacey said groggily. "My hand slipped."

"Your hand slipped, my ass…," he grumbled, managing to scoot away and drift back to sleep.

Within minutes he was again awakened by Kacey, this time talking in her sleep about cheese and then alphabetizing all of the different types. "*G* stands for gouda, and…"

He clamped his hand across her mouth in hopes of silencing the shrew, but instead she continued mumbling under his hand, all the while stretching her body beneath the blankets.

Could he help that his eyes naturally went to the curve of her breasts? Or that his blood heated just at the sight of her creamy skin clad in her tank top and short shorts?

He told his eyes to move.

He begged his mind to stop playing images of what she would look like without that tank top covering her.

Truly, he was trying to be a gentleman, and then the inevitable happened, not because he was planning on it, rather because they were in a bed, and he was exhausted and she was...there.

Really, it didn't have anything to do with his feelings or love for all things Kacey.

With a curse he pulled his hand away from her mouth and crushed his lips against hers. His hands gripped her shoulders, and then he was on top of her, straddling her. Aggression poured out of him as he slammed her arms against her sides and continued his attack.

Kacey whimpered, and then sprang to action, thrusting her tongue into his mouth with such a fiery hot need that he was half-tempted to fall to his knees in ecstasy; then again he was already on his knees, straddling the goddess as she reached behind his head and pulled his neck closer to hers. Lying across her, he knew it was going to happen, probably because it was the next logical step.

Logic, logic, what was the meaning of that word again? And then...then someone was at the door.

"What the—?" He pulled away from Kacey, abruptly landing on the floor in a tangle of sheets. "Yes?" His agitated voice was clipped.

"Sorry, honey, it's Mom..."

"Oh no!" Kacey shrieked, tripping on the same sheet and crashing down on top of him. Her eyes widened, and her mouth opened. Travis slapped his hand across it and gave her a death glare.

"I just woke up, Mom. Did you need something?" What the hell was the time?

"Oh, no. I just thought I heard some commotion, like a person screaming, or snoring, or...I don't know. It's probably my imagination, but I wanted to make sure you were okay."

"I'm fine, Mom," he said, silently pleading for her to leave.

Kacey moved on top of him and then placed a wet kiss across his lips.

He was going to strangle her.

And then she straddled him.

"And I know how you don't have your bunny anymore." His mom's muffled voice came through the door. "Funny how I hadn't thought of that until Kacey brought it up tonight."

"I don't...," he said between kisses. "Need..." Oh God, her mouth was so hot. "...the damn bunny!" he all but yelled.

"I know, honey. You were just so attached after you went off to college, and I know how you named it Kacey. Hmm. Why did you name it Kacey? I forget. She didn't give it to you. Strange."

Kacey froze on top of him, the kissing stopped, and he wished to God she didn't have such great hearing. Kacey gave him a panicked, almost horrified look.

Swell. He was scaring his bed partner.

"Oh well," his mom said when he didn't answer. "See you for breakfast. It's in two hours, so you have some time. Bye!"

TWENTY-FOUR

Kacey struggled to keep her hands at her sides, when truthfully, all she wanted to do was strangle the man she was still straddling.

"You named your bunny after me? You hated me in high school. What gives?" She crossed her arms.

Travis looked away. "Don't flatter yourself, Kace. I named the bunny after you because I figured it was the only name that would evoke fear in even the scariest of monsters."

"So it had nothing to do with me?" Kacey wondered why she was suddenly upset.

"Oh, it had everything to do with you." Travis reached around and pulled her body tighter against him as he leaned forward and kissed her again. "After all..."

His lips tortured her neck, he groaned into her hair, and Kacey hated that she was so easily seduced by the man she had been trying not to fall for the entire trip. "I wasn't allowed to physically torture you. I was brought up to be a gentleman. So whenever you…frustrated me"—he nipped her ear and claimed her lips again—"I'd come home and beat my bunny."

"You took out your sexual frustration on a bunny?" Kacey's voice was breathless.

"Who said I was sexually frustrated?"

Crap. Now what was she going to do? Lie? Kiss him again? Knee him in the balls? "I, uh," she stuttered. "I just assumed that was the life you led, almost like a eunuch. You know, because you didn't date much and took that Jezebel to prom with you."

Travis rolled his eyes. "I'll let my cousin know you said hi."

"She always was such a dear." Kacey and Travis's cousin, Lucy, had had a falling out that night, when they both showed up in the same dress. Lucy, with all her naturally endowed gifts from God, had nearly fallen out of hers, while Kacey had needed tissue stuffing in hers to fill it out. It wasn't her fault she was a late bloomer! The entire night was ruined when Lucy, in a fit of lust—and most likely alcohol—made a move for Jake. They were, after all, only second cousins, once removed. It didn't make it any less creepy, or wrong, or sad to watch as she tried to molest him on the dance floor. Ah, high school. Good times.

Kacey shook her head and gave Travis sweet smile, pushing at his chest so she could get up.

"Where are you going?" Travis grasped her wrist. She had to get out, had to leave him before she attacked him and lost all control.

"My room."

"You can't go to your room. What if someone sees you?"

"Who's going to see me?" The birds? The tiny squirrels outside his bedroom window?

Travis blinked several times before answering. "Anyone could see you, and if you come out of my room looking like that, they'll be suspicious."

"Your family knows we hate each other." Kacey grunted.

Travis, the devil, gave her such a seducing smile she wondered if her heart would stop beating. "Yes, but my family knows of my certain reputation, that of a playboy, not a eunuch, as you've so lovingly described me."

"Right, well, since you're paranoid, I'll just shower here, and we can escape out the back. Sound good?"

Travis groaned into his hands. "Too good, Kace. Too good."

Not wanting to hang around, or even allow his double meaning to penetrate her already jumbled thoughts, she skittered away toward the bathroom.

"Right, then." *What was I going to say? Something snappy. Something funny. Damn his abs! They have no right to be so ripped!*

Kacey pushed through the door and closed it hard behind her. Lock? Lock? Where was the lock?

"There's no lock, Kace." Travis's deep timbre explained the situation. "They haven't gotten around to actually fixing up the bathroom yet, so it's kinda still in shambles, but the water's hot, and the towels are clean. Just don't go making it smell all girly in there."

How the heck was she going to do that? Just naturally give off her womanly musk by bathing in the steam of his bathroom? Idiot.

"Fine!" She went to the shower and turned it on. Steaming water came pouring out. Perfection. Within two seconds, she was stripped and in the shower, dreaming of bacon and scalding coffee.

Which was why she didn't hear the door open. Or Travis's voice when he asked if she was okay.

Or the shriek that came from him when he slipped on her thong and grabbed the shower curtain on the way to the floor.

Naked. Gloriously naked. No doubt, he was going to be a little upset over the fact that she'd left more than her musk behind.

Travis cursed for a great while and then finally set his eyes on her. All of her.

Following his lead, she cursed like a sailor. His eyes scanned her boldly without shame. They stood in silence, neither of them wanting to make the first move, or even to breathe, it seemed.

"What the hell!" a male voice roared.

Horrified, Kacey looked up into murderous green eyes and gulped. "Hi, Jake."

TWENTY-FIVE

This isn't what you think!" Kacey managed to grab a nearby towel and cover her nakedness, though it was hard to see the point of it all, considering both men had openly gaped at her. There had to be something ethically, or at least religiously, wrong with two brothers ogling one woman's goodies in the bathroom.

"Oh?" Jake crossed his arms. "Because you don't want to know what I think right now. How could you!" He shoved Travis against the wall.

"How could I?" Travis roared. "What the hell kind of question is that? When you've been running around this weekend screwing everything with a skirt?"

"One time!" Jake shouted.

"You're supposed to be pretending to be engaged!"

"It doesn't even matter anymore!" Jake pushed him

against the wall again, his arm coming up beneath his chin. Obviously, Travis was letting him, considering Jake was younger and clearly not as strong as Travis.

"Why the hell not?" Travis's voice was strained.

"Grandma didn't say! She just wanted Kacey back! Besides, she knows we aren't engaged, all right? I did it for my reputation. Apparently dating strippers is bad for the company. It was the board's idea anyway. It's a win-win! I needed to save my reputation, so we pretended to be engaged. Do you think I *want* to be married?"

Kacey stood there, stunned. She knew the marriage wasn't real, but for some reason his words still stung, as if he were breaking up with her all over again. And what was worse was that she was watching the entire exchange almost naked.

"What was the point of bringing her down here if it wasn't real anyway? And why was Grandma faking a stroke!" Travis shoved Jake, causing him to fall onto the floor with a thud.

"How should I know? I was being the dutiful grandson!" Jake pointed at himself and sneered.

"Um, guys?" Kacey raised her hand.

"Not now!" they yelled in unison.

"Guys."

They ignored her and continued to fight over whether or not Grandma was sick, Jake was lying, and why it was so important to bribe Kacey to come down to Portland. All in all, it was the worst five minutes of her life.

And then...

Bets, Wescott, and Grandma burst into the room.

Lovely.

Kacey prayed for lightning to strike.

No such luck.

"What is the meaning of this?" Wescott roared, then turned a bright purple when he glanced at Kacey in the towel.

"She was naked!" Jake pointed to Kacey.

Travis rolled his eyes. "In the shower, where people usually are naked."

Jake sneered. "And you were staring at her because you find human anatomy fascinating?"

Travis lunged for Jake's throat, but Wescott pushed between the two. "Stop! Now, I don't know what has you boys so upset, but you're adults. Sit down and discuss it. Don't start throwing punches, especially when Kacey's standing there in nothing but a towel."

Both Travis's and Jake's eyes flashed to her. She wanted to die of embarrassment.

"I'll just, um...I'll be in my, or his..." She pointed to Travis and shook her head. "The guest room."

Travis was shaking with rage. It didn't help that every time he closed his eyes to try to calm himself down all he saw were mental images of Kacey without any clothes, standing in his bathroom.

Jake was grumbling next to him.

"Both of you," Wescott said, pointing. "Speak. Now."

"At the same time?" Jake sneered.

"Smart-ass," Travis muttered.

Grandma stood behind their father, her arms folded. A tiny smile formed across her lips.

"I'll take it from here, Wescott," she instructed.

Their father lifted his hands in the air and walked out, pulling their mother with him.

"Listen here!" Grandma snapped, making both men jump. "I needed Kacey to come down here and that's my business and mine alone. I told Jake to bribe her if necessary. Obviously, he used my stroke as an excuse, as well as money, which was fine by me, as I plan on leaving that girl an inheritance anyway. Though I'm honestly disappointed that Jake used a fake engagement to save face in front of the board. Grow a pair, son."

Travis opened his mouth to speak.

"Don't," she snapped. "I'll deal with you later, Travis, but right now my scorn is for your little brother." Travis tried not to look pleased when Grandma's eyes blazed in Jake's direction.

"How could you! I asked one simple task of you, and you're running around lifting skirts!"

Travis cleared his throat. "In his defense, some of the girls were wearing pants."

Jake glared.

Grandma continued to lecture. "Now, Jake, I think it's safe to say you've made a mess of things, especially in front of Kacey. I want you to pack up your things and stay the night in the condo downtown. You don't fly out until Monday, and that will give me adequate time to do damage control with your parents. Besides, from the looks of it, the newspapers have enough photographs of you two running about that they'll be satisfied you're settling down."

Travis was only half-listening. He still didn't understand why they needed the pretense of a fake engagement. If Grandma wasn't dying, the only people who were getting duped were his parents. Well, them and the rest of the Twitterverse who followed Jake's updates religiously.

Grandma said some more choice words to Jake and told him to leave.

He did, much like a dog with its tail between its legs.

"And you!" Grandma poked Travis in the chest. "I was counting on you!"

"Counting on me?"

"Yes, you fool! I gave you every opportunity, and you were doing so well the other night!" Grandma plopped onto the bed next to him. "Do you know how difficult it is to fake a stroke when you're in your prime? If I have to lie down one more time..."

"Pardon?" Was she insane?

"You've loved her a long time, my boy." His hands began to shake in his lap as his grandma patted his back. "I know it was hard for you growing up, and no girl has piqued your interest since. I just thought, well...I thought having her here with your brother would make you jealous enough to finally do something about it."

"Well, you got the jealous part right. You're lucky I didn't kill him the other night when I punched him."

Grandma shook her head, and suddenly Travis felt like she was very frail. "What aren't you telling me, Grandma?"

A little tear ran down her cheek, but she pushed it away with her wrinkled hand. "I haven't given up on Jake, so don't for a second think that, but you, you're different." She looked up, her eyes glassy. "You remind me of your grandfather so much, Travis. You need a good strong woman by your side. I think Kacey is that woman. I've always thought so and now I know it. Do yourself a favor and talk to her."

Travis laughed bitterly. "And say what exactly? That I'm in love with her and have been for as long as I can remember? Beg her to not love my brother, but love me, be with me?"

"That's a start," his grandma said. "Besides, there is something neither of you boys know."

"Oh?"

"Kacey was like a granddaughter to me. I've kept in touch with her as much as possible over the years, though I admit I've been lazy in my writing. These old hands don't work as well as they used to." She leaned her head on his shoulder. "When her parents died . . . Oh, Travis, it was the worst tragedy. She became a shell of the girl I once knew. I figured if I let her heal and deal with it on her own, she'd find her way back. I knew her well enough to know that if I coddled her, she'd push away. It didn't help matters that Jake lied to all of us about how close they truly were these past four years."

Travis's blood ran cold. "I figured. I mean, she hinted as much earlier."

"Oh, honey, Jake and Kacey haven't spoken in years. He kept tabs on her, but they never got together. Ever since her parents' death she's been nothing but a childhood friend, an acquaintance. I used to send her newspaper clippings from her parents' business, but I don't know if she ever truly read them or looked. It was as if she died right along with them."

"That explains a lot." He was suddenly sick with worry. What the hell had really happened between those two? It couldn't have been just her parents' death. No. There was something else, some underlying tension.

"In their will they named me her guardian."

"I'm sorry, what?" Travis was sure he wasn't hearing his grandmother correctly.

Grandma chuckled. "I'm her legal guardian. Naturally, she's an adult now, so it hardly matters. They drew up the papers when she was still quite small. But Kacey is just as much mine as she was theirs. I've always watched out for her, always wanted what was best for her, and in my mind, the best was for her to be part of our family."

"Just not by way of Jake?" Travis nudged his grandmother.

"Heavens, no." She chuckled. "Kacey knew there was something going on, knew I wasn't really sick. I told her to use this time to find herself, and I think she was beginning to."

"Until I kept screwing it up?" Travis asked.

"I wouldn't say you screwed it up, but you did make a mess of things. You're so hot and cold around her. But I'll tell you what. I'll give you exactly twenty-four hours alone with the girl to figure things out."

Travis laughed and reached behind his neck to rub a sore spot. "Yeah, and how are you going to do that?"

She rose to her full height and pulled at her tight jacket. "I'm Grandma. I can do anything I want."

The woman had a point.

"Be happy, Travis." She kissed his nose and walked toward the door. "Your parents and I will be gone within the hour. I hear the cottage at Seaside is lovely this time of year. I may even take pity on your brother and let him tag along rather than rot in that dratted condo downtown."

Travis lay back against the bed and stared at the ceiling.

Manipulative little thing, his grandma. To think she had gone to such extremes just because she wanted him to be happy, well, him and Kacey.

He wasn't sure how long he stared at the ceiling fan, but it was a while before he managed to jump in the shower and get ready for the day.

Travis bounded down the hall. The house was eerily quiet. He silently hoped Kacey hadn't somehow run off, leaving him alone in the house.

He knocked on her door.

No answer.

He knocked again, then pushed it open.

Her bags were still in the room, but she wasn't there. Her perfume, however, danced off the walls, filling his nose with her scent. Great, now he'd be uncomfortable for the entire search.

"Kacey?" he called as he went down the stairs. He went into the living room, the kitchen...Where was she?

The door to the patio was open. He went outside and called for her again.

"I'm in here!" she answered, then waved from the tree house.

Of course she was. If he had been thinking rationally, he would have realized that the first place to look should have been the tree house.

Whenever she'd had a bad day at school she would rush over to their house, drop her backpack on the kitchen counter, snatch a cookie from the jar, and climb up into the tree house.

Sometimes it was hours before she'd emerge.

But when she did, Kacey was always happier, as if the day at school no longer mattered.

He sighed and climbed slowly up the ladder until he pulled himself up into the tree house.

Kacey was sitting in the corner, her arms wrapped around her knees.

"Sorry." She bit down on her lip and sighed. "I just needed to think, so I came out here."

"Yeah, well, that makes two of us. I don't suppose you snatched cookies from the kitchen too?"

She reached to her side and pulled out a bag with three chocolate chip cookies. "Of course."

He took one from the bag and smiled. "Kace."

She looked up.

"I had a really good speech for you. I mean, it was fantastic—something that would bring you to tears..."

"No doubt," she agreed, taking a bite of her cookie.

"But sitting here, looking at you, all I really want to do is kiss you and make the sadness go away. I know what happened earlier was awkward, but I hope your feelings weren't hurt. What Jake said was..."

Kacey laughed. "What Jake said was exactly what I would expect. I know he doesn't want to get married, and we both know I'm not insane enough to want to marry him either."

Travis exhaled in relief.

"But..." Kacey shook her head.

He didn't like the sound of her voice.

"But I don't know. It hurts all over again for some reason. Isn't that silly?"

He knew he probably wasn't going to get another opportunity, so he asked, "What happened between you two?"

Her face froze, and her breathing threatened to stop. "He, um..." She nervously pushed away hair from her face and bit her lip. "We...had..." A tear ran down her cheek.

Alarmed, Travis grasped her wrists and pulled her into his lap, rocking her back and forth. "What? Tell me." He rubbed her arms with his hands.

"We slept together."

His heart stopped. Anger and frustration as well as jealousy jerked through his body with such force he wasn't sure if he wanted to go shoot his brother or blame himself, even though it wasn't his fault. Still, he felt responsible for Kacey. He always had.

"In college?" He was thankful he was able to ask without screaming.

She nodded in his arms. "It was horrible."

Thank God.

"We were still so young, and it was a stupid mistake, and we both felt so bad and stupid. It was so confusing! The next morning all I wanted to do was call my best friend, but he wasn't my best friend anymore. I didn't know what he was, and then that day was when your parents called to tell me that Mom and Dad had had an accident. I couldn't tell anyone. I felt so ashamed." She began to softly cry in his arms, as he kissed her hair and rocked her.

Kacey wasn't sure why she was spilling her deepest secrets to Travis, but it seemed time to let everything out into the open. She was tired of keeping it inside, tired of trying to be strong when really she felt so scared and weak most of the time.

"I tried calling him, but he wouldn't answer his phone. Finally, someone picked up. It was a girl."

Travis cursed under his breath.

"Nothing was the same. He hugged me and said he was sorry about my parents, and that was it. We never talked about it. We never fixed what we broke, so we just slowly grew apart as if we hadn't caused this giant divide in what had been a lifelong friendship. He was the only tie I had to your family, so when he pushed me away, I felt...I felt like an orphan."

She began to sob harder into his chest. He whispered encouragement into her ear. "I would have died that year without Grandma."

"What do you mean 'without Grandma'?"

Kacey smiled despite her tears. "Remember that summer she said she was touring the United States?"

He chuckled. "Oh yes, I received a postcard every other week."

"Well, those postcards were bought at a bookstore, and Grandma spent the entire summer with me."

"What?"

"Yup." Kacey wiped more tears away and smiled. "She saved me, said she'd always be there for me and take care of me. That's why it was so weird when she stopped writing last month, and then Jake came in with this huge story about how she was sick and dying and... well, I had to come even if it meant I was manipulating everyone to do so."

"I understand." Travis used his thumb to wipe an escaped tear from her cheek. Kacey's breath hitched. Her eyes glanced at his lips, then back up to his gaze.

"Kace..." His lips descended slowly, even though his body was going a hundred miles an hour. "I'm going to kiss you now."

"Okay."

TWENTY-SIX

Kacey knew she shouldn't feel nervous; it wasn't as if they hadn't kissed before, but now that everything was out there, she felt even more vulnerable.

What if he rejected her too?

Dang, she hadn't realized how insecure she was until this very moment in Travis's arms.

His lips touched hers.

It wasn't even really a kiss.

He pulled back, his eyes hooded with desire.

"I can't."

"What?" Her heart froze in her chest. "You can't kiss me?"

"No." He shook his head and laughed. "It wouldn't be right to kiss you in the tree house."

Kacey stiffened. "Why?"

"I saw you and Jake have your first kiss in this tree house."

"We were ten."

"It still counts."

"I cried afterward!" Kacey pushed against his chest, but his arms held her braced against him.

"I don't want you to cry this time," he murmured in her hair, and then kissed her neck. His lips were warm and soft as he took her skin between them, gently sucking. "Let's go."

He pulled away, leaving Kacey completely shaken.

He expected her to walk in her condition? She'd just shared her innermost secrets with the man, he'd kissed her, and now she was supposed to climb down a ladder without falling on her head?

She slowly crawled to the hole where the ladder hung and nearly fell out of the tree house completely when she lost her footing.

"Sure you aren't drunk?" Travis laughed.

Kacey glared and continued climbing down. Once she reached the last rung, her leg slipped through the hole in the loose rope ladder, and she toppled to the ground, her leg still caught.

Embracing the moment, she laid her head against the grass and closed her eyes, lacing her hands behind her head.

"Comfortable?" Travis hovered over her.

"Immensely. I did that on purpose, by the way."

"It was so graceful it had to have been on purpose."
He winked and held out his hand. She reached up and
pulled him down on top of her, not that it took much
effort.

Travis leaned over her, straddling her. "We're out
of the tree house now."

"Yes, yes, we are." Kacey's voice was shaking.

"So I guess I can kiss you now."

"You guess?"

"I want to kiss you now."

"That's better," she murmured as his lips descended
toward hers.

It felt strange that such a simple kiss could make her
entire body tremble with need. But his kisses did that to
a girl. His tongue reached out and parted her lips as he
opened his mouth to her. Muscled arms wrapped around
her body, pulling her off the ground enough for her to
arch into his embrace. Kacey pulled at his neck, wanting to bring him down to the ground. Heck, she wanted
to roll around with the guy if he'd let her. Moaning, he
pushed her to the ground and pulled her shirt out of her
jeans, his hands just barely touching the ground.

"Damn," he murmured.

"Huh?" Kacey said breathlessly.

"Grass, damn grass!"

"What?" Kacey wasn't sure she was catching on.
Why was he cursing the grass? And why did he stop
kissing her?

Travis's lips formed a smile as he pulled back. "I'm allergic to grass."

Kacey lifted up onto her elbows and grinned. "Pretty sure everyone's allergic to grass."

Travis shook his head and looked away, a slight blush staining his cheeks. "No, not like this. We need to get some Benadryl."

"You're kidding."

"I wish I were." He showed her his forearms, and sure enough, they were beginning to welt.

"You're going to let me drug you with Benadryl?"

"Kacey, I swear if you tell anyone I willingly allowed you to drug me—"

"Your secret's safe with me." Kacey crossed her heart. Knowing the whole time she was lying.

"You are such a little liar." Travis cursed and began scratching his arms. "I can't believe the one time I get you all to myself, I get an allergic reaction."

"At least you didn't stutter," Kacey offered.

"Wow, that was so incredibly helpful. I feel like such a man." His scratching continued until finally he yelped and pulled off his shirt.

Kacey covered her mouth with her hands to keep from laughing out loud. His entire upper body was turning puffy. Poor guy. "Let's go get you some drugs."

He rolled his eyes and held out his hand to pull her to her feet. "So much for being romantic."

"Who says Benadryl isn't romantic?" Kacey asked once they were walking back to the house.

"Who says it is?" Travis countered.

"Watch. You'll see."

"Not sure I want to see, but all right."

The itching was getting worse. Travis was about ready to play the part of a small child and rub himself in calamine lotion. Anything to get rid of the itching and red welts.

He'd never felt more unattractive.

Kacey made him take a quick shower, which at first he was more than excited about, but then he discovered she meant alone.

Well, as alone as a person could be when one's skin decides to become a puffy monster. It was as if he were turning into two very swollen people.

When he was finished, he sat dejectedly on the downstairs couch and waited. Kacey came rushing in with some sort of concoction, no doubt meant to torture men.

"What is that smell?" He pulled away, but she slapped him across the shoulder.

"Sit still."

Kacey gave him a glass of water with a pink pill, then began meticulously rubbing the gross-smelling paste onto his body.

"You're trying to get even with me, aren't you?"

The foul-smelling paste began to burn on his arms. Good God, she would be the death of him.

"It will make everything numb," she explained, massaging it into his arms, which felt quite nice until the word *numb* began to penetrate his senses.

"No!" Travis pushed at Kacey. "I don't want to be numb! If I'm numb, it means I can't..."

Kacey arched her eyebrow. "Can't?"

Crap, he wasn't getting out of this one. "Um, feel. I can't feel...things."

"What's so important that you need to feel?"

He slapped her hand away and reached in, running his hand behind her neck. "If you have to ask, then you don't deserve to know."

Kacey laughed and kissed his nose.

Like a mother would do to a small child.

Forget the numbing cream. Now he was losing his masculinity.

"Chin up." Kacey ran her tongue along his lower lip and sighed into his mouth. "It's not like I'm rubbing any of this stuff on your man parts."

"Man parts?" he sputtered.

She nodded and laughed. "Now, sit still while I give you a rubdown."

That was more like it.

And then she dipped her hand into the bowl and grabbed more paste.

Ah, again with the torture.

"How long do I have to keep this on?"

"An hour."

"An hour?" Travis mumbled a curse. "And what am I supposed to do for an entire hour? It's not like I can move my arms or anything. I'll get this crap everywhere."

"You"—she put the bowl down and wiped her hands on the towel—"don't have to do a thing."

Smiling, he leaned back, feeling quite smug that he was going to get rewarded for such good behavior. Travis yawned and shook his head. Damn, he was tired.

Kacey bit her lip and began kissing across his stomach.

He yawned again and closed his eyes.

Her tongue made tiny circles on his skin, blazing a hot trail all the way up to his chest. He tried to lean down, to catch her tongue in his mouth, to pleasure her the way she was pleasuring him.

She pulled back and shook her head, her nails digging into his back as she pulled him closer, careful not to get any of the paste on her.

Her hands skimmed up his neck and dug into his hair. She tugged at his lower lip and whispered, "I've always wanted to have you to myself."

"To torture me?" he said hoarsely.

"Absolutely. After all, you tortured me when I was little, so it's only fair to have a little retaliation." She licked his ear. He nearly fell off the couch. He was having a damn hard time keeping his hands from moving to any part of her body. He felt like he was going to explode. The only good thing was that he knew no numbing cream had gotten on the lower region of his body.

That, he knew with absolute certainty.

Though, if she kept kissing him like that, he was going to be begging for something to keep him from embarrassing himself.

"Kace." His mouth found hers. He parted her lips and twirled his tongue in her mouth, tasting every part of her, taking his time and feeling the hot sensation of her mouth on his.

Feeling more at ease, he leaned back, allowing her to straddle him. He kept his arms firmly at his sides.

Her kisses relaxed him somehow, made him feel comfortable and...

"Crap."

"Pardon?" Kacey's head popped up, giving him a glorious view down her shirt.

"The Benadryl." Oh God, was he slurring? No, no, this was not happening, not when things were going so great.

"What about it?" Kacey went back to work, kissing down his stomach.

"Itsh making me shleepy." Travis began to see double. Kacey suddenly grew two heads, and his arms felt so heavy he was sure they had detached from his body.

"Kacshy?" Maybe if he just closed his eyes for a minute—no longer—he would get rejuvenated and...

"Travis?" Kacey shook him, and he moaned and let out a snore.

Too much Benadryl.

"And this is what happens when people don't build up a tolerance!" she said to herself. She shrugged and picked up the bowl and towel. As she walked into the kitchen, she heard another snore and couldn't help but giggle. Poor guy.

Returning to the living room, she placed a cup of coffee on the table and sat next to him on the couch. He looked so peaceful.

He looked perfect.

Kacey sighed.

Was it too good to be true? Why did the fact that there seemed to be no roadblocks in the way scare her more than when he seemed unreachable?

At least when they'd hated each other she hadn't needed to worry about her heart. But now it seemed that he had won her over without even trying. It was the way he cheered her up and spent time with her. Even going as far as rescuing her from the reunion. In fact— she bit her lip—Travis had always been there. In the background.

She sighed and looked at the blank TV. Her eyes narrowed as she took in the DVDs on the side.

Family Memories.

Quietly, she tiptoed over to the DVD player and threw in the disc. She didn't have anything else to do, so she might as well travel down memory lane. It figured that Bets would have all of the memories on DVD now. Those poor boys didn't stand a chance.

She carefully sat back down and pressed Play.

NSYNC began playing in the background, and then Jake and Travis appeared on-screen. And they were dancing.

Not just any dance. No, because that wouldn't be even close to as funny as what she was currently watching.

Travis had on a curly blond wig. And he was playing lead singer.

Jake was in the background shaking his butt.

But the best part? They were both old enough to know better and still deathly serious about their little music video.

As the song came to a close, Grandma Nadine made an appearance in a leopard-print leotard and began playing air guitar.

Kacey snorted and covered her mouth with the back of her hand.

The only thing she could think of was how she was

going to get a copy of this and sneak it to the press. Jake would kill her.

And it would be totally worth it.

The movie skipped to Christmas 2007.

She remembered that Christmas. It was two years before her parents' deaths. She shifted on the couch, tucking her feet underneath her, and watched the perfect little Christmas take place.

She and Jake were sitting under the tree. Her braces were glowing in the candlelight of the room, and Jake looked like a lady-killer even at the ripe old age of sixteen, with his curly brown hair and megawatt smile. She giggled at the memory, transfixed by what she saw.

Travis was in the background, sulking, or looked to be sulking. His eyes were downcast, and he was playing with a brightly wrapped package in his hands. The video zoomed in. He was shaking and mumbling something to himself.

"Just give it to her," Grandma Nadine urged from the side.

Kacey watched in horror as she read the red tag. *To Kacey.*

Swallowing a knot of emotion, she watched as Travis wiped his hands on his pants and slowly got up and walked toward her.

She wanted to go back in time and scream at herself, "Look at him! Look!"

Instead, sixteen-year-old Kacey flashed him a look of annoyance and then got up and made some excuse about needing more spiced cider.

Travis froze.

Jake sneered. "What? Did you actually think she'd accept a gift from you? After everything you've done?"

Travis shook his head and licked his lips, and the package slowly dropped out of his hands onto the floor. He shoved his hands into his pockets and walked off.

Jake rolled his eyes as Grandma Nadine went after Travis.

And then Jake did the most asinine thing she'd ever seen in her life. He ripped the tag off the package, and when Kacey walked back into the room, he held it out to her as if he had gotten her a present.

"For me?" Kacey squealed with excitement. "Oh, Jakey!"

Oh, gag me, she thought, but couldn't tear her eyes away.

Slowly, she watched as her sixteen-year-old self unwrapped the package and gasped with excitement, throwing her arms around Jake's neck.

"It's so perfect!"

And in that moment Kacey knew exactly what the present had been.

Tears flowed freely down her face as the movie played.

It was a framed picture of her and her parents on a family vacation, and underneath it was the word *Love*.

She clicked off the TV and began to sob into her hands.

It was the very same picture that still sat next to her bed at night. The same picture she'd wept into when her parents died, the same picture she'd talked to when she'd had a bad day. And it had never been from Jake.

But Travis.

She looked over at him now. His eyes were completely open, but she was unable to decipher if he was upset or just cautious as to how to proceed.

"You…" She swallowed down the tears. "You gave me the best present I've ever had. When my parents died…" She couldn't even finish, her body racked with sobs.

Travis cursed and immediately pulled her down to him, spooning her and kissing her hair. "Shh, baby, it's okay. It's going to be fine."

It had always been Travis. Always. She flipped around to face him as he brushed the tears away from her eyes.

Then his mouth was hot on hers, possessive, fierce. It melted every part of her and made her knees weak even though she was lying down. He kissed her tears away, his kisses burning a trail down her cheek until he found her mouth again, searching and pulling.

• • •

Embarrassment had washed over Travis when he'd opened his eyes. It was as if he were reliving the moment all over again. Reliving the pain of being rejected and then made fun of left a bitter taste in his mouth.

All he had wanted back then was to say he was sorry, to give Kacey something she could treasure before she left for college.

Jake had ruined everything, but in the end Travis hadn't cared that Jake took credit. It had sucked, and he'd been pissed, but when he'd seen the look on Kacey's face, he'd known it was worth it. Regardless of who'd given her the picture, at least she had it, and for that he'd been thankful.

He'd just wanted her to be happy.

His only desire had been to see her smile.

Mission accomplished. He left it alone, walked away, and hadn't spoken to her since that fateful day. He'd watched from afar at all the holiday events where Kacey made her presence known and he spoke to her at the funeral, so maybe it wasn't that they hadn't talked, but the meaning behind the words was completely different. That was the day he stopped trying.

"Travis." Kacey kissed him roughly across his lips. He should have cared that he had gross numbing cream on his arms, but it didn't matter. All that mattered was that she was now in his arms, exactly where she belonged.

"Travis," she said again, this time pulling away.

"What?"

"I can't feel my lips."

"Huh?" He looked down. Sure enough, some of the cream had gotten onto her lips, and they were swelling at an alarming rate. "Um, Kace, maybe you should take some Benadryl."

"Why?" Her eyes widened.

"Um, just take my word for it, 'kay?"

He lightly pushed her away, reached for the pill bottle, and tossed her a pink pill. The very same one that had sent him into dreamland for at least a half hour.

She took the pill and grimaced as the water touched her lips.

"Shower." He looked at his arms, then at her lips.

She blushed.

"What? Suddenly turning into a prude on me?"

"No." Kacey bit her lip and forced a piece of hair behind her ear. "It's just that, well, the stuff I used, it has clove and some other things in it, and water just makes it worse. You have to use oil to get it off your skin."

"Oil," he repeated, mouth slightly ajar. "What type of oil?"

"Coconut oil."

"Right." He gulped and turned away, lifting his arm above his head to scratch his neck. "So we have to rub down with oil."

She nodded.

"But I can't actually..." He nodded in her direction, and she gave him a blank stare. He looked up at the ceiling. "I can't actually touch you because then the oil and the numbing cream will get on you."

She bit her lip and winked.

"So I can look but I can't touch?" Why did he need to keep torturing himself? No matter how many ways he said it. *No* still meant *no*. He would have to watch her lather herself with oil while he stood there like an idiot, keeping his hands to himself.

"Maybe it would be best if we did this separately. You know... you go into one room and I go into the other." His body jerked in opposition.

"Travis." Kacey put her hands on her hips. "Where's your sense of adventure?"

"I lost it along with my manhood the minute I fell asleep and began drooling."

"C'mon, you can do it."

"Oh, I know very well I can do it, thank you very much. I'm just unable to perform at this given moment in time. Believe me, my body has no problem understanding what I can and cannot do."

Kacey's eyes scanned him from head to toe, her

eyes stopping exactly where a lady's eyes should never linger. "I see."

Yeah, anyone could see. She'd have to be blind not to see.

Blood began to pulse through his system into all the wrong places. Could a man die with want?

"We'll go fast." She placed her hand in his.

"Yes, because every man dreams of going fast when he's in the presence of a beautiful woman as she slathers oil across her naked breasts and moans and—"

"Travis?"

"Yeah?" he said hoarsely.

"We aren't making a porno, so there won't be any moaning."

"Hey, it's my torture, and I'm imagining moaning. Let me dream."

She lifted her hands into the air as if giving up and marched ahead of him up the stairs.

He counted each stair as his foot hit, hoping and praying that somehow he would get through this without exploding or doing anything remotely embarrassing. His track record proved that the odds were not in his favor. Damn *Hunger Games* reference. He cursed and stomped up the last two stairs to the master suite shower. It was the biggest one in the house and had two shower heads and the rain effect that made you feel like you were, well, getting rained on.

He stepped into the bathroom and watched as Kacey grabbed a tub of coconut oil and rubbed it between her hands.

His fantasy was immediately crushed. "It's all hard."

"That's what coconut oil is," she said and winked. "It warms up and turns into liquid when you rub it in your hands." She quickly demonstrated and then gave him a chunk of it. "I only have the numbing cream on part of my face, thanks to you, and on my arms—again thanks to you."

"No problem," he said through gritted teeth as he watched her apply the oil to her hands.

"Strip," she commanded when he stood immobile, gawking like a teenager.

"Sorry, what?"

"Strip." She nodded to his shirt. "Now."

"But it's only on my arms and—"

"Travis, don't be a baby. Just take off your clothes like a man so this woman can rub you down."

Sweating. He was actually beginning to sweat at the thought of Kacey's hands anywhere near his body. Nothing could be more embarrassing than being painfully aroused and unable to do anything about it, with the woman of his dreams patting him down with oil. Especially when knowing that she was the reason he was so turned on.

Cursing, he lifted his shirt and threw it to the

ground. His pants quickly followed, and then he reached for his boxers...

"I-I..." Kacey's mouth dropped open and she covered her eyes. "I just meant your shirt."

Hell.

What was he supposed to say? Sorry, I was too distracted by your lush mouth to understand what you were saying? Sorry, other parts of my anatomy are clouding my decision-making skills?

So he said nothing; instead he grinned and held out his arms, knowing full well she had to get extremely close to put the oil on.

Her face flamed red as she stepped into his space and began very slowly rubbing oil up and down his arms. He closed his eyes as her hands took on a seductive rhythm. He had to fight to keep from leaning forward and taking her on his parents' bathroom floor.

"Umm." Kacey's voice wavered. "Your forearms are fine. You can rinse them and your hands."

He opened his eyes, and she was a breath away from his lips. "Okay." He stepped into the shower and rinsed off the lower part of his arms and his hands. The welts were gone, and they were no longer numb. He wrapped a towel around himself and walked back out.

"Now what?"

"You still have some here." She touched his shoulders with the oil and began to rub. It felt so damn good, he wasn't sure he could keep on standing. And then he realized she hadn't ever put any numbing cream on his shoulders.

She hadn't reached that far because he'd had on a T-shirt.

His eyes flew open.

She was grinning.

"Tease."

"Absolutely." She kissed him hard on the mouth. He laughed and pulled her directly into the shower, clothes and all.

"Oh sorry, you're gonna have to take those off now." He shrugged as she swatted him on the arm. The little tease lifted her hands above her head. Slowly, he pulled at her shirt until it was off. His heart hammered in his chest as he viewed her lacy black bra.

"These too." He pulled at her jeans, jerking her against him. She giggled and tugged at his towel. It fell to the ground. Grinning, he unbuttoned the first button of her pants and unzipped them. She wiggled out, and soon she was standing in front of him, a beautiful, sensual goddess. Damn! He didn't deserve her. But he wanted her so much that in that moment he didn't really care.

He pulled her under the shower. The water teased down her body, little droplets dripping off her lips and running down her neck, only to stop in her lacy bra and slide down her sleek stomach.

He bent down and held a droplet captive between his lips as he kissed her chin and closed his eyes.

She tasted like home.

Like forever.

TWENTY-SEVEN

Clearly, she was out of her mind. Never had she been naked with a man before. Ever. She didn't count Jake because, after this particular moment, she wasn't really sure he had been a real man. Not after seeing Travis and his naked body.

People could write romance novels about that body.

All rippling muscle stretched across his chest. She sighed happily in his arms as he licked water droplets off her neck.

Not to mention...well, the unmentionable parts that ladies were so not supposed to mention. She giggled nervously. Jake couldn't hold a candle to him, mainly because Jake wasn't Travis. Travis wrapped his arm around her neck and dipped her underneath the showerhead again. He reached for the soap and began lathering it across her chest.

He backed up. "Damn, I wish I had the heart to take this off too." He pointed at the bra and smirked. "But you look too pretty in it." With one fluid movement, he was kneeling in front of her. Her knees nearly knocked together, she was so nervous as he placed kisses across her stomach.

With his teeth, he nipped at her hipbone and bent down to kiss behind her knee, slowly raising his eyes to look at her. Travis placed his hands on her hips. "Perfect."

His hands didn't budge. He didn't even try to take off the rest of her clothes; instead he continued to kneel in front of her. He closed his eyes and rested his forehead against her stomach.

She caressed his head for a few minutes as the water cascaded down his back. Then he looked up at her again, his eyes smiling right along with his mouth.

He ran his massive hands up her thighs and then continued lathering her body. She wanted him so badly, but he never made a move to do anything more than kiss her.

Travis reached for the shampoo and washed her hair, taking special care in massaging her scalp. She leaned her back against him and closed her eyes. Naked muscle encased her body, and she wanted to stay there forever.

"Rinse," he whispered in her ear as he pulled her backward underneath the showerhead again. His fingers worked magic as he rinsed the shampoo from her head, and then those same warm hands wrapped around her waist and pulled her more tightly against him. "We should get out."

Not the words she was thinking he would say.

"What?" She didn't mean to snap or sound irritated.

"I think"—he nibbled her ear and breathed into it—"that we should get out before we christen my parents' bathroom."

Rejection washed over her. Trembling, she slowly moved away. He grasped her and lightly pushed her against the cool tile wall.

"Not like this," he murmured in her ear as he nuzzled her neck underneath her hair. "Besides, it's our first time together...Do you really want to remember it being in my parents' shower?"

On second thought.

She giggled and kissed him full on the mouth. His eyes wavered as his hungry gaze swept her up and down. With one final hard kiss, he pushed her away and told her he would be a minute.

She hopped out, wrapped a towel around herself, and heard the shower turn off. Travis stepped out, a cocky smirk placed firmly across his handsome face.

"Something funny?"

"No." He kept smiling and rubbed his chin.

"Why don't I believe you, then?"

"Because I'm lying." He leaned his arm against the wall and settled his full weight to the side.

"So?"

He shook his head. "Nope, not gonna tell you. You're just going to have to see, but aren't surprises the best?"

"No. No, they aren't," she said dryly.

He blew her a kiss and then smacked her on the butt as he walked out of the bathroom. Cocky one, Travis Titus. Who would have ever thought that the little boy with the stutter had game? Or kissed like a movie star? Not that she'd ever kissed a movie star before, but she figured kissing Johnny Depp was pretty much like kissing Travis.

It had to be.

It was too good to be anything but that.

She looked at her reflection in the mirror. Every piece of skin visible was flushed. Her fingers clutched the side of the sink. A clanging noise sounded as she gripped the sink harder. The ring. Jake's ring to be exact, stared back at her, mocking her. Instead of guilt, she felt minor annoyance. Kacey reached down and slid the ring off.

Decision made, she padded over to Jake's old room. Everything was just as he left it. Trophies were scattered across his dresser. A few pictures of the Pussycat

Dolls hung on the wall, and his bedspread was the same faded red. So many memories were part of this room. But it was over. Done. Tomorrow she had to leave, but she hoped Travis would ask her to stay. Actually, she hoped he would make the big gesture. One thing was for certain. She was saying good-bye.

Good-bye to Jake, good-bye to the pain and the memories, and hello to a bright future with the boy next door. She bit her lip to keep from squealing with excitement as she thought of her time with Travis. She set the ring on the dresser and ran to her room to put on some fresh clothes. Whatever surprise Travis had waiting for her, she wanted it, as soon as possible. Especially if he was giving and she was receiving.

Kacey bounded down the stairs in the general direction of the kitchen, where she assumed Travis would be located. After all, they hadn't eaten anything but cookies all day and it was nearing lunchtime.

The sound of a pot clattering confirmed her assumptions. She walked into the kitchen and burst out laughing.

Travis was on his hands and knees, putting bits and pieces of hard macaroni into a bowl.

"Trouble cooking?" She tilted her head and smirked.

He looked up and scowled. "Nobody ever said multitasking was so difficult." He threw one last piece of macaroni into the pot and stood. "Luckily, we have more than one box of this stuff."

"You do know you're supposed to boil the water first." Kacey pointed at the dry macaroni.

"I know." Travis laughed unconvincingly and dumped the noodles into the trash and placed the pot underneath the faucet

Kacey took advantage of the opportunity to gaze at his tight jeans. She felt herself smile when he reached forward and grabbed a towel to wipe off the table. It was almost like she was in a trance. So much, in fact, that when Travis turned around she had to snap her head back up.

She felt her face flame with heat as a knowing smile tugged at the corners of his mouth. "Find something you like?"

"No." She looked away and began inspecting her nails. "So why macaroni?"

"Why not?"

Men.

Travis shrugged. "I have it on good authority that it was the only food you'd eat until you turned eight."

"Please." Kacey rolled her eyes. "I ate other things too."

"Name them."

Kacey searched her memory, but the only thing she could come up with was even lamer than macaroni. "I may have had an obsession with SpaghettiOs."

"With or without meatballs?" Travis asked as he lunged for her and wrapped his arms around her body, trapping her within his hold.

"With." She leaned up and kissed his chin. "Why? Are you going to make me those too?"

He shrugged. "If I ruin the macaroni, we may have to rely on the microwave to fix up some SpaghettiOs." He kissed her forehead, then moved down to her cheek. "I have a confession to make."

"What's that?" Kacey shuddered beneath his touch.

"I can't cook."

No, but you can kiss. "Well, I guess that means I can't sleep with you."

"Thought you'd say that." His mouth found her neck as he tilted her back. "But we had a good run, didn't we?"

She wondered if that was a rhetorical question as his lips pressed against the base of her throat.

Travis pulled away. "Sorry, I tend to get carried away when I'm hungry."

Kacey raised an eyebrow.

"For food," he clarified, and then cleared his throat. "Um, anyway, let's, uh, let's just finish this up and we can get going."

"Get going?" Kacey grabbed the next box and began pouring it into the pot Travis had placed on the stove. The water started boiling.

"Yeah, I have a plan."

"Oh," Kacey said, laughing, and threw the box at Travis. "So the food wasn't the surprise."

"Hell, no." Travis shuddered. "I'm not sure if I should be offended or thankful that you think I lack that much originality." He seemed to think about it a moment, then nodded. "Thankful. I'll take thankful. Now pour in that orange stuff so we can get on to the surprise."

"Carbing up for something, are we?" Kacey teased.

Travis growled and pushed her against the counter. "You have no idea." His lips found hers in an aggressive kiss. Just as Kacey wrapped her arms around his neck, she heard steam hitting the stove.

Travis cursed and turned to the pot of macaroni, which looked pretty pathetic with the orange stuff in it. "I forgot to drain the water."

"Yup." Kacey nodded.

"Pizza?"

"Chinese?"

"Thai?"

"Italian," they said in unison. Kacey went to the house phone while Travis got on the Internet on his phone to find some Italian takeout.

A quick thirty minutes later and they were sitting over chicken Alfredo and opening up a bottle of red wine.

"So...good," Kacey murmured between bites.

"I can't cook, but I can order...," Travis boasted

as he held a piece of bruschetta with goat cheese to her lips.

It was the type of meal she would never eat on a first date.

Possibly not even on the second.

Way too much garlic.

It was comfort food at its best, and she couldn't imagine a more perfect meal to share with Travis. They'd ordered enough to feed a small country, but there was something about having so many choices laid out around them.

"I can't do it," Kacey said as she exhaled and took a gulp of wine. "I'm done. I seriously cannot eat another bite."

Travis put his hands behind his head and leaned back on his chair. "That's too bad."

"Why?"

He shrugged. "Part of your surprise is dessert."

Did his version of dessert include lots of skin, whipped cream, and chocolate? Because at this point Kacey was beginning to think she would really like some more food. Mouth watering, she leaned forward. "Well, what are you waiting for?"

"So, you're game, then?"

He was talking about going upstairs, right?

"I am if you are." Her heart skipped a beat as Travis walked around the table and pulled her into his arms.

"Music to my ears. Now, go grab a sweatshirt."

"Huh?" What the heck kind of foreplay was this?

"For dessert," he clarified, a mocking twinkle in his eyes.

Kacey bit her lip and stepped out of his embrace. "Fine, but this better not be a trick."

"Please." Travis held up his hands. "Like I've ever tricked you."

"Says the one who put frogs in my bed when I was ten."

"In my defense, they were dead."

"Yes, Travis," Kacey said, rolling her eyes. "That makes it so much better. Dead frogs. Seriously?"

"Just grab your sweatshirt." He suddenly looked nervous and insecure as he stuffed his hands in his jeans pockets and looked at the ground.

"Okay." Kacey took off at full speed and grabbed the first sweatshirt she could find in her bag. When she ran back down the stairs, Travis was already grabbing the keys and leading her outside. "Okay, where are we going?"

"It's all part of the surprise."

"Right." Kacey hopped into the truck.

"And my charm."

Rolling her eyes, she pulled a piece of gum out of her purse and waited while Travis's truck pulled out of the long driveway.

It took all of ten minutes for them to reach their destination.

And Kacey honestly couldn't have guessed it.

Not even if someone had given her hints.

Because it was the place where prom had been held her senior year of high school. It also used to be her parents' restaurant before they'd died. So many memories threatened to escape from her. She had to hold her breath to keep them in. Swallowing, she forced herself to exhale slowly as the lights flickered in front of her. It looked exactly as she remembered it.

Nestled beautifully on the Columbia River, it had been one of the hot spots for locals. The beer selection had been legendary. It had had so many wines from around the Columbia River and Yakima Valley that people often had joked that the best place for all-day wine tasting was a table at River's Edge.

"River's Edge," she whispered and looked down at her hands. They were clenched together as if to keep the pain in. All the memories…her parents' deaths, the times she and Jake would come here and try to convince her dad to give them just one glass of wine, even though it was illegal…

He never would, but still.

Her many stolen kisses by the waiter's entrance in the back.

It was also the only place Travis and Kacey had talked in the last five years.

She remembered it like it was yesterday. Her parents had left the business to her, naturally, but she'd wanted nothing to do with Portland or her old life, so she had sold it to a family friend and taken the money to buy a car and pay off her parents' debts. It had also been an escape, which is exactly what Travis had told her the day she'd signed the papers.

"What the hell are you doing, Kacey?"

She remembered the rabid look in his eyes, like he was ready to tear something apart but couldn't find an object. Now that she thought about it, he had been really good-looking at the time, but she had been so frustrated with him, so angry that he would make light of her pain, he seemed ugly and unbearably frustrating.

"It's my life!" she'd screamed.

"It's their legacy!"

"I don't want it!" She'd beat against his chest over and over again. But he hadn't budged. Instead, he'd held on to her as if he never wanted to let her go. He'd then whispered in her hair that it would be okay.

"Let it out, baby girl."

"I'm not your baby." She'd sobbed into his chest.

"Don't I know it," he had said sadly as he wiped large crocodile tears from her puffy cheeks.

"Everything okay back here?" Grandma Nadine had called, right before she'd walked around the corner.

"Fine, it's fine." Kacey had frantically wiped her cheeks and pasted a smile on her face. "No biggie. You know how Travis and I can get." She'd lamely

punched him in the shoulder and walked off. But she hadn't remembered until now what Grandma Nadine had said to Travis when she'd thought Kacey was out of earshot.

"She'll come around one day, Travis. Don't give up."

"Damn, Grandma," Travis had mumbled. "That girl wasn't ever mine to give up in the first place."

TWENTY-EIGHT

Travis watched the display of emotions wash over Kacey's face. Hell, as long as he lived, he would never get tired of watching those eyes squint when she was thinking, or the way she held her lip captive between her front teeth when she was trying to keep herself from saying something she'd regret.

And finally, the worst of all, her tells. The way she clenched her hands in her lap as if that simple gesture would hold all the walls firmly in place.

"Kace, say something." He reached for her shoulder and gently placed his hand across it.

"The last time I was here was with you."

"Yup." Figures she'd remember that first.

"You were so angry at me."

"Kace," Travis said, turning off the truck. "You

262 RACHEL VAN DYKEN

were angry at yourself. I was angry at you for giving up—or at least in my mind, giving up something that I thought you wanted. But mainly, Kace, I was angry that when things got rough, you ran."

"What did you expect me to do?" Kacey screamed, causing Travis to jump.

"Fight. I expected you to fight."

"Against what, Travis? Myself? There was nothing left to fight for! I lost my parents. I lost my best friend. I lost everything!"

Travis scowled and pulled back his hand. He couldn't touch her, not with what he had to say. "You didn't lose everything. You still had my family, and you still had Grandma. Geez, Kacey, you had me. You lived! But that was the day I watched part of you give up, and you let a part of yourself die. Maybe that's why Grandma wanted you here in the first place. You really do need to find yourself, Kace. And if that means I lose you . . . again, in order for it to happen, so be it."

"What?" Her head whipped around to face him. "What do you mean lose me again?"

Shit. "That day, the day you walked away from me, from us, from everything. I uh . . . I followed you."

"To?"

Travis gulped. "Seattle."

"Why?"

Travis closed his eyes and leaned his head against

the back of the seat. "To bring you home, Kace. To bring you home."

"I don't understand."

Of course she wouldn't. Travis groaned aloud and fought the urge to hit the steering wheel or at least strangle something. "You never belonged apart from us..." He gulped. "Apart from me. You never belonged apart from me."

"What are you saying?"

"I'm saying..." Could he do it? Could he say he loved her? Travis looked at her moonlit face and chickened out. "All I'm saying is, I was an idiot and chased after you to bring you back home. It was stupid that you would run to another city after your parents died. I know you needed a fresh start, but why couldn't you lean on us? Why couldn't you allow us to support you?"

"I can't talk about that." Kacey looked away again.

Damn his idiot brother. He'd do anything to know what else happened that night besides sex. No way did sex ruin people the way it ruined Jake and Kacey. Was she really telling him everything? Part of his heart clenched at the thought.

"I bought it," he blurted, much like an eighth grader with no skills with the female sex, or communication for that matter.

"Pardon?"

"The restaurant. I bought it."

"Today?" Kacey gave him a horrified look.

"No." He felt suddenly embarrassed. "The day you signed the papers, you signed them over to my business partner. Three years ago I bought him out. It's all mine."

"Why?" Kacey's lip trembled.

"Because I'm a good businessman?" And he got an enormous trust fund when he was eighteen.

Kacey rolled her eyes.

The inside of the truck fell silent except for Travis's heavy breathing. The windows would be steamed any minute. He wondered if she could hear his heart hammering in his chest. "Because of you, Kace. Everything I do, everything I've done in my life, it's all because of you."

There, he said it. Now she could rip out his heart and stomp on it.

With a sob, she lunged across the console and into his lap, grabbing his lips between hers in such a forceful kiss he was breathless.

"You knew," she said while kissing his jaw. "You knew how much this place meant to me, Travis."

Adrenaline mixed with lust slammed through him as she wrapped tighter and tighter around him. It was hard to think straight, let alone do anything but strategically plan for ways to remove her clothing in the fastest way possible.

"I knew." He shuddered as she licked his ear.

"I think I l—"

"What the hell kind of place is this?" a man's voice shouted outside the window.

Alarmed, Travis turned, then relaxed and grinned. Old man Casbon was smiling from ear to ear and already pulling open the truck door. So much for privacy.

"Mr. Casbon," Kacey sputtered. "Didn't know you'd, um, be here."

"Yeah, well, the woman always sends me out for dessert. Got a phone call a bit ago saying she needed me to bring her some chocolate to her cottage. Hearty appetite that one. Besides, I know the owner." He nudged Travis and continued. "She had an itch for some sort of chocolate soufflé, so I drove on out to grab her whatever her heart desires."

"Sounds like love." Sadly, Kacey hopped off Travis's lap and leaned against the truck.

"Oh, girlie, it is. Though sometimes I wonder if I rate above that chocolate she likes. Say, Travis..." He turned to face him. "Got any more of that stuff left?"

"Sure thing. Follow me." Travis turned off the truck and led them into the restaurant. It was nearly closing time, meaning there were only a few people scattered about.

He hoped that Kacey wouldn't be too alarmed by the changes he'd made. When her parents owned the place it'd had a sort of Italian café look. Nowadays, it looked more like an old-world café. It boasted original wood floors, thick rugs, modernized furniture, old clocks and pictures, as well as a few hanging lanterns.

Kacey tightened her grip on his arm. "I really like it."

Her eyes lit up as she broke away from him and began walking the perimeter. His favorite part of the restaurant had to be the outside. The balcony overlooking the water was beautiful. It was decorated as a plantation-style deck complete with ceiling fans. His personal favorite.

Kacey walked outside, so Travis turned to Mr. Casbon. "Soufflé, right? I'm on it." He ran to the back and nodded to the manager as he grabbed a to-go box and stuffed in a few treats for Grandma.

Mr. Casbon pulled out a fifty.

Travis shook his head. "Nah, you'll need it for next time. It's on the house. I know the owner."

With a wink and a pat on the shoulder, Mr. Casbon shuffled out, and Travis went in search of Kacey.

When he reached the deck, he noticed her sitting in the chair closest to the water.

"This was my dad's favorite spot. He'd say he could see all the way to China from this spot right here."

"Hmm." Travis kneeled down next to her. "Not China, but maybe, just maybe, Vancouver."

Kacey sighed heavily. "I don't even know where to start. Do I say thank you for doing something I didn't have the guts to do? Do I say I'm sorry for treating you so horribly? Do I apologize to my dead parents for being less than what they brought me up to be—"

"Whoa! Wait right there." Travis jerked her to her feet. "Don't you ever say that. I will throw you over my shoulder and jump into the river next time you say such stupid things."

Kacey's eyes began to tear.

"Oh, baby, you can cry. Cry all you want, but you need to hear this, hear it from me, okay? This wasn't your dream. I know that. And you probably should have gone away for a bit to try to heal. I did this for you, for me, for your parents. I loved them too, you know. And it worked out in the end, didn't it? Your parents..." He swallowed so he wouldn't begin to get choked up. When he felt he had control over his emotions again he continued. "I count myself lucky every day I get to see you breathe, let alone walk and talk at the same time. Because each day you do those things is one more day that your parents didn't. To me that's living. You are living, and that is what your parents would want, Kace. They wanted you to live, to love, to hurt, to laugh, to cry. They wanted it all because they lived it all. Here, look at this..."

Travis lifted the chair Kacey had been sitting in and flipped it over, reading, "X marks the spot. Here lies my treasure."

He turned to look at her. "My treasure is right next to me." A red arrow pointed directly to the other chair, and then, as if there was ever any doubt of who the message was talking about, a tiny picture of Kacey as a baby was taped to the bottom.

"Did you put this here?" Kacey choked.

"No." Travis grinned. "Your parents did, or at least I'm assuming they did, considering it was like that when we bought the place. I've just kept it in pristine condition, which would have been easier if they had taken the precaution of laminating the picture. No worries though. I've got stalker in my genes. I just swapped the photo out with another one from your baby album."

"Which you got from..."

"Mom..."

"How does she even have those?"

Travis shrugged. She didn't need to know his family had an entire shed full of the stuff Kacey refused to look through after her parents' death. "We had it around."

"This is..." Kacey lifted her hands in the air and huffed.

"A lot to take in, I know. I can be like that. So, now I'm going to feed you."

"Ah, so that's your evil plan. Make me emotional, then feed me."

"Of course." He kissed her nose. "I hear chocolate works wonders. It's also an aphrodisiac—at least that's what I hear."

"Lucky you." Kacey punched his arm.

"No, Kace." He breathed into her ear and licked the side of her neck, loving the way her skin tasted salty and sweet at the same time. "Lucky you."

"Arrogant bastard," Kacey said, playfully pushing him away.

"Always. Now sit. I'll be right back."

Kacey was suddenly thankful for the sweatshirt as the wind picked up. But she didn't want to go inside for warmth. She wanted to stay planted exactly where she was and never leave.

Ever.

Suddenly the thought of going back to Seattle seemed too depressing to dwell on, and her flight was early the next morning. She leaned back against the chair and played with a sugar packet from the table. Dread filled her stomach as she thought about leaving.

What if she stayed?

What if she stayed here?

Kacey laughed as she looked around her, at the place she'd run away from. The memories made her heart hurt, but they also gave her hope, and the more she looked, the easier it seemed to breathe. As if her stress-filled life was directly correlated with the lie she was living.

She'd actually been a business major with an emphasis in entrepreneurship until her parents died.

She'd switched to kinesiology the next year and took extra classes to finish her degree and trainer's license.

Well, she had a lot to think about, and it was all because of Travis.

The silly little boy who stalked her by the tree house.

The same one who threw rocks at her and pulled her pigtails.

And she was desperately in love with him.

Apparently, she was also good at conjuring up the man himself, because seconds later, he was approaching her table with a large tray.

His white apron was damn sexy too.

"Do you happen to have a chef's hat?"

"My staff would kill me for pretending to be anything less than a waiter, believe me. I'm allowed to wear the apron only on holidays, and even then it's a big deal. I won't get into it. But there's usually a lot of clapping and champagne."

"Do you want me to clap now?" she asked cheekily.

"Well, does my current look give you reason to clap?"

"I don't know." Kacey tilted her head. "Turn around."

He did a circle.

"Now stop!" She giggled when she had a nice view of his tight butt. "Yup, I'll clap for that." She also added in a whistle and a catcall.

"I'm not a piece of meat, Kacey. Geez, I have feelings too."

"Pity."

Travis rolled his eyes. "Okay, I've brought several selections for the lady, as well as a wine pairing for each selection. What is your desire?"

"All of it."

"And what will you give me in return?"

She gulped and shakily met his gaze. "Everything."

Travis stared at her lips, his eyes taking on a hungry glint as his mouth curled into a seductive grin. "I'm sure that can be arranged. But first, we eat."

"You want to eat before you ravish me. Is that it?"

"Kacey, I've been ravishing you in my mind all morning and afternoon. Believe me, you have no idea. But first, I feed you."

"Thanks." Kacey felt herself flush with pleasure as he poured her a glass of red wine and scooted over a plateful of different types of chocolate.

TWENTY-NINE

Travis displayed eight different types of chocolate from all around the world. "The trick is to take a small bite and then pair it with a glass of wine, or espresso if you prefer, but I think we both know what happened last time you had caffeine."

"I ended up in your bed."

"Espresso, it is." Travis grinned.

Kacey laughed and reached for a piece of dark chocolate. "I like it here."

Travis told his heart to stop clenching in his chest every time she hinted toward staying. "In Portland?"

"The restaurant." She shrugged. "It's as if I never left."

"They would be proud of you, Kacey." He reached across the table and grasped her hand. "I know I am."

Kacey shook her head. "What would they be proud of? The girl who hasn't finished college? Who lives on her own and has one sad goldfish as a pet?"

"No." Travis went to kneel next to her. "They'd be proud of your spirit, proud of the woman you've become. You're strong, you're brilliant, not to mention beautiful."

Kacey's head snapped up. "Do you really think I'm beautiful?"

"No. I think you're breathtaking."

Kacey flushed.

"I think you're life-altering."

She tried to pull away.

"I think you're uniquely, wonderfully . . . you."

Her lips trembled.

"I think I'm going to kiss you."

"I think I want you to," Kacey whispered as his lips descended toward hers. She tasted like bittersweet chocolate and wine. His hands moved to touch her skin, then glided over her cheeks and dipped into her hair.

"Thank you . . ." Her voice was husky. "For saying that." She pulled away and sniffed as her eyes began to water. "The last person who told me I was beautiful was my mother."

"That," he said as he kissed her nose, "is a shame. You should be told you're beautiful every day. Because every day it's true, and every time I see you, you grow in your beauty. Just because people don't say the words doesn't mean it's any less true, Kace."

She bit her lip and looked down. He kissed her forehead and reached for the chocolate. "Chocolate makes everything better."

"Where have you been all my life?" she said, watery-eyed.

"Home," Travis answered, a note of seriousness in his voice. "I've been home, waiting for you."

They drove home in silence. A light rain pattered across the windshield. Travis wasn't sure what had shifted between them, but something had changed. Maybe he had been too vulnerable with her. His emotions felt raw, but then again, Kacey's probably did as well.

It was dark by the time the truck pulled back into the driveway. They had spent at least three hours talking and sharing childhood memories. Several times Travis had wanted to drown himself in the river. After all, most of their childhood memories were of him stalking her or being hateful and Kacey crying.

But they'd still had fun.

He didn't remember ever spending so much time with a girl and wanting the day to never end.

Not to mention the night.

He turned the truck off and ran to the other side to open Kacey's door.

"Tired?" His voice cracked.

"You'd think after all that wine and chocolate, I

would be." Kacey hopped out and gave him a shrug. "You up for a movie?"

I'm up for anything. "Whatever you want."

"Great." She bounced to the door and turned around. "But it's my choice."

"No Care Bears."

"No *Alice in Wonderland*."

They shook on it like they were five and burst out laughing as Travis let them into the house.

Everything was blanketed in darkness. In all his haste to start his romantic evening, he hadn't left any lights on. The door clicked closed. Suddenly it felt very small in the giant living room. As if the air were being sucked out the windows. Travis told himself to calm down. But he was painfully aware of the girl standing next to him. The one that really did get away. The girl next door.

He sighed, not meaning for it to be so loud.

And the next thing he knew, Kacey's mouth was on his.

"What about the movie?" he asked lamely, his body tensed in protest.

"Forget about the movie." She wrapped her arms around his neck and sighed into his ear.

"Forgotten."

He lifted her easily into his arms and carried her up the stairs, stopping only once they were inside his room.

Slow motion, everything was in slow motion. The music in the background wasn't even enough to drown out the roaring of blood in his ears. He must have left his iPod on from this morning when his alarm went off.

He swallowed, then reached out to touch her arm.

That simple gesture, the feel of her skin, was enough to make him dizzy. "Kace..." How was he supposed to want her? To love her as she deserved, when all he could think about was wiping his brother from her memory completely.

Kacey looked up, her eyes clear and bright. She moved her hand slowly across his chest. He closed his eyes and allowed himself to feel—everything.

He knew his breathing sounded ragged. He knew his control was slowly fading into a puddle at her feet, but he didn't care.

Nothing made him more nervous than the look she'd just given him, as if he could singlehandedly save the world, cure cancer, and still be home for dinner, all within the span of twenty-four hours. It was a responsibility he wasn't sure he was ready for, but they had nowhere else to go.

They couldn't return to being friends.

And he didn't want to.

Though he couldn't help but worry that at some point, he was going to screw up. He wasn't sure how, but he had a feeling things would go horribly wrong if he rushed things with her. Their friendship was fragile as it was.

Travis opened his eyes. They were alone in his bedroom, and suddenly he felt like he was in high school again. Reliving his most vivid fantasies.

He had to say no. He needed to take things slowly.

Kacey pulled his head down to hers and kissed him so hard he nearly lost his balance, not to mention his heart.

The words, *I can't* and *let's take this slow*, no longer mattered as he grasped her arms and braced them above her head against the wall. With a moan, she leaned back her head, exposing her neck and breasts.

He took full advantage.

He kissed down her neck, licked across her cheekbone, dipped his tongue in her mouth, and groaned when she bit his lip and tried to fight him.

"Make me forget him," she whimpered.

"My pleasure." He nipped her lip and pulled her into his arms, then hastily threw her onto the bed.

She burst out laughing.

Which he naturally took as a bad sign, considering women did not laugh during foreplay, or at least in his experience they didn't.

A tear ran down her cheek. "I'm sorry. It's just…" She kept laughing and reached behind her, pulling out his little bunny. "It seems that I've just sat on your bunny, you know the one you took out your sexual frustration on, the one that has my name? Interesting turn of events, don't you think?" Crap. He thought he'd hid that bunny a long, long time ago. How the hell did it get out from under his bed?

"Give it here." He held out his hand.

"No." She hid it behind her back. "Take off your shirt first."

"Oh, so it's going to be like that?"

She nodded.

Damn, how was he supposed to say no to such a cute face? "Fine, but this is another one of those blood-oath moments. Never, under any circumstances, are you allowed to tell another human being that I took off my shirt in order to steal my bunny back from you. Not to mention that this is all taking place before I plan on making you scream out in pleasure." With jerky movements, he took off his shirt.

Kacey's grin grew. "The pants too." She nodded at his jeans and tilted her head.

"We're going to have one of those relationships, aren't we?"

"What?"

"The type where we bicker."

"Of course." Kacey leaned up on her elbows, then slowly unbuttoned her shirt, leaving only one button closed.

His mouth went completely dry. His hands were paralyzed near the button of his jeans.

"Besides," she said as her hands slowly caressed her own stomach and she arched her back. "Think of how much fun it will be to kiss and make up."

Never in his life had he ever taken off a pair of jeans so fast.

"The bunny." He held out his hand.

"The boxers." She held out hers.

"You've got to be kidding me."

"Do I look like I'm kidding?" She hugged the bunny close to her chest, making him insanely jealous. Over a damn stuffed animal.

"Fine." He jerked off his boxers and threw them at her. The bunny came flying toward his head. He ducked and with a curse tackled Kacey on the bed.

"Now it's my turn."

"Turn?" Kacey said breathlessly.

"Yes, to torture you, just like you've been torturing me, for not only days, but for my entire life."

Kacey beamed up at him, then kissed him lightly across the mouth. "I surrender."

Travis attempted to keep his joy in check, considering it was probably inappropriate to sing the "Hallelujah Chorus" in bed, naked.

Damn.

His fingers reached for the final button to Kacey's shirt. He pulled it off and told himself to act mature, even though he felt like a small boy seeing a girl's breasts for the first time.

But it was Kacey.

His Kacey.

And he wanted to love her, to treasure her, to make her see what he saw every time he looked at her.

Perfection.

His lips caressed hers. Her tongue reached out and touched his, just slightly, but it could have been lightning for as much as it affected his body.

He needed little help or encouragement as he stripped her of the rest of her clothes, then fought the urge to shout again as their skin made contact.

It felt like a dream. His hands made slow, languid movements up her thighs as he sighed against her lips. He'd wanted her more than anything. His entire life. How many people could actually claim that? That for their entire existence, the one person they wanted to share eternity with had never changed, never faltered. Her. It had always been her, and he was damn well going to show her how much he loved her.

Never in a million years would Kacey have imagined that she'd end up in Travis's bed—in his arms. His eyes blazed as he took in her naked body and then shuddered as he bestowed a kiss on her stomach. "Do you even realize how damn beautiful you are?"

Kacey groaned with pleasure as he tilted her hips toward his and reached behind her head, pulling her in for a scorching kiss. His kiss was so different from

Jake's, different from any guy she'd ever been with. It held promises of more than a one-night stand. It promised her forever, and she hadn't realized until right now how badly she'd needed that commitment.

He was so careful with her, as if she were this long-lost treasure he was just discovering. Every kiss, every touch, was tender and slow. *Torture* could not even begin to describe what it felt like for his warm hands to run down her body.

His mouth hot, he kissed her like a man starved. Like every moment he'd ever lived, every breath he'd ever taken, had been saved up for now.

Kacey hadn't realized. Never knew that Travis was what she was missing. In every other relationship there was always something lacking. Even with Jake. With Travis, she finally felt complete, loved, whole, beautiful. She sighed.

"That feels good." Kacey licked his lower lip and chuckled against his mouth.

"Woman, you're going to kill me." With a shudder, he groaned and closed his eyes as he pulled away.

"Such a way to die, eh?" She gripped his back, scratching all the way down to his firm backside, and then trailed kisses down his jaw. His body was so firm and tight. The man was gorgeous, and he was hers, all hers.

"Absolutely." Travis growled, taking her mouth again and pinning her arms against the bed. His touch was dominant, possessive—something that should have scared her; instead it made her hot as hell. All she wanted was for him to claim her, to brand her as his and only his.

Every touch, every caress, was like a gift. Kacey wanted to stay there forever. She'd made her decision. She was going to stay. Even if it meant abandoning everything in Seattle. Even if it meant conquering old demons. For once in her life, a man she cared about, whom she truly loved, was offering her everything. He wanted to fight for her, to rescue her, and for once in her life she truly believed that a happy ending was possible.

Travis closed his eyes, allowing his body to memorize the moment. Her skin against his, he ran his hands up and down her arms as he settled himself on top of her. She was searing herself upon his soul and she didn't even know how permanent this was—he would do anything to never let her go.

"Travis," she whispered against his lips, wrapping her arms around his neck. Needing to go slow, he kissed the corner of her mouth and made his way to her ear. His teeth grazed the soft skin of her neck.

She gasped.

"You're so damn sexy." He pulled back and looked into her eyes. He was changing everything. This moment was changing everything and he never wanted to go back.

She moved beneath him, making it so she was at her most vulnerable. Her eyes said, "Take me," and he knew. He couldn't stop. He didn't want to. Because in that moment, she needed to know whose she was. His. He clenched his teeth.

With a soft sigh, she pulled his head down and kissed him, and he was gone. Lost in a sea of passion and desire. A pull so strong that he couldn't stop himself from entering her—from making her his.

Kacey moaned his name as he plunged greedily into her. She took him in, shaking as beads of sweat ran between their bodies.

He stopped, cursing his own enthusiasm. Damn, but the woman would be the death of him. He should have been gentler, but hell if he could stop now that he felt her around him, now that he knew they fit like perfect puzzle pieces.

"I'm fine. I'm fine." She smiled seductively, reaching for his head and coaxing it toward hers.

Their foreheads touched as he pulled her even tighter against him, and her legs naturally went around his waist. And they sat there, in an intimate embrace, just looking at each other. And again, his heart slammed with the idea that he was finally home, finally exactly where he wanted to be. In her arms.

He closed his eyes and began a slow rhythm of lovemaking. She smiled faintly as he pulled her tightly against him and claimed her. The only thought that crossed his mind was that he would be happy to stay inside her forever.

The moment was gone too soon. His body was already wanting to take her again and again until they were both exhausted. He sagged against her and sighed, his body still humming with the aftermath of the life-shattering encounter.

"I love you," Kacey whispered against his cheek as she gave him a kiss. It should have been expected. Hadn't he thought the same thing over and over again? But for some reason he froze. Severe dehydration after sex did that to a man. So he stared at her, a blank stare, and then pushed away and sat up. Suddenly feeling like a nervous idiot.

"Travis?" She rubbed his back.

"Oh God, I'm such an idiot." He needed to say those words, but there was something so wrong about only admitting his true feelings after she'd just given her body to him. She was so much more than sex, so much more than one moment.

She jerked her hand back. "What?"

"I'm an idiot. I'm so sorry, Kace." How could he explain to her the depth of his feelings? She needed to know it wasn't about sex. It was about something so much more. Something he was unable to describe.

He turned and looked at her face, unable to meet her gaze. He should have been the one to say it first. He was better than that, and she deserved better than this. He nervously glanced away.

Suddenly insecure, he walked to the bathroom and shut the door quietly. He just needed time to think, time to decide the right words to say so he didn't screw up the best thing that had ever happened to him.

Kacey was numb. For the second time in her life she experienced utter loss. A loss so huge that she couldn't even cry.

Was she cursed to always have bad sexual experiences? Not that the experience itself was awful. It was the exact opposite—perfect, wonderful. Life-altering, and then nothing.

He'd stared into space.

He'd put his head in his hands.

And he'd walked away.

Just like Jake.

The knot in her throat made it hard for her to breathe. She grabbed her discarded clothes and ran out of the room.

She locked the door to the guest room and slid against it, the tears finally coming, and with them, pain she never knew possible.

The pain of a heart being broken, a girl being rejected by yet another man in the Titus family.

And suddenly she felt exactly like a stripper, like one of those girls Jake salivated after. Quickly, she packed up her things, changed her clothes, and peeked out into the hallway.

Travis was nowhere to be found. It was nearing midnight. She could see if any flights were going out and just hang out at the airport. Anything was better than facing Travis, than seeing the disgust on his face.

She hurried down the stairs and out the front door and ran directly into Grandma.

"Grandma," she blurted, suddenly feeling ashamed and guilty.

"Honey, where are you off to? Where's Travis?"

Kacey fought hard to keep the tears from falling down her cheeks, but the minute Grandma reached out and touched her, she shattered into a million pieces.

"He doesn't love me," she wailed on Grandma's shoulder.

"Yes, he does," Grandma said simply.

Kacey shook her head and tried to clear her throat. "No, he doesn't. It was just like Jake and then..."

"What?" Grandma peeled Kacey from her shoulder and held her head between her hands. "What happened with Jake, honey girl?"

"We slept together, in college, my first time." She hiccupped. "The night my parents died. And he f-froze. He just sat there afterward. I was so vulnerable and he just sat there, and then he left w-without saying goodbye." Tears freely flowed down her cheeks. It was as if everything that had happened so many years ago was finally coming to the surface. All the hurt, the anger, the betrayal.

"And Travis, you and he?" Grandma asked softly.

Kacey nodded and continued. "And he just sat there! He called himself an idiot and went into the bathroom!"

Grandma put her hands on her hips. "I may be old, but that is no way to leave your bed partner."

"Grandma," Kacey said, managing a tiny smile. "It doesn't matter. I'm leaving."

"You can't!" Grandma grasped her hands tightly within hers. "You need to talk to him. He loves you. I know him. I do! He's just scared!"

"And I'm not?" Kacey yelled. "I'm terrified!"

Grandma gave her a peculiar look. "Does Travis know how Jake reacted that night?"

Kacey slowly shook her head, feeling a little guilty for allowing her hurt heart to put them in the same category.

"Go," Grandma said, surprising her. "Get on your plane. I'll take care of this."

Kacey shook her head. "There's nothing to do but pick up the broken pieces."

"There's always something to do." Grandma handed her the keys to the BMW. "Just leave it at the airport, and I'll have Wescott take me down there to retrieve it tomorrow."

"Thanks, Grandma. I love you."

"I love you too, honey." Grandma kissed her cheek and walked quite briskly into the house. The last thing Kacey heard before she started the car was Grandma yelling at the top of her lungs at Travis.

Kacey pulled out of the driveway, feeling completely raw as she left the house, full of memories for the second time in her life, knowing with certainty that it was not in her future.

"Sorry, Mom, Dad." Kacey wiped the tears from her eyes. "I guess I'm just not good enough."

THIRTY

Travis stared at the running water in the sink for what felt like hours. Really, it was probably thirty minutes, but he needed to get his speech perfect. Words often failed him, but he was going to try to convey the raw emotional need he had to be with Kacey, and not just for one night.

But forever.

"Travis!" Grandma's voice echoed into his room. What the heck was she doing back?

"Coming." He ran into his room and put on a pair of jeans just in time for Grandma to come bursting through the door.

"You are officially my least favorite grandson."

Travis smirked. "So I was your favorite before?"

"You are a jackass."

"Grandma, I hardly think swearing is appropriate—"

"She's gone."

Travis felt his world tilting. He sat on the bed and put his hands over his face. "What do you mean she's gone? She was just here."

"She left."

"Why?"

"Because you're a jackass."

His heart constricted. "What did I do? I mean, I didn't say *I love you* back, but I was so ashamed of myself for not having said it first, for taking her to bed and not telling her how much..." His voice went hoarse and then silent.

"Well, she thinks you're ashamed of her."

"What?" Travis bolted from the bed. "That's impossible! I didn't say anything hurtful!"

"I know." Grandma sighed. "That's the problem. You didn't say anything at all."

"What?"

"Just like Jake."

"Pardon?" He clenched his fists and began to sweat.

"He and Kacey... She never told you?"

Travis shook his head. "I know they slept together, but..."

"When all was said and done, Jake grabbed his stuff, said he was sorry, and walked out of her life."

"But..."

Grandma patted his hand. "You, my dear boy, had

the exact same reaction. Your motives were different. I know this and you know this. Kacey, however, feels like you think you made a mistake, and now she's at the airport."

"You let her go!" he roared, ashamed that he was yelling at his grandmother.

"No." She turned and walked to the door. "You did."

Travis didn't know what to say. Instead he pushed past his grandmother and ran down the stairs. It wasn't until he was outside that he realized he didn't have a shirt on. Cursing, he ran back into the house and grabbed a T-shirt from the laundry room.

His truck wouldn't be fast enough. He would never catch her in that thing. It was huge and hard enough to weave in and out of traffic.

He ran into the garage, nearly out of breath. The black-and-white Ducati sat quite comfortably in the middle.

"That'll do." He grabbed a helmet and sped off in the direction of the airport.

The whole time he weaved in and out of traffic he prayed he wasn't going to be too late. How could he be so stupid? He hadn't been thinking.

He still smelled like Kacey.

Her perfume was intoxicating, and it seemed every time he angled his head, he could smell her on his skin. Feel the touch of her lips against his.

"Damn." He pulled into the Portland airport and rushed to short-term parking.

He almost forgot to take his helmet with him and tripped trying to get the bike to stand alone, but finally he was through the entrance and looking frantically for Kacey's brown hair.

She had to be flying Alaska Airlines, either that or Southwest. He ran to the ticket counter. "Have you seen a girl with brown hair, brown eyes, really cute...?" Oh God, he was officially turning into the guy in the movies who breaks down at an international airport.

The lady shook her head. "I'm sorry. Our last flight left an hour ago."

"Right."

He went to the Southwest counter. "Have you seen—"

"Sir, you need to get in line."

"Listen, I'm not here to fly. I'm here to—"

"Sir! Get in line!"

Travis slammed his hand against the counter. Which, apparently, the lady didn't like. Within minutes, security guards were escorting him back outside.

Fabulous.

"I'm looking for my—"

What was she? His friend? Never. She would never be just a friend. She was more than a girlfriend. She was his lover...his—well, he wanted her to be his wife.

He smiled, despite being escorted out of the airport. He grabbed the security guard closest to him and grinned. "I'm going to marry her!"

"Good for you, son." The guy gave him a perplexed look. "Now we need you to leave."

Dejected, Travis went to the bike, then pulled out his cell and dialed Kacey's number. It went straight to voice mail.

Which meant only one thing.

She was flying, in the air, back home, and he hadn't even gotten to say he loved her.

THIRTY-ONE

Kacey laid her head back against the wall.

No flights out tonight meant she had to sleep in the airport. Sure, she could go to a hotel, but for some reason she wanted to feel sorry for herself. Well, there was that and the small opportunity she had to get an earlier flight than the one Jake was on.

That was just what she needed.

To sit next to Jake after sleeping with his brother.

Her life was like a dramatic TV show. She shook her head and shivered.

The airport was desolate. It was doing nothing for her horrible mood. Maybe she really should go somewhere else so she didn't end up crying by herself in the corner. That would be the ultimate of lows.

Pulling out her cell phone, she pressed Menu, but

the screen was black. She shook it—not that shaking a phone really did anything.

Dead.

Just like her heart.

Figured.

She threw it back into her purse and sighed. Maybe if she just closed her eyes for a bit she could get some sleep.

But the minute they fluttered closed she heard a voice.

"Hey…"

Her eyes flickered open. "Jake?"

"I know. I know. I'm supposed to be at the condo or wherever, but I got bored, and Grandma left saying something about having dessert with the neighbor away from the watchful eyes of the family, leaving me even more bored. Then Mom and Dad were treating it like another honeymoon, if you know what I mean. Anyway, I decided nothing was worse than that, so I drove home."

"Oh." Kacey shifted in her seat and broke eye contact.

"But then," Jake continued to talk, "Travis was gone and Grandma was muttering something about her damn grandson. I can't help but think she was referring to me."

Kacey snorted.

"What?" Jake nudged her. "No flippant remark? No agreeing? What's wrong? You sick or something?"

She shook her head and then burst into tears.

"God, I'm sorry. I'm so sorry. I didn't know you were sad. I'm such a selfish bastard sometimes. What's wrong? Are you sick? Are you okay?" He pulled her into his arms and held her.

It felt foreign, not at all like Travis. It was comforting to an extent but only as a friend, not a soul mate.

She shuddered, trying to gain her breath. "Nothing. It's fine. It's..." She continued to sob, even though she was willing herself to stop.

"Kace?" Jake whispered into her hair. "What's wrong? What happened?"

"Travis."

"I'll kill him." Jake pushed her away and rose to his feet. "Did he do this to you? Is that why you're crying? That son of—"

"No, no." Kacey sniffed. "It was me too. It was both of us. But in the end it was him."

"Huh?" Jake crouched to her eye level. "Why don't you start at the beginning?"

He had no clue. This perfect specimen of a man had no clue the hurt he caused. Well, he was about to.

"Actually..." Her voice wavered. "It starts with you."

"Me?"

She nodded. "Yup, the night you left me and never came back."

Surprisingly, she was holding herself together quite well, considering.

"You're referring to the night I live to regret every day of my life. That night?"

She wasn't sure if that was a compliment or a really cruel thing to say.

Jake cursed and wrapped his arm around her. "I was scared."

"What?" Of all the things he could have said, that was the least expected.

"Yes, I know. Jake Titus, scared? But it's the truth. I knew I'd messed up. I knew we were friends, and of course we were attracted to each other. I mean, how could we not be? We were inseparable, and let me tell you, it's nearly impossible for girls and guys to be friends."

Kacey sighed into his shoulder.

"I knew I'd messed up and I didn't know how to fix it. For once in my life I didn't have a plan. I had no idea what to do. Should I apologize? Should I do it again?" He chuckled. "Should I say I loved you? I just didn't know, so I did the only thing I could at such an immature age."

"You left," Kacey finished.

Jake nodded. He looked at her watery eyes and cursed. "I was an ass."

Kacey laughed. "That we can agree on."

"I never said I was sorry."

Her lip trembled.

Jake reached out and tilted her chin. "I am though. I'm so sorry, Kace. I never meant to hurt you. I was stupid and young and, well, sometimes it's easier to be selfish and cruel than to be real. I chose the stupid route, hoping it would just make everything go away."

"I'm sorry too," Kacey mumbled. "I should have done more, said more, or even said no. I just, I don't know…"

Jake pulled her to her feet. "Kace, let's both agree that bad choices were made, but let's move past it. I don't know what Travis did, but I do know one thing. That kid has been obsessed with you ever since you were old enough to run away when he threw rocks." He leaned in and kissed her cheek. "It will work out, promise."

Kacey nodded, still not trusting her voice to speak.

"And I think we've waited long enough. Let's drive home."

"It's four hours."

"We'll pay someone." He shrugged.

"Heartless billionaire."

Jake threw his head back and laughed. "Heartless, no. Billionaire, someday." With a wink, he wrapped his arm around her and led her back through the airport.

And directly into the lion's den.

Paparazzi cameras went crazy. The flashing

lights blinded Kacey so much that she tripped. Jake grabbed her arm and, with a curse, tried to cover her with his jacket as they walked to the line of waiting taxis and cars.

He looked down the street and cursed. "Come on. This way."

Kacey followed in an emotional haze as Jake led her back inside and pulled out his cell phone.

"I don't care if it's past midnight. Just get a car down here now." He threw his phone onto the chair and sat down.

"I'm sorry, Kace. I had no idea. I mean, we've been here for the whole weekend without actually running into the paparazzi. I only told the ones I hired."

Kacey sat with a huff and put her hand on his back. "It's okay. It's not like you're a normal person. You hired people to take pictures of us? You really are an ass sometimes, Jake."

Jake lifted his eyes to glare at her.

"But it's not like you had to hire anyone. People follow you everywhere." She shrugged, then gave him a small nudge. "You are Seattle's most infamous bachelor, not to mention a celebrity in these parts."

"Right." He looked down at his hands.

"Jake," Kacey said as she rested her head on his shoulder. "It's going to be fine. The car will be here soon and then we can go home. Besides, isn't this what you wanted?"

"Home," he repeated and shook his head. "I thought it was. But not like this, Kacey."

With a sigh, he nodded and said, "Home sounds good. Thanks, Kace. Sorry for dragging you into all this. You know they're going to think we're together."

"Ah." Kacey waved her hand in the air. "It's just like high school all over again."

"Except this yearbook gets national attention."

Kacey nodded. "And I'm pretty sure any pictures taken of me today will make it look like you're dating an emotional pill popper."

"Yes, there's that too."

"Thanks."

"No prob." Jake flashed her a grin. "Come here." He pulled her into a hug and kissed the top of her head. "You know it will all work out, right?"

"Yeah, I know. We'll just have to sneak into the car and…"

"No," Jake said, squeezing her shoulder. "With Travis. God, it sucks being passed over for my older, nerdier brother, but apparently that's what's happening."

Kacey wasn't confident enough to think that she and Travis were going to make it through this rough spot, even if she did get to talk to him. She still couldn't read his mind.

Did he miss her?

Was he just as upset as she was?

Should she have stayed?

"Get the hell off my woman!" a male voice yelled.

"Wasn't he kicked out?" a woman shrieked.

Kacey looked up to see Travis charging them both, his hands in fists and a woman pointing at him as if he were some sort of criminal. Her eyes were wide with fear.

To be fair, Travis did look a little menacing.

"What are you talking about?" Jake pushed up to his feet. "She's not your woman. If she were your woman, why the hell would she be sitting here with me?"

Bad move, Jake. Bad move.

"You lying bastard!" Travis lunged for Jake.

Both men fell to the hard ground with a grunt. Travis was on top, and Jake, unfortunately for him, was on the bottom.

And soon cameras were flashing all over again.

Kacey yelled, "Get off him! There's nothing going on!"

"You left her!" Travis punched Jake across the jaw.

A loud thunderous yell emerged from Jake as he wrapped his hands around Travis's throat. "So did you, you bastard! At least I apologized."

Travis's fist came crashing into Jake's jaw. Jake hooked his foot inside Travis's leg, like some sort of MMA move, and then Jake was on top. His fist pulled back to hit Travis, who had suddenly stopped fighting. And then security was pulling them apart.

Travis's eyebrow was cut and Jake was spitting blood.

And the cameras caught it all.

Every bloody thing.

"Come with us," a security guard ordered, grabbing both men.

"Wait! Wait, they, um…" Should she claim them, both of them? Reluctantly, she realized she had to. "They—they're with me."

"That true?" a security guard asked Jake.

He nodded.

And the next thing she knew, Kacey was getting arrested along with them.

Of course.

Paparazzi followed them, asking questions. "Jake, is this your new girlfriend? Isn't that your brother? What's going to happen to Titus Enterprises? Is this a reflection of how the company is being run since your father's retirement?"

Kacey felt sick to her stomach.

They were led into a cold, dark room that she could only assume was used to torture would-be terrorists.

The minute the door closed, she glared at both of them.

Both brothers.

Two men she had known her entire life.

One a friend, the other something so much more.

Her heart ached in her chest. She looked away
and huddled in the corner. She couldn't say what she
wanted to say, not now.

"I came after you," Travis mumbled in a low voice.

"Shut up," Jake said and groaned.

"Imagine my surprise when I see you in Jake's
arms on the receiving end of his kisses. Seriously,
Kace? Hours after we have sex? Really? I thought…"
His voice trailed off. "I thought we were more."

Furious, Kacey jumped to her feet and charged
toward Travis. Jake scooted as far away from his
brother as possible. Kacey slapped Travis hard across
the face.

"That is less than what you deserve."

Jake chuckled in his corner. "Ouch."

Kacey turned to him. He squirmed in his seat,
breaking eye contact. "As for you!" She pointed at him.
"We are on very shaky ground, my friend, very shaky
ground."

"She called me friend," Jake boasted aloud.

Travis cursed and held his head in his hands. "I'm
sorry," he said, his voice cracking. "I'm so damn sorry."

Kacey closed her eyes to fight the tears. "You
should be."

"I'd like to say something." Jake cleared his throat.

Travis turned a murderous glare in his direction.
"I'd rather you not."

"Regardless," Jake said, pushing up from his seat

and pacing the room. "I think it must be said that both of you are being stupid."

This? From Jake? Kacey scowled. "And what? You're suddenly the voice of reason?"

"Voice of reason." Jake shoved his hands into his pockets. "I kind of like the ring of that."

"I'll bet," Travis mumbled.

"Speaking of bets..." Jake walked over to Travis and lightly kicked his foot. "I think you won this one."

"Bet?" Kacey repeated. "What bet?"

"I was eight." Travis seethed.

"You were in love."

"You made a blood oath!"

Jake laughed. "Again with the blood oaths. Let's get one thing straight. An oath taken by spitting is not even close to being a blood oath."

Travis swore and glanced at Kacey. "I had to see you. The way you left..."

Kacey was still stuck on this whole bet business, and just as she was getting enough courage to ask...

The door burst open.

"Make that two of my least favorite grandsons." Grandma seethed.

Jake flinched and sat down next to Travis.

"Arrested at an international airport for fighting!" Grandma Nadine put her hands on her hips. "Shame on both of you! To think I had to find out on national television where my sweet boys were."

"She said sweet; that's a good sign," Jake said under his breath.

Grandma swore.

"Grandma!" the men said in unison.

"Poor Kacey," Grandma said, walking over to Kacey and opening her arms. Kacey went into them willingly, comforted that Grandma was there but also finding it mildly amusing that both boys were getting the cold shoulder. Just how immature would it be to stick out her tongue?

"You, my dear, are coming with me." Grandma grabbed Kacey's purse.

"What about us?" Travis asked.

"I told the lovely security guard to let you sit and stew for a while. He'll release you in three hours."

"But—"

"No," Grandma said, pointing a finger in the air. "When this is all over with, I'll let you speak to Kacey, Travis. Until then, I suppose now is as good a time as any to settle the score with your brother."

THIRTY-TWO

Damn, she's scary," Jake muttered.

"Tell me about it." Travis kept his eyes trained on the door, willing Kacey to come back through.

"So." Travis felt air whoosh by his ears as Jake took a seat next to him. "We gonna have this out, right here? Right now?"

Why wasn't she coming back? Why did he have to act like such an idiot? Why couldn't he have just told her he loved her when she needed to hear it most? It was hard to remember that Kacey could be insecure. Hadn't she just said nobody had told her she was beautiful since her mother had?

To sleep with her and then say nothing?

He hit his hand against the chair he was sitting in.

"So, no kiss and make up?" Jake asked.

"Sorry." Travis swallowed the lump in his throat. "It's not you..."

"It's not you, it's me? Are you breaking up with me, bro?"

Travis laughed despite the strong urge to strangle his brother. "No, and I'm not giving you the speech, though if I knew it would humble you, I'd damn well try."

"I'm humbled after tonight. Believe me."

Travis looked into his brother's eyes, the same ones that usually reflected so much arrogance it made Travis want to become violent. Instead of their usual cockiness, all he saw was regret, and maybe a little shame.

Jake smiled sadly and shrugged. "I ruined the perfect girl. She wants you. She told me she wants you. Nobody else."

"Not even the great Jake Titus?"

"God, I hate it when you both use my full name. I can't even imagine how bad it's going to be when it's two against one."

"Welcome to my childhood." Travis slapped him on the back.

"I'm sorry, you know," Jake said, shaking his head. "For everything. If I could take it back—"

"I wouldn't want you to take it back. In your own sick way, you drove her right into my arms."

"And the humility just keeps coming." Jake laughed. "Go after her."

"Didn't you hear Grandma? We're stuck in here for three hours."

"Ten bucks says Grandma's lying." Jake nodded to the door. "Look for yourself."

Travis got up from his seat and walked out the door. The guard nodded his head but said nothing. "Well, I'll be..."

"Conniving little thing, our grandma," Jake said, suddenly at his side. "Go get her."

Travis wasn't even sure which hallway to go down, let alone know where Kacey would be. "I have no idea where Grandma would take her."

"Really? No idea? None at all?" Jake gave him a stupid look and frowned.

Travis searched his brain for any sort of recollection of where Grandma would take Kacey. Obviously, she'd want her to be able to relax and be happy and comfortable and...

"Home."

"Are you sure he'd be okay with this?" Kacey asked, once she dropped her bags in the living room of the six-thousand-square-foot ranch house.

"Oh, honey, why else would he give me a key?"

"He didn't give you a key. You lifted ten rocks to find the hide-a-key."

Grandma shrugged. "Same thing."

"Right." Kacey looked around the room and

wanted to cry. Everything seemed so familiar, yet different. It felt like home, even if it was someone else's house entirely. After Grandma had taken Kacey away from the airport, she had told her about Travis as a little boy.

How he had watched her, tried to protect her. She said he'd felt like it was his duty to make sure she was always safe. So when her parents died, he'd tried to preserve everything, even going as far as to put her parents' belongings in the shed when Kacey sold off the house. He'd kept only a few things he knew she would want one day.

Some of those things, like her dad's favorite hunting trophies and stuffed animals, were mounted on the wall of his living room.

She swallowed the giant lump in her throat when she walked to the east end of the room and saw a picture of Travis and her dad, shaking hands and laughing, on one of their hunting trips.

Funny, how she had forgotten how close Travis and her father were until now. They'd been hunting buddies for as long as she could remember. Jake hated hunting. He said it was cruel to shoot animals, and actually had gone as far as to tell Kacey that her dad hated the furry things for doing that.

It hadn't mattered that her father had always eaten everything he'd hunted.

Jake had always thought it a stupid sport.

It hadn't been stupid to Travis, though. Her dad had come home after every hunting trip with funny stories about what Travis had done and how proud he'd been of him.

Her eyes fell to the planked-wood floor. The moon shone in through the French doors that led to the outside balcony. Travis had done a beautiful job building the house.

"Shall I leave you?" Grandma said from behind her.

"You don't have to." Kacey's voice shook.

"I think he'd rather I left." Grandma nodded toward the door and gave Kacey one more hug.

Kacey's eyes fell on Travis.

She wanted to run to him.

To throw her arms around his neck and beg him to never let her go again. But at the same time, what he'd done was still so raw and hurtful. Especially the way he'd reacted at the airport.

Grandma walked by her grandson and mumbled something that made Travis laugh. The door closed behind her and they were left alone.

"Kacey," Travis began, then walked purposefully toward her, gaining speed the closer he got. "Kacey," he mumbled again as he pulled her against his body and kissed her across the mouth. "I'm so damn sorry."

Kacey melted in his arms.

"I need to explain."

"You do." Kacey tried to pull away, but his arms locked around her body.

"I was scared—"

"Why do I scare all men?" she interrupted, frustrated and hurt.

"Let me finish." He smiled, and she became even more irritated that her stomach flopped at the sight. "Holding you in my arms, kissing you, making love to you. It was everything I've ever wanted, and then suddenly I felt like such an ass because I got lost in it all without saying the one thing I've been dying to say for my whole life."

"What's that?"

"I love you." His voice trembled. "You and only you. I love you so much that I can't breathe."

"You're breathing right now," she pointed out, still trying to be mad at him while her heart was thumping wildly in her chest.

"Well, that's because I'm using your air. It's because you're in my arms. Kacey, I'm never letting you go."

"Good." She reached for his neck and pulled his head down so their mouths could touch. His lips parted. Home. "I love you too."

She felt his mouth form a smile beneath their kiss, and then he lifted her into his arms and twirled her around the room. "Does that mean you'll stay?"

"If you ask nicely and promise not to throw things or pull my hair."

"You know I can't promise those things. I'll probably pull your hair, jump on you, and push you against the wall. And I'm pretty sure in a few minutes you'll be screaming my name."

Kacey felt her knees turn to jelly.

"But"—he placed her back on her feet—"I can promise to love you forever."

"Are you asking me to live in sin with you, Travis Titus?"

"No." His eyes darkened as he got down on one knee in front of her. "I'm asking you to be my wife."

"Kacey?" Travis was still on his knee. "Aren't you going to say something?"

"I thought a long pause was necessary after what you put me through tonight."

"I don't like long pauses."

Kacey shrugged. "Too bad."

Travis raised an eyebrow.

"Yes, I'll marry you...Satan."

"Aw, see? We already have pet names!" Travis jumped to his feet and picked her up again.

"Where are we going?"

"To celebrate," he answered gruffly.

"Where?" She giggled.

"The bedroom. Where else?"

"You can't propose to a girl, then sleep with her," Kacey pointed out. "It doesn't work that way!"

Travis paused and placed her on her feet. "Wine on the porch?"

Kacey nodded her head. She didn't trust her voice not to squeak with excitement.

"You're beautiful when you smile like that." Travis touched her cheek with his hand.

"You make me feel beautiful." She looked down.

"Don't do that. Don't look down when I give you compliments."

Kacey met his gaze. "I'll try not to."

"Come here. I want to show you something." Travis grabbed her hand and led her into a room off the main living area. It looked like a study. Every wall was lined with books. In the middle of the space was a giant oak desk sitting on a circular rug. The room had a private entrance to the porch as well.

"I've kept this, for you, all these years." Travis reached into the desk and pulled out a manila envelope.

"What is it?" Kacey reached out to grab it, but Travis pulled it back.

"Promise me you won't be angry?"

"No."

"Figures." He chuckled and handed over the folder. "I'll be outside when you need me, okay?"

She nodded as he closed the door behind him.

The envelope was thick.

Shaking, she poured the contents onto the desk in front of her. The first thing she saw was her parents' will.

She hadn't looked at it; nor had she been there for the reading. She'd just had Grandma tell her the specifics.

Good thing too, because it stated in no uncertain terms that Grandma was her legal guardian if her parents ever died before her eighteenth birthday.

No wonder Grandma never lost track of her.

Grandma really had been her godsend.

Sighing heavily, she placed the will aside and pulled out a tiny envelope with her name on it.

The paper inside was college-ruled notebook paper, something she hadn't written on for years.

The letter was addressed to her.

Kacey,

    I don't know why I'm even writing this. You're probably going to think your old mom's insane for putting something like this in our belongings, but I was sitting at school during my prep period and thought I should give you some words of encouragement.

    I heard from another teacher that you and Jake broke up today.

    I know it's hard. Senior year is never easy.

    But, honey, don't you think he's a better friend than boyfriend? The boy doesn't even pass a mirror without looking in it! You know you're smiling because it's true! I know we pressure you sometimes, but goodness gracious, you could marry Travis, and we would still be proud.

That was me trying to cheer you up. I know how much you despise that boy, even though he's been there for you without you even realizing it.

I guess what I'm saying is, it's important to keep your options open. It's important to live and not get so hung up on the past. The past is called the past for a reason. If you are constantly looking behind you, your eyes aren't on the road ahead. You don't drive a car that way, so why would you live your life that way? Isn't life more important than driving that beat-up Subaru?

I love you so much. As a mom I have to allow you to make mistakes, to learn and to grow, but you need to know that my love for you is unending. Regardless of what you've done, my love is unconditional. Where you've been helps you grow, and, my little treasure, I want you to grow!

Well, the bell just rang. I may not give this to you until you get married. I know you're rolling your eyes right now, but let's just say you probably aren't ready to hear all this from me just yet. But one day, one day this letter will make sense, and I hope it finds

you on that very day. In fact, that's my prayer
right now.

Love you,
Mom

Kacey wiped the tears from her cheeks with the
back of her hand but cried harder when she saw several
other letters in the same pile. Her mom had written her
letters and never given them to her. Mom was always
strange like that, writing down her thoughts, then forgetting that she wrote them down in the first place.

Kacey always saw her mom writing little things
down in her notebooks, but she had no idea they were
ever for her.

She tucked the letters back into the manila envelope and walked outside to the porch, where Travis was
sipping wine.

"You saved all of this for me?"

Travis looked into her eyes and nodded. "I don't
know what any of it said, Kace. I never looked. I just
knew, one day, you would want all of it, and selfishly, I
wanted to be the man to give it to you."

Kacey sat on his lap and leaned against his chest.

"I have a confession to make." He laughed
nervously.

"What did you do?"

"I got drunk."

"Now?"

Travis laughed again. "No, not now. I got drunk a few weeks ago, and I complained to Grandma about how no woman would ever compare to you. I'm pretty sure I was feeling sorry for myself, and I never make a habit of doing things like that. Nor do I make a habit of drunk-dialing my own grandmother."

"Do you think that's why she faked her stroke?" Kacey asked, taking the wineglass out of his hands and sipping from it.

"It's possible." Travis exhaled. "Either way, I don't care. I'm thankful."

"Me too." Kacey nestled into him and sighed. "Me too."

"Maybe now she'll direct her attention to Jake while we enjoy a honeymoon far, far away from the family."

Kacey laughed. "You mean you don't want your mom, dad, Mr. Casbon, and Grandma to join us?"

"We'd get kicked off the plane in seconds. Admit it."

Kacey giggled. "I'd rather have you to myself anyway."

"There's one more thing." Travis sighed heavily.

"What?"

"Jake owes us a million dollars."

"Huh?" Kacey jerked back and looked Travis in the eye. "What the heck? Why?"

Travis grinned smugly. "I bet him a million dollars, when I was eight, that I would marry you."

Kacey burst out laughing. "Shall we call him tomorrow?"

"We shall," Travis agreed. Then his mouth found hers, and immediately she stopped laughing, too distracted by what his mouth was doing.

She'd left home to escape the pain, not knowing that one day, this day, she'd return to find her own true happiness.

EPILOGUE

I don't know why you're still so upset... It happens to every guy from time to time." Kacey covered her mouth with her hand and averted her eyes. Groaning, Travis reached for the doorknob and glared.

"Really? That's what you're going to go with? It happens to every guy?"

Kacey shrugged and leaned against the doorway, "Hey, I'm just defending my fiancé. It's not your fault you can't perform."

Cursing, Travis pulled her against his body, "Sweetheart, I don't really think performance is my issue."

"No." Kacey grinned up at him and kissed his nose. "But admit it. When the bear appeared on the giant screen, you screamed like a little girl."

"Did not." Travis snorted. "The girl scream you heard was from the six-year-old behind us. Seriously, what parents take a child to a horror movie!"

"Really?" Kacey's brows lifted. "Do you even realize how badly you set yourself up, or do you just not care that everything you say makes it easy for me to make fun of you?"

"I—"

"You screamed. Loudly. The nice pimpled high schooler working at the theater had to make an announcement for the parents to take out all small children."

Travis shrugged. "I hate scary movies. So sue me."

"You hate furry animals."

"It had fangs and slaughtered an entire family."

"Movie, Trav, it's a movie."

Well, what could he say to that? He'd already lost half his manhood in that theater when he unintentionally screamed. In his defense, the giant bear on-screen wouldn't have shocked the hell out of him like it did if Kacey knew how to eat popcorn properly.

A kernel was resting quite nicely on her left breast. He knew it was her left because he watched it like a spider watches a fly. Watched and waited for it to fall, so he'd have the totally lame excuse to rescue said kernel and then maul his fiancée in the movie theater.

It was not his fault he'd always wanted to make out at the movies with a hot girl. And if Kacey didn't want him to be so damn distracted, she shouldn't keep wearing such low-cut shirts!

"Are you sweating?" Kacey felt his forehead.

God, he needed sex. Swatting her hand away, he laughed uncomfortably. "Nope. I'm fine. Should we go in?"

"Yeah?" Kacey frowned. "Nobody's answering the door?"

Travis shrugged and walked into the house.

Nothing in his life could have prepared him for that moment.

Some things just can't be unseen.

"Grandma!" he and Kacey said in unison.

She was on the couch feeding Mr. Casbon chocolate-dipped strawberries, which would have been odd yet semi-normal for the woman had she not been showing an ungodly amount of pink lingerie.

"Took my advice," Kacey whispered.

"Victoria's Secret!" Grandma pointed to her bra and winked.

"My eyes!" Travis turned and began waving wildly in the air. "Grandma, put more clothes on. God. Do you even own a sweater?"

"I hope not!" This from Mr. Casbon.

"Holy hell, I want to die right now," Travis muttered under his breath while the room erupted into laughter.

"No, you don't," Kacey whispered.

"Pretty sure I do."

"I picked a date."

"For my insanity? Thanks, yeah, a person experiences that after seeing his grandmother naked!"

"I'm not naked!" Grandma shouted while Mr. Casbon answered, "Too bad."

Kacey wrapped her arms around Travis and said, "Open your eyes."

"So I can see my grandma in various states of undress?" he all but yelled.

Kacey kissed him hard across the mouth, pushing his hands out of the way. Getting caught up in the moment, he wrapped his arms around her and opened her mouth with his tongue, tasting her, memorizing her.

A throat cleared.

Kacey pulled back.

"Oh right." She cleared her throat. "I picked a date."

"You keep saying that, but…"

And then the lights flickered on.

Jake stood on the opposite end of the room with a skank wrapped around him. Typical. His parents held a cake, and glasses of champagne were in everyone's hands.

"I'm confused."

Kacey tugged at his hand and laughed. "Good. I was hoping you would be."

What the hell was going on? Grandma stood,

adjusted her shirt—clearly she hadn't been acting—and took a glass of champagne from a nearby table.

He turned to face Kacey. "I still don't get it."

She grinned. God, she was beautiful. How could he have ever survived without her?

"It all started this way, Trav. You and me getting caught by Grandma, not even realizing it was a setup in the first place. I wanted to relive it. Relive the moment that shocked us both into realizing we had feelings. The manipulation, the lies, it all started here. Even when we were kids it started here. And I want it to end here."

Holy shit, was she breaking up with him?

"Here." Kacey squeezed his hand, her eyes welling with tears. "I want to get married here, at your parents' house. This fall."

"You mean it?" Travis choked on the words. They'd been going back and forth on where to get married. Up until now Kacey had been convinced they should go to Vegas, leave out all the crazy family antics.

Kacey nodded, her face breaking out into a gorgeous smile. "I love you, Travis Titus. Marry me here?"

"I'd marry you anywhere."

"Backyard." She nudged him, then reached up and whispered in his ear, "Tree house . . . where we had our first kiss, the room where we were first together . . . here, Travis. I want to get married at home."

With a shout, he picked her up and swung her in his arms, raining kisses all over her face. "It's a deal."

"To the happy couple," Jake announced as Travis set Kacey down. "To my brother and friend. I'm happy for you guys." His eyes looked sad, his body worn—no way was Jake going to last in the type of lifestyle he was living. He already looked like he was one drink away from dying.

"Cheers!" everyone said in unison.

"He needs a woman," Travis muttered under his breath.

"I've got just the one." Kacey nudged him with her elbow. "She's going to bring him to his knees."

"Wanna bet?"

"Not a bet...a wager." Kacey turned toward him and winked. "I wager he'll be begging her to marry him by the time we say I do."

"And if you're wrong?"

She bit down on her lip and winked. "I guess we can come up with the terms tonight..."

"At the house."

"Yeah."

Travis set down her champagne and grabbed her ass. "Or now?"

"Tree house?" she said, breathless.

"Tree house."

What is it about a junior-high crush that can send an otherwise intelligent woman into a tailspin? TV reporter Char Lynn wishes she knew.

Please see the next page for an excerpt from

THE WAGER

PROLOGUE

Summer 2002

Jake! Catch me. Catch me!" Char yelled as she did the trust fall at junior high camp. She'd had a crush on Jake for years. Now that she was in eighth grade, things were looking up. Legs shaved, she knew she looked good, and Jake was just about to know how good when she fell into his arms—literally.

"Um, sure," Jake called from behind her. "I'm almost ready."

"Okay." Suddenly nervous, Char took a few deep breaths. "Falling!'

"Fall away!" Jake called.

The wind whipped at her back as Char planked and fell the few feet backward. But she kept falling;

nothing was there. She hit the grass with a thud and looked up.

Amy Stevens was twirling her hair between her fingers and laughing at something Jake was saying. The guy had the attention span of an ant.

"You jerk!" Char hit the ground next to her with her fist, "Jake? We're partners; it's called a trust fall for a reason. You're supposed to catch me!"

His eyes widened. "Oh crap. I'm sorry, Char. Amy here needed help with the directions and doesn't have a partner, so I told her she could join us."

"Oh, but—"

"Wow, Jake, good thing I offered to be your partner. It's going to take two of us to catch that girl. She's like a swollen whale." Amy laughed and nudged Jake.

He stared at Char. His cheeks reddened a bit, but he didn't say anything. He didn't defend her. He did nothing.

Maybe that was the worst part.

The nothingness.

He could have joined in and laughed, which at least would cause Char enough anger to punch him in the face. But instead, he looked at her with pity—as if what Amy said was true.

As if he believed it too but didn't know how to tell her.

Char looked down at the itchy grass as tears welled in her eyes.

"Hey, you guys ready for the trust fall?" Kacey, her best friend, walked up to them and smiled. Sometimes Char hated how easy it was for Kacey to be best friends with Jake.

Jake pulled her in for a hug. "We were just warming up."

"Cool." Kacey looked down at Char. "Come on! Stop being so lazy and lying around."

Amy burst out laughing. "Exercise, Char, know what that is?"

Kacey glared at Amy and held out her hand to Char. "Ignore her. She's just grumpy because your boobs are bigger than hers."

Rolling her eyes, Char got to her feet and took one last look at Jake. She was done crushing on him. Absolutely finished. After all, what girl wants to fall in love with a boy who doesn't come to her rescue when she needs it most?

She wanted a man, like the ones she saw in movies and on TV. Jake Titus could just . . . die for all she cared.

ONE

Present day

Grandma, what the hell are you doing?" Jake took in her two larger-than-life suitcases, giant pink Coach handbag, and what looked like a dead animal on her head, and cursed again.

"Language, Jake." Grandma Nadine squared her shoulders and pushed past him to the ticket counter.

Oh no. Oh, hell no. Merciful God above. Jake looked around for Aileen, his latest conquest and plus one for the engagement party for his brother, Travis.

"Yes, I need only a one-way ticket," Grandma announced loudly to the Alaska Airlines clerk at the kiosk. Jake watched in a mixture of horror and panic as his grandmother bought a ticket on the same flight as him. *Please let her credit card be declined. Please, please.*

"Here you go!" The evil lady handed over a boarding pass and smiled at Grandma. Jake glared at the woman and then at his grandmother.

"No." He shook his head when she approached him, all smiles. "You aren't coming."

"I am." Grandma waved her ticket in front of his face and smiled. "Now, get my bags."

"But—"

"Jakey?" Aileen strutted toward him. Skirt shorter than what should be allowed in any public place, let alone an airport, she fluffed her hair and walked to his side. Her bleached-blond hair was held up by at least two cans of hair spray, and since she was unable to walk in straight lines, it was safe to assume she was still drunk from yesterday.

Grandma smiled brightly. "How lovely! It seems your whore has arrived."

Jake groaned and covered his face with his hands. There was no way out of it. His grandmother was going to get him shot.

A&E women scorned, here I come.

"Excuse me?" Aileen put her hands on her hips and did a weird head nod at Grandma, nearly teetering off her high heels. Oh, this wasn't good. Not good at all.

Grandma reached out and patted Aileen's arm. "Sweetheart, I'm the one with hearing aids, not you.

I called you a whore. Would you like me to spell it out for you too?" She nudged Jake. "What did you do? Find her at a high school career fair?" And then in a horrifyingly loud voice she began spelling "W-H-O-R-E."

Was his grandmother really spelling *whore* in an international airport? To his girlfriend? Sex buddy? What was she?

Shit, he didn't even know her last name.

Probably a bad sign.

"I'll have you know that—"

"Jake, I'm hungry. Take me to get food." Grandma looped her arm in his and began pulling him, with more strength than an eighty-six-year-old woman ought to possess, toward security.

"But what about me?" Aileen pouted behind them.

Grandma stopped in her tracks and turned around. "Honey, I'm sure you can find another nice little plaything between now and the time your flight leaves. This one's taken."

Aileen snorted. "Didn't take you for having that kind of taste." This directed at Jake. He opened his mouth to say, *This is my grandma*. Instead, Grandma smacked a large kiss on Jake's cheek, then pinched his ass.

"Oh, honey, you have no idea what this one is into." She winked. Good God, she just winked and alluded to Jake—he couldn't even finish the thought. Horrified, he saw Aileen's eyes widen. He opened his mouth to speak but was smacked on the ass again as his grand-mother pulled him in the other direction.

Karma, it was finally coming for him. And it was in the form of an eighty-six-year-old woman with lip-stick on her teeth. Hell.

TWO

Breathe, Char, just breathe. In and out, there you go."
Char tried to even her breathing but was finding it very
difficult, considering her sister continued to slap her
across the back every time she opened her mouth.

"Hand me the paper bag?" Char jerked the bag out
of her sister's hands and began breathing slowly into
it. Finally, after two minutes of her thinking she was
going to die, the panic attack alleviated.

"All better?" Beth whispered.

"No." Char bit her lip and looked down the aisle.
The very same aisle Jake Titus had walked down minutes earlier. He'd even looked in her direction, offered a
polite smile, and then proceeded to go to his seat.

A smile.

That was all she was worth. One polite smile. It

didn't help that the plane chose that exact moment to hit the worst turbulence of her life.

But the icing on the cake, what really made this day the worst day of her life, was when the flight attendant's boobs accidently—right, accidently—fell out of her shirt and into Jake's face.

The man needed to be neutered. He was like walking sex, and everyone around him knew it. Even if he wasn't a real celebrity, he would still attract women like rats to cheese.

She'd been a rat once. "Bastard," she mumbled under her breath, clenching her hands into tiny fists.

But that was years ago. She was jaded now. Wiser, and stronger.

Yes, stronger. She was a public figure, for crying out loud! She could and would act like everything was *fine*.

And it was.

It was, it was, it was.

"Char?" Beth nudged her. "You're rocking back and forth again. Do I need to get the bag?"

"Nope." Char felt a smile curl at her lips. "I'll be right back."

Beth put out her arm to block Char's way. "No, absolutely not. You've got that crazy look in your eyes. And I really don't want you to go to prison. As your sister and future maid of honor, I cannot with good conscience let you by me."

"I'll buy you a new Louis Vuitton purse."

"On the other hand, you are an adult and you can make your own decisions. Carry on." Beth lifted her arm. "Black, I want the black one."

Char rolled her eyes and made her way toward Jake's seat.

The FASTEN SEAT BELT sign was no longer on, so Char was in the clear. She'd practiced this speech ever since that fateful day last year when they'd reconnected. Char had wanted more than a one-night stand, and Jake, well, he'd wanted a one-night stand and a thank-you. She never told Kacey, and swore she'd take it to her grave—that is, unless she saw him again and then all bets were off.

What would she say to him if she ever saw him again? How would he react? Would he apologize for being an ass? Or would he even remember her? He didn't seem to recognize her! Then again, her hair was longer now. But faces don't change.

If only they did.

She really should ask God about that one. Jake needed more than a new face. He needed an actual heart inside that muscled body.

Her eyes darted to a few rows behind him. A girl had a cup of water sitting on her table. "Hey, honey, can I borrow this?"

"Oh my gosh!" The girl looked about twelve, and she began clapping her hands wildly. "Aren't you *that* news lady?"

"Why, yes." Char usually loved being recognized, but not now. Now she needed to be incognito. "You must watch the news a lot, huh?"

"No." The girl sighed. "But my mommy and daddy laughed really hard when you fell out of your chair that one time. They said you were drinking alcohol and that's why you fell."

Fanfreakingtastic. Had everyone seen that You-Tube clip? It had been the night after she'd hung out with Jake. Hung out because she felt sorry for him, which was bad choice number one, followed by bad choice number two, which was a bottle of tequila and waking up in a hotel suite with nothing but a thank-you note and a killer hangover. She was lucky she'd made it to work on time.

Then again, luck didn't get you more than two million hits on YouTube and a spot on the *Today* show with Kathy Lee and Hoda, who graciously forwent their wine and offered Char tequila shots in honor of her night of horror.

"I wasn't drinking," Char explained. "I was... tired, and overworked and—" Holy crap, she was officially going to lose it in front of a twelve-year-old. "You know what? Never mind. How's five bucks sound?"

"Five bucks?"

"Give me your water and I'll give you five bucks."

"Make it ten."

Char glared.

The girl glared back. Fine. Ten bucks to make her feel better about Jake being an ass? Deal. She'd take that bet.

Char reached into her back pocket and pulled out a twenty. Shit.

The girl swiped it from her hand before Char could do anything. Grumbling, she grabbed the cup and made her way toward Jake's seat.

Two more rows.

Finally. She stopped at Jake's row and cleared her throat.

He didn't look up.

She cleared her throat again.

Finally, he slowly raised his head. His mouth dropped open. "Char?"

"Jake," she purred.

"How are you? I mean, it's been forever!" His smile didn't reach his eyes.

Actually, it had been eleven months, one week, and five days. But hey, who was counting? Not her.

"Hasn't it though?" She leaned against the seat.

"We should catch up." He eyed her up and down before coughing and looking away.

"We should," she agreed, and then before she lost her nerve, she dumped the entire cup of water down the front of his pants. "But I don't date assholes who abandon me after sex."

"What the—" He made a move to stand up just as

she buzzed the flight attendant and announced loudly, "Sorry, it seems Jake Titus just peed his pants. Could you please help us?"

Snickering ensued around them. Char smirked at a gaping Jake. He reached across the seat to the striking elderly woman sitting next to him.

"Well, well." Char leaned on the seat and whispered, "Looks like you're going for every type of woman these days, eh, Jake?"

"Oh, he truly does," the lady piped up. "Did you know that he had the balls to take a whore to his brother's engagement party!"

Holy crap. Please let the elderly lady be talking about someone else, and not referring to her.

"I, uh…" Char took a moment to compose herself. "Actually, I believe it."

"And you know what else." The woman released Jake's hand and leaned forward over his seat. He rolled his eyes but otherwise kept silent.

"What?" Whoever this crazy lady was, Char liked her. A lot. Pity that Jake was going to break her heart.

"His high school sweetheart is marrying his brother. He tries to pretend it doesn't bother him. But a grandma knows these things…" She patted Jake's hand.

Ah, grandma. Wait. Was this the infamous Grandma Nadine Kacey was always talking about? Even though Char grew up relatively near the Titus family, she'd never actually met the old woman before—until now.

"So"—Grandma leaned back—"I'm going to fix him."

Jake groaned.

"You mean you're going to neuter him."

"Oh, honey." Grandma choked on her laughter. "There would be nothing better for the boy than getting neutered. Did you know I even looked into a male chastity belt?"

Jake groaned again. "Dear Lord save me from the female sex."

"Sex." Char snorted. "Kind of what got you in this predicament in the first place, wouldn't you say?"

The flight attendant chose that exact moment to walk up. "Where's the young man who peed his pants?" She had a nice pair of Depends in her hand.

Both Grandma and Char pointed to Jake.

Classic.

Karma. He knew it by name. Oh how he loathed it. That's what was happening to him. After all, a guy can only whore himself around the world so many times before God starts smiting or killing, or in Jake's case, plaguing him with emotional women.

"I did not—" Jake cleared his throat and whispered, "Have an accident. This woman here"—he pointed to Char—"accosted me."

The flight attendant looked between the two of them. "With what, sir?"

"Water." Grandma answered for him. "She threw water on him."

"Um." The flight attendant shifted nervously on her feet. "Sir, did you um, that is to say, were you wanting to report her?"

"To who?" Char laughed. "The air marshal? What's he going to do? Taser me for throwing water on this one's favorite anatomical part?" She thrust her finger in Jake's face and laughed. "Seriously! It's not like I said *bomb*."

"Oh hell." Jake pinched the bridge of his nose as the word *bomb* was repeated and then murmured several seats behind him until, like a literal bomb, the plane was in an uproar.

"Ma'am!" The flight attendant raised her hands in front of Char's face. "Calm down. I need you to calm down. Do you have a bomb?"

"What?" Char's face fell. "Why the heck would I have a bomb?"

Good. At least she had enough sense to stop talking when—

"If I had a bomb, it's not like I would be stupid enough to announce it anyway!"

Just kidding. No sense, no logic. How could he forget? It was *Char* they were talking about. She adopted blind dogs and cried during the stupid Sarah McLachlan animal rescue commercials. Clearly, common sense wasn't one of her strong suits.

"Ma'am! I need you to stop raising your voice." The flight attendant motioned to someone behind her. Within seconds, a man in jeans and a white T-shirt appeared. Well, it wouldn't be fair to call him a man since he probably ate small children for breakfast. Even Jake shifted uncomfortably and avoided eye contact.

"You the one talking about bombing the plane?" the man asked.

"What?" Char looked to Jake for help. And honestly, it probably would have been the right thing to do, all things considered.

But she *had* thrown water on his pants and accused him of having an accident.

And there was also that one time in high school when she told everyone that the reason he didn't play sports was because he was afraid everyone would see his girl parts in the locker room.

So yeah. Perhaps he wasn't feeling very Samaritan-like.

"Jake!" Char smacked him on the shoulder. "Help me out here!"

With an evil grin, he opened his mouth to talk, but his grandma slammed her hand across it before any words could come out.

"Both of them. They both have bombs." Then Grandma Nadine promptly burst into tears.

Real, honest-to-God tears.

The next thing Jake knew, he was getting zip-tied and force-fed peanuts by a man who had larger hands than Jake's face. Which he knew only because the minute he was escorted back to his seat, he nearly passed out—swell, a nervous breakdown. Just another thing to add to what had to have been the worst few months of his life.

Next thing he knew, Char was spouting out nonsense about how Jake needed protein. For some reason—perhaps it was the fact that the room was spinning—he couldn't respond fast enough to say that he hated peanuts.

He was still trying to decide what was most horrifying, the fact that a man was actually trying to force-feed him something that sounds like *penis* or that the man's fingers were softer than anything he'd ever felt against his lips. Which really begged the question, why were his fingers even touching Jake's lips? And why did it feel so—

Holy shit. He gripped the armrests and cringed. Was he switching playing fields?

"No more penis—I mean peanuts." Damn.

Char peered around the man and gawked. "Did you just say no more pe—"

"No!" Jake laughed and tried to move as far away as possible from the man sitting between them. "I said peanuts."

"No, you didn't." Char grinned.

"I did."

"You didn't."

"Can we please take these things off?" Jake said as he jerked against the armrests. The zip ties wouldn't budge and were making permanent marks on his skin. "It's not like we really have bombs! My grandma's insane, like literally insane! You have no idea what she's capable of."

"*That* apple didn't fall far from the tree." Char huffed.

"Do you mind?" Jake peered around the air marshal. "I'm trying to get us out of a difficult situation. The least you can do is help or apologize!"

"Apologize?" Char's eyes widened. "Apologize?" Nostrils flaring, she leaned as far as the zip ties would let her and glared at Jake. "I'm surprised you even know the meaning of the word."

Jake snorted. "I know what it means, but I'm not the guilty party."

"Holy crap, I want to slap you across the face so hard—"

"Slap me across the face so hard? Who the hell talks like that? Same old Char, all bark and no bite. Besides, your hands are literally tied. I can say whatever the hell I want and you have to sit there and listen... In fact—"

"Don't you do it, Jake Titus. Don't you dare do it! I'll, I'll—"

Jake yawned. "I'm waiting."

"I'll—"

"So it happened like this." Jake turned to the air marshal and cleared his throat, but for some reason it wasn't clearing. His mouth felt like he was swallowing cotton. "Thar..." His tongue felt huge. "Thar, I—"

"Holy crap!" Char yelled and kicked in her seat. "Um, Jake, um, Mr. Air Marshal Guy—"

"Randall, the name's Randall." The guy held out his hand; then, realizing Char was still zip-tied, chuckled and blocked Jake completely from Char's view. Weird. It was almost like he was having trouble breathing. Maybe it was the altitude. He tried swallowing again. Shit, it was getting harder. What the hell?

"Jake!" Char yelled louder this time and kicked the air marshal next to him. "Look, Randall? We've got a problem. You're about five seconds away from having a death on your hands."

"Dweath!" Jake croaked. Holy freaking shit, was Char going to murder him? The plane was crashing? Well, it wasn't as if he had anything to live for now that his grandmother had cut him off.

He could see the newspaper article now. Jake Titus, millionaire bad boy, cut off from entire family and dies in a plane crash with peanut crumbs on his face. Not that they would find the peanut crumbs, considering his body would probably be incinerated and...When had his life gotten so depressing?

He blamed his brother's impending marriage. Everything had gone downhill since the engagement.

"Pardon?" The air marshal stiffened up, jolting Jake from his morose daydream or nightmare, however one wanted to look at it.

"Look!" Char nodded her head in the direction of Jake. So, this is how he was going to die? By Char's hand, a woman scorned. Well, technically it would be by the air marshal's peanut hands. How the hell did he end up starring in his own TV melodrama?

"Sir, calm down." The air marshal's eyes widened as he stood and hit his head on the ceiling, cursed, and then ran up the aisle. Jake's eyes followed him. Damn, what was his problem? Was he really that concerned about Jake's impending death?

"So…" Char chuckled. "You allergic to anything, Jake?"

"Ha-ha!" He croaked. "Yeah, wright. What, you gonna poison me? Sorry, babe. I'm kind of on tha wright fide of pwerfection."

"Yeah, there went my apology."

"For what?" Jake straightened in his seat. Maybe if he moved he could breathe easier?

With a triumphant grin, Char shrugged and looked away.

Was it hot in that airplane? What the hell was happening with his mouth? His hands began to itch something fierce; he looked down and froze.

His very swollen, Mickey Mouse hands.

"HOLY SHWIT!" He jerked violently against the seat. "My wands, my wands!"

"Wands?" A lady turned around and stared at them both.

Char nodded solemnly. "Please excuse my friend. He's under the impression he's the tooth fairy."

Full-on panic set in as it got harder and harder to breathe. Was it an allergic reaction, or was he just freaking out? Nothing like this had ever happened to him before. He looked up the aisle and noticed Grandma strutting down it with some sort of object in her hands. Great. Now he was going to get knifed by his own grandma. Would flying experiences never be normal for him?

"Don't worry, Jake!" Grandma pointed at him and nodded. "Grandma's got this." She raised her hand high in the air. Jake closed his eyes. Maybe it was just a bad dream. Maybe he wasn't really zip-tied. Maybe he was having a nervous breakdown and—

"Son of a bwitch!" Jake wailed as a needle went through the hole in his jeans directly into his thigh. Well, if he didn't die, he would surely pass out from the pain. So many things to look forward to.

When the pressure subsided and the needle left him, thank God, he opened one eye, then two, to see Grandma standing in front of him with what can only be described as a torture device in her hand.

"He was allergic as a small boy. I wonder if the stress did him in..." She *tsk*ed and then motioned to Char. "Thank you, my dear. I don't know what we would have done if you wouldn't have told Randall here that Jake was going to die."

"You're a hero, ma'am." Randall's lower lip quivered as he nodded his head and looked down at the ground.

You've got to be shitting me.

All eyes turned to Jake.

He could have sworn the plane around him fell to a deathly silence. To be fair, it was extremely small since the flight from Portland to Seattle was less than an hour.

"Jake." Grandma sighed. "Don't you have something you need to say to Char?"

You're insane? You almost killed me? I want to strangle you? Grumbling, he turned to look at her—really look at her. Damn if she wasn't still irritatingly beautiful.

Where the hell did that thought come from?

Must be the allergic reaction.

Long chestnut hair fell in waves across her shoulders, her blue eyes widened just a bit, and then his gaze fell to her full pink lips. Only they weren't drawn in concern; no, if anything, she was trying not to laugh.

"No." Jake glared. "I think she knows exactly how I feel about her."

Char's smirk fell as her eyes turned icy. "He's right." Her eyes flickered back to Grandma. "He said all he needed to say the night after he slept with me and then left me a note on my pillow saying thank you. Isn't that right, Jake?"

He should have seen the slap coming. But to be fair, he was still in shock that Char would air their dirty laundry in front of God and everyone.

So when he felt air whoosh by his ear, he did what any man would do, he ducked. Too bad his grandma wasn't one to give up too easily.

The second slap was a backhand and it burned like hell.

"I've raised you better than that!" Grandma Nadine thrust her finger in Jake's face and shook her head.

With a huff, she straightened her jacket and ordered Randall, the weepy air marshal, to untie Char, explaining that really, the issue was not with her but Jake all along.

The next hour was the longest of his life.

His breathing was raspy. His face was most likely still swollen from both the reaction and his grandma; never had he felt less like a man. And it was all Char's fault.

ABOUT THE AUTHOR

Rachel Van Dyken is the *New York Times* and *USA Today* bestselling author of Regency and contemporary romances. When she's not writing, you can find her drinking coffee at Starbucks and plotting her next book while watching *The Bachelor*. Rachel keeps her home in Idaho with her husband and their snoring boxer, Sir Winston Churchill. She loves to hear from readers! You can follow her writing journey at www.rachelvandyken.com.

Fall in Love with Forever Romance

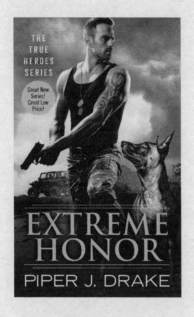

EXTREME HONOR
by Piper J. Drake

Hot military heroes, the women who love them, and the dogs that always have their backs. EXTREME HONOR is the first book in Piper J. Drake's high-adrenaline True Heroes series.

Fall in Love with Forever Romance

#1 *NEW YORK TIMES* BESTSELLER
RACHEL VAN DYKEN
THE Bet

"LAUGH-OUT-LOUD FUN! RACHEL VAN DYKEN IS ON MY AUTO-BUY LIST."—JILL SHALVIS, *NEW YORK TIMES* BESTSELLING AUTHOR

THE BET
by Rachel Van Dyken

Lose a bet, lose your heart. Kacey should have run the minute Seattle millionaire Jake Titus's mouth said he wanted to marry her. Instead, she made a deal with the devil in hopes of putting her past behind her once and for all. The #1 *New York Times* bestseller from Rachel Van Dyken is now in mass market.

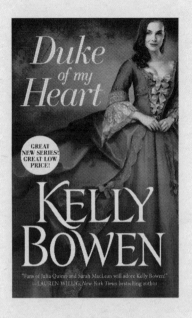

DUKE OF MY HEART
by Kelly Bowen

Captain Maximus Harcourt can deal with tropical storms, raging seas, and the fiercest of pirates. But he's returned home to a crisis and has only one place to turn. So now he's at the mercy of the captivating Miss Ivory Moore, known throughout London for smoothing over the most dire of scandals.

Max has never in all his life met a woman with such nerve. And such magnetic appeal...